A Burning and Shining Light

The Life and Ministry of the Rev. David Brainerd

by Denise C. Stubbs

Soli Deo Gloria Publications
. . . for instruction in righteousness . . .

Soli Deo Gloria Publications
P.O Box 451, Morgan, PA 15064
(412) 221-1901/FAX 221-1902

*

*

ISBN 1-57358-070-8

*

Cover art by G. Carol Bomer

To my loving husband, Berry, for his constructive criticism, support, and encouragement, and for sharing with me a common love and admiration of the Puritans

Contents

v

Contents *vii*

Acknowledgments

I would like to thank my dear friend Nancy West for introducing me to the Puritans, and for her insightful suggestions concerning the manuscript. Also, many thanks to Susie McAllister, Betty Lee, and Kerry Carr for their excellent editorial assistance, and to David Freeland for his invaluable help on the cover and map design. Lastly, I would like express my appreciation to the Rev. Albert N. Martin for his encouragement in pursuing this project.

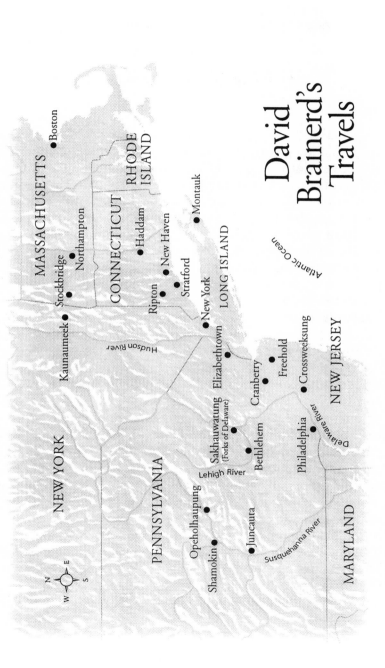

David Brainerd's Travels

Preface

J. I. Packer once asked the question, what can "we late twentieth-century Westerners, with all our sophistication and mastery of technique in both secular and sacred fields" learn from the Puritans? He answered, quite insightfully, "maturity." "Maturity is a compound of wisdom, goodwill, resilience, and creativity. The Puritans exemplified maturity; we don't. We are spiritual dwarfs." Dr. Packer went on to explain that the Puritans were "great souls serving a great God. In them clear-headed passion and warm-hearted compassion combined. Visionary and practical, idealistic and realistic too, goal-oriented and methodical, they were great believers, great hopers, great doers, and great sufferers. But their sufferings, on both sides of the ocean (in old England from the authorities and in New England from the elements), seasoned and ripened them till they gained a stature that was nothing short of heroic. Ease and luxury, such as our affluence brings us today, do not make for maturity; hardship and struggle however do, and the Puritans' battles against the spiritual and climatic wildernesses in which God set them produced a virility of character, undaunted and unsinkable, rising above discouragement and fears, for which the true precedents and models are men like Moses, and Nehemiah, and Peter after Pentecost, and the apostle Paul." (*A Quest for Godliness.* Wheaton: Crossway, 1990, p. 22)

As Dr. Packer so eloquently expressed, we can

learn much from the Puritans because they possessed a maturity that we sorely lack. We see this so markedly in the life and ministry of David Brainerd. To imagine a man so dedicated to Christ, so driven by devotion, and so characterized by self-abandonment might be quite beyond our abilities. So foreign are these attributes in today's giddy generation that the world of David Brainerd leaves many perplexed and bereft of any ability to relate.

But we do not think our generation so irreparable that we can learn nothing from this young man who gave so much to serve his Lord. As Dr. Packer said, we can learn something of spiritual maturity if nothing else. And this is our hope for those who read the following pages, that they might be struck by the love David Brainerd had for his Lord and for his fellow man and that they might, in turn, be inspired to live in a similar fashion.

In the following pages, you will not find frightful stories of physical persecution, murder, or war, as you might in the biographies of other early Americans. Such drama is not the appeal of David Brainerd's life. Instead, you will read of the spiritual struggles of a young man coming to grips with his own sinfulness and his desperate need of God's grace, of the difficulties and trials that accompany the call to be a missionary, of the joys of seeing the lost come to know Christ, and of the rare determination to put one's calling above ordinary desires and common comforts.

As to the mechanics of this biography, any person who has tried to write a non-fiction dramatic narrative can well understand that the fine line between literary license and historical truth is not so easy to walk.

We hope the reader will forgive any embellishments that are meant only to give life to the story and fluency to the narrative. Some scenes were added to give closure to a particular account and to move the story forward. For example, we do not know exactly what caused David Brainerd to begin considering mission work to the Indian people, so we took a bit of literary license to fill in the details. We also created some scenes as composites of various experiences. For instance, David Brainerd met a number of white people who opposed his ministry among the Indians. These people are represented by the "trappers" in chapter 11. Lastly, we do not know exactly what David Brainerd's feelings were toward Jerusha Edwards. We do not even know when he met her for the first time. We have assumed that he knew her before his final trip to Northampton. This assumption is based on entries in his journal wherein he considered marriage. He referred to "someone" who had proven to be very dear to him. We believe that person to have been Jerusha Edwards. Any other elaborations in description or dialogue, we hope, will be graciously accepted as an effort to enliven and not to detract from the truth. You can be sure that David Brainerd's life, as recorded in his journals, has been faithfully portrayed.

David Brainerd was a burning and shining light, and it is said that the candle which burns the brightest dies the quickest. Such was the case with this eminent saint, who served the Lord faithfully, who preached the Gospel fearlessly, who overcame the struggles of the wilderness, of spiritual opposition, of sickness, and of doubt to proclaim Christ and Him crucified to the natives of North America. Here is a man whose love burned like a raging fever, whose light shone like a beacon on a hill, and whose life ended in the golden days of youth. For a brief season, the world and the church benefited from his light. May that light continue to shine from the pages of this book, and may we rejoice, not only in the man, but in the God he loved so well.

To God's Glory,
Denise C. Stubbs

The Life and Ministry of the Rev. David Brainerd

Time Line of Events

April 20, 1718 – Birth

March 1732 – Mother's death

April 1738 – Moved to live with local pastor, Mr. Fiske

July 12, 1739 – Conversion

September 1739 – Yale College

Winter 1742 – Expulsion from College

November 1742 – Approved by Missionary Society of Scotland to be a missionary to the North American Indians

April 1743 – Begins work at Kaunaumeek

May 1744 – Forks of Delaware

June 1744 – Ordination

October 1744 – First missionary journey to the Susquehanna River

May 1745 – Second missionary journey to the
Susquehanna River

June 1745 – Crossweeksung

July 21, 1745 – First baptism among the Indians

September 1745 – Third missionary journey to the
Susquehanna River

May 1746 – Indians move to Cranberry

August 1746 – Fourth missionary journey to the
Susquehanna River

November 1746 – Leaves Indians because of sickness,
delayed in Elizabethtown

March 1747 – Last time he sees his congregation at
Cranberry

May 1747 – Arrives in Northampton at the home of
Jonathan Edwards

October 9, 1747 – Death at age 29

1

The Journey Begins

David Brainerd pulled the high collar of his dark blue jacket tight against his neck. The wind had picked up, sending an unseasonable chill through the Pennsylvania mountains. The young missionary looked around as he gathered his supplies to continue the long journey to the Susquehanna River. The forest surrounding him had grown dark as the clouds massed together like an army preparing for battle. Jagged rocks that lined the path seemed to huddle in the shadows, bracing for the downpour. Even though springtime had already announced her arrival with the green of newly sprouted leaves and a sprinkling of sunny daisies, the flowers lost their youthful shine and the green of the trees appeared almost black in the fading afternoon light. David frowned. He didn't look forward to trudging through the treacherous mountain terrain in a storm.

"We'd better get moving," David said to his interpreter, an Indian called Moses Tinda Tattamy. Moses was busy putting out the fire where he had cooked rabbit for lunch. Without looking up, he merely grunted. He, too, dreaded the thought of traveling in a spring storm. The Indian looked into the sky. It had taken on an ominous appearance as the clouds turned a greenish-gray color. His weathered face, which made

1

him look older than his 50 years, mirrored David's concern.

"It looks like it will be a bad one," he said as David mounted his horse. "I don't think we'll get far before the rains come."

"Then we need to get going if we want to find shelter before nightfall," David responded, eager to be on his way.

Moses climbed onto his horse and headed up the trail behind his companion. They had traveled less than an hour when Moses' horse suddenly stopped, refusing to be coaxed a step further. Moses tugged and nudged, but the horse wouldn't go forward. A few minutes later, David's horse moved to the side of the path and began rubbing its nose in the damp grass. Despite David's insistent pulls and tugs, the horse would not move back onto the path.

"What could be the matter?" David asked, glancing back at his interpreter.

"They're probably sick," the Indian replied. He jumped down and examined his horse's eyes and felt its stomach. "Sure enough. They are sick. The stupid beasts probably ate some poisonous berries back where we stopped for lunch."

"One thing is for sure," David said, slipping from his saddle. "We can't ride them. It looks like we'll have to walk."

They had not walked more than a few hundred yards when a thunderclap ripped through the mountains and the rain began to fall. David pulled a heavy cloak from his saddle bag, wrapped it around his shoulders, and continued to make his way up the trail. The path, which had been smooth earlier, soon transformed into a tangled mass of muddy tree roots and clumps of craggy rocks. David's high leather boots quickly became caked with mud and grew heavier with each step.

Pushing his horse ahead of him to squeeze through some brush, David glanced over his shoulder. He squinted as the driving rain lashed against his face. Through the relentless downpour, he could barely see the bent form of his interpreter stumbling his way through the rocky terrain behind him. Not wanting to get too far ahead, David paused to give him time to catch up. Taking advantage of the brief rest, the missionary bent over, trying to catch his breath from the hard climb. Moses looked up and motioned for him to go on. But David hesitated, deciding it would be best to wait. He didn't want to become separated from his companion in the angry storm. Annoyed that the missionary had refused to push forward, Moses shook his head and hurried up the trail until he stood beside him in the pouring rain.

"It doesn't look like it's going to let up," David yelled so he could be heard amid the thunderclaps. "We need to keep moving."

Panting from the climb, the Indian nodded and continued to plod up the mountain. David followed, pulling his cloak tight around him as he tried to keep his footing on the slippery trail.

The mid-afternoon faded into early evening and still the rains bore down on the weary travelers. Frustrated and sore from the steady climb up the mountain path, David stared at the mournful horses that slushed through the mud ahead of him. With their heads hung low and their drenched manes plastered against their necks, they lumbered up the trail as if they barely had the strength to take another step. David shook his head. They had been walking for hours now, but the storm only grew worse. It would have been so much easier if they could have ridden the animals, but they didn't appear any better. If he and Moses didn't find shelter by nightfall they would have to stop and spend the night exposed to the fury of the northeasterly storm. They couldn't possibly continue walking all night, at least David knew that he couldn't. He felt weaker with every step.

Trying not to think about the rain and the many miles still ahead of them, David and Moses made their way along a trail that skirted a high wall of sharp rocks. Before them, a sea of misty blue-green pines, hemlocks, and budding maples stretched for miles. David looked wearily into the distance. The pounding rain covered the dismal landscape before him like a silvery sheet, gray and forbidding under the massive storm clouds. David groaned and walked on.

Soon the path disappeared in a thick cascade of mud, making it difficult for the men to get their footing. Trying to be careful to stay on the path, they inched their way forward. Swirls of shadows danced wildly across the face of the mountain as lightning lit up the sky. David and Moses did their best to calm the horses, but the men soon became concerned that the lightning flashes and crashing thunder would send them bolting into the forest. To keep the animals from running off, they grabbed hold of the reins and kept the frightened horses close beside them as they continued their hazardous journey.

Just as the travelers rounded a sharp bend, thunder clapped and bellowed across the darkening sky. The mountains trembled as if frightened by the sudden sound. Through patches of sky in the trees that arched over the pathway, David could see the storm clouds thickening into an impenetrable barrier. He shivered. The temperature dropped even further, turning the spring day cold and sending a chill through David's thin body. His head began to ache, and his stomach cramped. He paused a moment to catch his breath, letting go of the rope that held his horse. Even though in the spring of life himself, David didn't have much strength, and his failing health was a constant struggle as he faced the rigors of the wilderness.

David's interpreter came up beside him. He had noticed that the younger man seemed to be laboring with every step.

"Are you all right?" he asked.

David held up his hand, indicating he was fine. Moses looked skeptical, but he knew there was nothing he could do to help the sickly missionary. So he readjusted the bundles on his back and kept moving up the slick path. David took a deep breath, not wanting to go on. For a moment, he watched Moses stumble along the flooded trail ahead of him. He took another breath, but it was cut short with a painful cough. He put a drenched handkerchief to his lips and tasted blood. Quickly, he stuffed the bloody cloth back into his wet pocket and hurried to take hold of the rope he had left dragging behind his horse.

Pushing forward, the two men staggered across rocks and underbrush, their boots feeling like weights tied around their legs. David thought he had never been more miserable in his life. He wanted to stop, but he had to keep moving. As the icy rain bore down on his face and shoulders, he tried to imagine warming himself beside a crackling fire. But the image soon faded. All he could think of was the persistent chilling rain and mud that clung to his clothes and soaked into his skin.

"Daydreaming won't help us find a dry place to spend the night," David thought, chiding himself for letting his imagination wander. "Only God can help us, and I pray that He will show us mercy."

David and Moses tried to hold themselves steady as they forged their way along the treacherous trail, but suddenly, just as they were cresting a ridge, part of the trail started to give way. David let his horse go on ahead, but before he could follow after it, the crumbling path forced him to lean against the rock facing. Moses' horse wrenched free and bolted up the path into the darkness. David reached to help his interpreter, but before he could grab his hand, Moses slipped down the collapsing path. Scraping and clawing at the gushing mud, the Indian finally grabbed hold of the edge of a large rock to keep from being swept over the cliff. He tried to grasp the low branches of a nearby tree, but he couldn't reach them. All he could do was brace himself between the massive rocks as mud washed over him.

Being careful not to slip, David slowly made his way to where Moses was trapped. The wind whipped against him, hurling the stinging rain against his face. Carefully, he wrapped his arm around a slender tree trunk near the Indian. He stretched as far as he could and clasped Moses' outstretched hand. Then, with all his failing strength, he pulled his interpreter onto the path. David fell backward, coughing uncontrollably. This time he didn't bother to pull out his handkerchief. He simply wiped the blood from his lips with the back of his muddy hand and slumped against a rock.

"We can't stop here," Moses yelled through the downpour.

"I can't go on," David said, his voice raspy from the coughing.

"Yes, you can," the Indian said. "Come on. I'll help you." Moses put his arm around the missionary's shoulders and helped him back up the flooded path. Together they eventually made it to safer ground.

Once they reached a more solid path, they hurried to catch up to the horses. They found them hiding under a large oak not far up the path, having been too weak to go any farther. The men picked up the reins and continued their weary climb up the trail. After another hour of walking, they were about to give up hope of finding a place to spend the night when David thought he saw a shadow in the trees off to his right. It looked like a small Indian hut. He squinted but wasn't sure if his eyes were playing tricks on him. It was difficult to see anything clearly in the pouring rain. Grasping Moses' shoulder, he signaled him to stop.

"I think I see a hut through the trees over there," David shouted over the crashing thunder. He pointed in the direction of the shadow.

Moses nodded and, prodding the horses, followed David through the trees to their right. They slid down a short bank into a heap of broken limbs and thick underbrush. Moses pushed their way clear as David, anxious to see what was at the top of the bank, drove the horses up the vine-covered incline. Pushing limp branches and dripping vines out of their way, they scrambled up the rain-soaked slope and peered through the trees. They couldn't believe their eyes! Partially hidden in a secluded glade was an Indian bark hut. David breathed a sigh of relief. God had answered his prayers.

The two men pushed their way through the bushes and sagging boughs until they found the entrance. Before going in, they looked for a place to secure the horses and soon discovered a wooded shelter beside the hut to tie the animals for the night. Moses quickly stacked some branches between two nearby trees to give the horses added protection from the rain. After making sure the animals were safe, the two men staggered inside.

The hut was dark and musty, but relatively dry, with only a few places where the rain was dripping through the bark-covered roof. David looked around the room for some dry wood for a fire but couldn't find any. Knowing it would be a vain effort to search outside, they huddled in the dark, dripping wet. Moses stripped, hung his drenched clothes on a pole near the door, and stretched out on the floor where he instantly fell asleep. David pulled a damp, smooth buckskin from his bags and, taking off his wet clothes, wrapped it around him. Grunting from the soreness in his tired legs, he bent down and curled up on the dirt floor. As the stale, humid air enveloped him like a blanket, he stared across the room into the darkness. He took a deep breath, rested his aching head on his arm, and thanked God for His mercy in providing them a place to sleep. He coughed, a deep scratchy cough that ripped through his lungs with searing pain. Wearily, he wondered if he would make it through the night.

David shivered as a fever began to steal through his tired body. He tried to take his mind off the pain by thinking about the wonders of heaven, about how glorious it will be to sing praises to the Lord with a chorus of angels one day. Sometimes he wanted to go home to heaven more than anything in the world, but like the Apostle Paul, David knew he still had much work to do. Even though being with Christ would be more wonderful than anything he could imagine, he didn't want to die until his work among the Indians was finished. Once the light had penetrated the darkness and Christ's glory shone in all its splendor in the lives of the Indians, only then would his work be complete. Until then, he wanted to live. He wanted to live so he could once again preach to the Indians who lived in spiritual darkness along the Susquehanna River. He wanted to live so the message of Christ could be spread throughout all the tribes of North America and beyond. He still had much work to do.

"No, it isn't time to die," he whispered in the stillness of the hut.

As the rain beat against the bark hut and the thunder pealed overhead, David pulled his buckskin blanket tight around him and remembered a time when even the mere mention of dying had struck him with terror. It was shortly before his fourteenth birthday in March 1732 when his mother died. At the funeral when it came his turn to throw dirt onto her coffin, all he could feel was fear, even though he really didn't understand exactly what he was afraid of. He had already lost one parent—his father had died when he was almost nine. David could remember the grief, the sorrow of no longer going hunting with his father in the forest that surrounded the family estate, of no longer sitting at his father's feet as he led the family in daily worship and instructed them with catechism questions. He remembered the sense of loss but not the feelings of fear that haunted him as he stood before his mother's grave.

Weeping quietly, he watched his brothers lower the coffin that cradled his mother's body, and suddenly he was overcome with thoughts about his own death. He immediately admonished himself for being distracted by concerns about himself instead of grieving over the loss of his mother. But her death compelled him to consider the fleeting quality of his own life and the inescapable day when he would follow her to the grave. Death was not something he simply heard about. He had seen its icy hand choke the life out of someone he loved dearly. He had looked on the faces of not one, but two dead parents, and he was only thirteen. And now he was alone. How could he possibly walk away from their graves without considering his own life, and his own death?

After the funeral, David left his brothers and sisters at the family's modest farmhouse and went into the woods where he could be alone. He often withdrew to the solitude of the forest that bordered the Brainerd property to think and pray. He found that he could think more clearly when he was removed from the distractions of the busy world around him. Sometimes he would read the Bible under the canopy

of trees, or a favorite book beside a stream that gurgled
its way through the forest. That day he gripped the
edges of James Janeway's *A Token for Children*. The
book was filled with stories of children who had come
to know Christ as their Savior. Many of them had died
very young, but they had died with the assurance that
they would be with Christ in heaven. David loved
the book, but it bothered him in a way. As he read
about other children who had come to know Christ,
he became frightened that he did not really know the
Lord. He was afraid that if he died, he would go to
hell.

David wanted to go where his mother had gone—to
heaven. He pictured her face the night she died. She
had closed her eyes and seemed to smile. He had
waited expectantly, but she didn't open her eyes
again. As he had stared at his mother's lifeless face, he
had known that one day he would follow her into
eternity. One day he would face God and be judged
for all the things he had said and done.

The thirteen-year-old boy, his head hung low and
his eyes searching the leaf-littered field before him,
walked toward a wooded clearing near his family's
farm. Consumed in thought, he reflected on Romans
2:7–9, where Paul taught that God will "render to every man according to his deeds; to them who by patient continuance in well-doing seek for glory and
honor and immortality, eternal life; but unto them
that are contentious and do not obey the truth but
obey unrighteousness, indignation and wrath, tribula-
tion and anguish upon every soul of man that doeth
evil." David trembled at the thought of hell, the eternal punishment of evildoers, the pain and torment of

all-consuming wickedness. His young face, already chiseled into a faint mold of determination that belied his years, hardened into a mask of solemn resolve. He decided then and there that he would do everything he could to keep from being condemned on the day of judgment. He would pray all the time, read the Bible every day, go to church every Sunday. No matter how often other boys teased him for being good, he would behave for his older brother who would watch over him now that both his parents were dead.

As the sun dipped behind the forest trees and long shadows cast their ghostly forms across the stolid clearing, David closed his eyes and pictured his mother's casket being lowered into the upturned earth. He would never forget the fear of standing on the brink of her grave and feeling death and judgment hot against his neck. Opening his eyes, he peered into the sky, tears streaming down his face. For just a moment, his determination to live a good life seemed to waver as a hint of doubt, of uncertainty concerning his relationship with God, seemed to hover over him like a stray cloud. But as quickly as it had come, it disappeared. The sober resolve, the unflinching sense of purpose, the confidence in his ability to obey God's law, remained as David vowed to use every hour as preparation for that final day when he would come face to face with God.

2

Conversion

The raging storm continued to pound its way through the mountains as David tossed and turned on the cold, hard floor of the Indian hut. The pain in his head had subsided to a dull throb, but the cramping in his stomach refused to relent, and finding a comfortable position became a fruitless effort. Frustrated, David sat up, wrapped the damp blanket around his shoulders, and leaned against the sturdy wall of the hut.

His mother's death and the fears of a thirteen-year-old boy seemed to belong to another lifetime. So much had happened since that day in 1732, so many changes. One of those changes, the most important that could happen in anyone's life, came shortly after David decided to prepare for the ministry.

It was not long after his twentieth birthday when the pastor of his local church in Haddam, Connecticut had invited David to move in with him to study for the ministry. The Rev. Phineas Fiske had known the Brainerd family for years. He had developed a great deal of respect for David, whom he found to be pleasant to converse with and serious about religion. Wanting to encourage the young man to pursue a career in the ministry, he asked him to move from his family home to live with him in Haddam. The older minister had prepared a quiet room for David, giving him permission to read any of the books in his library.

In the spring of 1738 when David arrived at the modest home nestled in the center of town, his heart fluttered at the prospect of studying theology and ancient languages. Since his mother died, he had spent most of his time working in the fields at the family farm, but now he would spend entire days reading the English Puritans and the early church fathers, studying Greek, Hebrew, and Latin, and, above all else, probing the depths of the Word of God.

His studies, however, involved more than just academic matters. Mr. Fiske would often discuss practical and personal subjects with him, answering David's many questions and advising him on matters such as relationships, civic duties, church functions, and ministerial plans for the future. One day while David was reading in the study, Mr. Fiske came in and sat down across from him. The old minister leaned back in his chair, sipped from a cup of tea, and cleared his throat. David closed his book and laid it on the table in front of him, his attention now focused entirely on the older man.

"How are your studies going?" Mr. Fiske asked, twisting his gray moutache with one hand and setting down his cup of tea with the other.

"Very well, sir," David replied, the respect he had for this older man not only in his words, but in the way he look directly at the gentleman as he spoke.

"That's just fine," Mr. Fiske replied. "I am pleased by the progress you are making." David smiled because of the unexpected praise.

"I know you have learned a great deal," Mr. Fiske

continued. "But as we have discussed before, there is more to learn than what you read about in books."

David nodded in response as the pastor paused before continuing. Mr. Fiske leaned forward.

"Mr. Brainerd, I have been impressed with the need to share some insights with you, if you don't mind receiving some advice from an old pastor like me," Mr. Fiske said with a grin.

"Of course not. I mean, I would appreciate any advice you can give me. I always do," David replied earnestly.

"Well, what I have to say may seem a bit strict by the standards of most people today, but I think it is biblical and will prove helpful to you," the silver-haired pastor said, his sober eyes never leaving David's face. "Many people think it best for young people to keep one another's company. The young are meant to frolic with the young, so they say. But this is not true. It is best if young people spend most of their time with older people, those who are mature in the faith."

David was about to interject something when Mr. Fiske raised his hand to stop him.

"You don't have to say anything. I know that you don't spend much time with other young people as it is, but that could change," the pastor said. "I just wanted to advise you to be cautious, to keep the company of wiser people. Then you will find your own life much improved."

David simply nodded as the pastor paused. Mr. Fiske seemed to be considering whether he had said enough or whether he should go on. He cleared his throat and decided he still had more to say.

"My dear Mr. Brainerd, no matter how pious and mature you might think you are, youthful friends, especially those who are not serious about their relationship with God, will always have a negative influence on you. No matter how much you might want to influence them for good, God has said in His Word that you are not to keep the company of those who mock true religion. Some young people might appear to be religious, but by their actions they are scoffers of the truth. Stay away from such as these, Mr. Brainerd. Instead, spend your time with serious, mature Christians, older people who have much experience in practical godliness."

Mr. Fiske cleared his throat again. "I just wanted you to think about that as you studied your Hebrew and Latin. The relationships we form are every bit as important as the knowledge we accumulate through study."

The old pastor smiled at David, a warm, paternal smile, then pushed himself from his chair. He patted David on the shoulder, then left the room, his back stooped from the burden of a long life. David watched him as he closed the door softly behind him. He smiled as he thought of the pastor's kindness to him and how, in many ways, he had become like a father to him.

David found that he could easily take the pastor's advice because he spent most of his time studying at home, doing his chores, and attending church. The only time he met with other people his own age was on Sunday evenings when they would gather together to pray and read Scripture. Most of the time they would discuss the sermon that had been preached that day and encourage one another in spiritual duties. Besides his Sunday night meetings, though, he greatly limited the time he spent with other young people.

David greatly appreciated Mr. Fiske's instruction and advice, but his time with the wise and generous pastor would not last for long. In the fall of 1738, Mr. Fiske died of a sudden illness. David attended the funeral and found, to his relief, that he was not plagued by the fears that had stirred him so deeply when his mother died. Instead, he found comfort, not so much for himself, but for Mr. Fiske, who he knew had gone home to be with the Lord. But did David have that kind of confidence concerning his own salvation? At the time, he couldn't say that he did. He wanted to have that blessed assurance that Mr. Fiske had, but it continued to elude him. Sometimes, usually after prayer and fasting, he felt certain of his salvation. But soon his heart would grow cold, or he would consider the perfect holiness of God and see how little he measured up to His standards. Then he would sink into the depths of uncertainty once again.

With disturbing questions about his salvation churning in his mind, David packed his belongings and moved back to the Brainerd farm. There, under a deepening shadow of doubt, he would continue his studies with the help of his older brother. Just as he had done at Mr. Fiske's house, David spent his days alone, in prayer, in study, and in a continual search for peace.

David's theological studies and diligence in religious matters did not bring him the peace he expected. The doubts continued to grow. He worried constantly about his relationship with God. Was he doing enough? Was he praying enough? Was he studying enough? No matter how much he tried, he could not find peace for his troubled soul. No matter where he went or what he did, fear of judgment haunted him.

Then one winter day in 1738, his fear seemed to reach a new height. After finishing his chores, he retreated to a solitary place in the woods that lined the borders of his family's property. As he walked among the trees, he began to feel very much afraid. He felt as if he were in grave danger, not physically, but spiritually. Thoughts of all the sins he had committed flooded his mind, recent as well as past sins. He remembered all the times he had lied, disobeyed his parents when he was young, and allowed his thoughts to wander in worship or in prayer. To make himself feel better, he tried to think of some good things he had done, but he couldn't remember any. His sins just seemed to pile one on top of another, filling his thoughts like an unscalable wall, or like wild ivy that kept extending its tentacles, choking everything in its path.

David quickened his pace until he came to a clearing in the woods. He had a sickening feeling that the ground was going to open beneath him and pull him into the fiery jaws of hell. Breathing heavily, he stopped in the middle of the clearing and dropped to his knees on a bed of dry leaves, his breath billowing in the cold air before him. The frosty breeze bit into his bare hands as he folded them on his lap. He tried to pray, but the words wouldn't come, and he knew that if he died right then and there he would go straight to hell. More than anything, he wanted to feel the freedom of standing in God's presence, but it seemed as if mountains were barring his way. After kneeling there for nearly an hour, rocking back and forth, trying to cry out to God, he gave up. Then, as if fleeing to escape an unseen foe, David ran back to the house. He went straight to his room, shut the door, opened his Bible, and began to read.

"If only I study more," he thought desperately, "then God will forgive me and save me."

As he sat on the edge of his bed, he read from Ephesians 2:8–9, and was reminded that everything he had always been taught about God's sovereignty in salvation was true: "For by grace are ye saved, through faith; and that not of yourselves, it is the gift of God—not of works lest any man should boast." A sinful person could not obtain faith on his own; it was a gift from God. David repeated the verse to himself, bewildered by its emphasis on man's dependence on God for salvation. The passage taught that because people are so sinful, they do not have the ability to put their faith in Christ. Only God can change their hearts and give them faith. As David reread the verse from Ephesians over and over again, he struggled with bitter thoughts about God. He didn't really understand faith nor did he want to be totally dependent upon God to receive it. Why couldn't he be good on his own despite his sinful condition?

David's distress over his sin, his fear of going to hell, and his hatred of God's sovereignty continued until summer. He would spend hours alone in his room, afraid to look anyone in the face. Imagining that they could see how terrible, how hopeless he was, he didn't want to be around other people. He was too ashamed to be near others who had found peace with

God.

His spiritual anguish continued to increase as the months passed. Then, one day in July, everything began to change. After praying, reading his daily devotions, and doing some work in the fields, he took a walk in the woods. The late morning air was warm, the sun glowed brightly, and the birds sang in the treetops. David put his hands in his pockets and stared at the ground in front of him.

"Being a Christian is just too difficult," he thought. He kicked some dark soil with the tip of his shoe and knelt by a tree. "I've done everything I can to be good, but it's impossible to be the kind of person God wants me to be. I can't do it!"

"I just can't do it," David shouted aloud, looking up at the overhanging boughs that threw their midmorning shadows across the clearing. Suddenly, he realized something he had never understood before. He stood up and put his hands on top of his head. "That's it," he cried. "I can't do it! No matter how much I pray, how much I study Scripture, how often I attend church, I can't be good as God wants me to be. I can't save myself! I need God to save me."

David walked deeper into the woods, picked up his pace, and looked around as if seeing the world for the first time. He breathed in the sweet aromas of summer, the delicate fragrances of lilac bushes, the lively potpourri of wild flowers, pine, and tender grass. All the distress, all the depressing thoughts, all the confidence he had in his own works began to disappear. He wasn't entirely free from questions and doubts, from the chains of his self-righteousness, but the ache in his heart began to subside, the emptiness receding like darkness before the dawn.

For the next couple of days, David's attitude toward his religious duties was much different. Previously, whenever he prayed or listened to a sermon, he had thought, "Now God has to save me." But after that afternoon in the woods, he prayed because he loved the Lord, not because he thought God owed him salvation. All his life he had believed God was obligated to save him because he thought he had done so many good things. But now, he realized that God didn't owe him anything.

"I have been heaping up my devotions before God, fasting, praying and pretending, and really thinking sometimes that I have been aiming at the glory of God," David thought. "But not once did I really aim at God's glory. I was only interested in myself and my own happiness. I realize now that I have never done anything for God. I have been a hypocrite, mocking God and worshiping myself."

David continued to think about all the ways he had tried to earn God's favor, about all the times he had prayed out of his own self-interest rather than out of a love for God. He had been like a child who cleaned his room or did his chores, not because he loved his parents, but because he wanted to go outside and play or get some kind of reward. Every time David had done something for God, he had thought God would do something for him. When he finally realized the game he had been playing, he was ashamed, and he wanted to change, not just in a small way, but thoroughly so that his life would be completely devoted to God.

The following Sunday afternoon, he returned once

again to his private refuge in the woods. Kneeling on the soft grass, he tried to pray, but no words would come. The mountains of darkness within his own soul, those barriers of sin that had kept him from worshiping God so many times before, loomed before him. After kneeling there for half an hour, he began to despair. "Why can't I pray?" he asked himself, his voice quivering. Trembling, he stood up and walked into a thick grove. The branches brushed his face and arms, but he didn't notice. He kept walking, hoping he would be able to pray. Then suddenly the mountains of sin that barred his passage to God began to fade, overcome, leveled by the power of God's sovereign grace. The fear that had haunted him, that had plagued him as he knelt on the summer grass, began to disappear, replaced by a joy, a sense of peace that he had never known in all of his twenty-one years. The burdens that had weighed heavily upon his mind were instantly lifted, like the sun piercing through the mangled branches above him.

"It wasn't like I saw any external brightness, for I saw no such thing," David wrote later in his daily journal. "Nor did I imagine seeing any light somewhere in the heavens, or anything like that. But it was a new realization inside of me, a new understanding of God, such as I had never had before. I stood still, wondered, and admired! I knew that I never had seen before anything so beautiful and excellent in my life. It was different from any conception I had ever had of God before. I was perfectly content just to be still and contemplate the wonderful glory of God. My soul was so captivated by the loveliness, greatness, and other perfections of God that I was swallowed up in Him. I totally forgot about myself, and only thought of God."

David remained within the grove until dark. All the frustration of trying to earn God's favor melted away. The fears of being condemned by God in His holy judgment subsided as he put his trust in Christ's righteousness instead of his own. His thoughts were filled with the excellence of Jesus Christ and the glory of his heavenly Father. He felt overwhelmed by the glory of God just as one might feel when he sees for the first time the purple majesty of a mountain range against the crimson hues of an evening sky. It's so beautiful it hardly seems real, and words fail to grasp its glory. All David could do was stand there and gasp at the unimaginable beauty of Christ. It was as if someone had spread all his favorite foods on the table in front of him, and he wanted to taste every delectable morsel. He savored every attribute of God—His love, His mercy, His holiness, His power, and His sovereignty.

The sun began to set, the grove grew dark, but he didn't notice. Filled with awe and reverence for God, he wanted to stay there and worship his Savior. As the darkness settled around him, he leaned against the harsh bark of a tree and let the tears roll down his face. He felt like the prodigal son who had crawled back home in shame and disgrace, expecting to be treated as a slave in his father's house, but instead being swept into his father's loving arms. God loved him no matter how many wrong things he had done in his life. God loved him enough to send His only Son to die for him on a cross. God loved him enough to send His Holy Spirit to change his heart, to reshape him—by the power of His grace—from a slave burdened by sin into a son reflecting the holiness of his heavenly Father. David knew he could do nothing to earn so great a love. God gave it freely, and, with faith given from above, he received his Father's gracious gift of salvation in Jesus Christ.

3

The Price of Ambition

A crashing thunderclap that sounded like the collision of armored warriors shattered David's thoughts, bringing him back to the cold darkness of the Indian hut. The storm was continuing its fierce rampage through the Pennsylvania mountains, keeping him from much-needed sleep. As he stretched out on the dirt floor of the hut, listening to the roaring thunder, the memory of that glorious afternoon in the glade faded from his mind. Wistfully, the young missionary wished that every day since the time of his conversion had been as peaceful. Sadly, one of the most difficult and frustrating periods of his life came the following year.

It began in the fall of 1739 after he arrived at Yale College in New Haven, Connecticut, not far from his hometown. Like many other young men, he attended the college to prepare for the ministry. Determined to perform well at school, he threw himself headlong into his studies and gave little thought to his physical health. Every night he would study late, robbing himself of essential rest, and as the fall quarter drew to a close, David's study habits grew even more intense.

One night in early winter, the hours ticked by as he read book after book to review for an upcoming exam. David leaned across the table to thumb through a pile of large volumes. Moving the candle closer for more light, he skimmed the titles, but the book he needed wasn't there. Carefully, he checked the stack on the floor beside him, but it wasn't there either. Sighing, he picked up the candle. Wax splashed on the table and dribbled on the floor as he walked toward the shelves in the back of the still library. From the shadowed cases, books filled with more knowledge than David would ever have time to read stared down at him in the dim light. The candlelight flickered across their antique bindings as he made his way through the dusty corridors of leather tomes. As he passed through the dusky passageway, no other sound could be heard except the echo of his footsteps. All the other students had gone back to their rooms hours ago, but David would study all night if he thought he needed more preparation. The exam would be difficult, and he wanted to do well. If he made high marks, he would finish the quarter at the top of his class.

As he walked among the massive shelves bursting with books, his chest suddenly began to burn, sending him into a coughing fit. He leaned against a bookcase to steady himself. He shook his head, frustrated with himself. The coughing spell brought to mind a resolution he had made the day he left for the scholarly halls of Yale College. Early in September, at the age of twenty-two, he had traveled from his home in Haddam with just a few clothes and some books. He had been nervous the day he had set out for college, concerned that the pressure of study would keep him too busy to spend time with the Lord and too busy to care for his physical needs, to rest and eat properly. He had recognized, before he even left for college, his tendency to let determination and ambition drive him beyond physical limitations. To guard against the temptation, he had told himself not to risk becoming sick by trying to do too much.

David shrugged off the memory of his resolution, telling himself that he had too much work to worry about his health. He wiped his mouth with a worn handkerchief and continued to walk through a dark hallway in the back of the library. He stopped in front of a section labeled "Church History" and ran his finger across the bindings until it rested on one with a frayed blue cover. He pulled the book free and walked back to the book-strewn table where he had been working. The candle he was holding burned low and began to sputter. He lit another one and settled back in his chair with the old book spread in front of him.

Behind him, a door creaked open, and the sound of footsteps echoed through the quiet library. David turned around to see one of his classmates walking toward him.

"Hello, David, I was just checking to see whether any candles were left burning in the library," he said in a hushed voice, unable to bring himself to speak loudly in a library even when no one else was there. "I should have known it was you."

"I had some reading to do," David responded, looking up from the book.

"You look worn out," his friend said. "When was the last time you ate something?"

David thought for a moment but couldn't remember. He shrugged.

"You need to take better care of yourself," the

young man chided. "You don't want to become ill, then what good will you be? You had better be careful. Some students in history class have come down with the measles, and I've heard it's spreading through the whole college."

"Don't worry about me," David replied wearily. "I'll get some rest soon. I just need to finish this one book."

"All right. Don't forget to blow out the candles when you leave," his friend said as he shut the library door behind him.

David read for another hour before returning to his room. There, in the chilly darkness, he collapsed onto his bed, not bothering to change his clothes.

At the beginning of the second quarter, he became so consumed with study that he grew increasingly depressed and frustrated over the little time he spent with the Lord. He did not feel close to God, and he knew his preoccupation with study had caused his fire for spiritual duties to burn low. His prayers were not as fervent as they had been, and he did not sense the presence of God as he had during previous months. He felt as if he hadn't seen his best friend since he had arrived at college.

One evening in late January, David took a walk to pray and be alone with the Lord. As the winter sun slowly set, he strolled along the borders of the college property, away from distractions and the chatter of students. It was freezing as the evening wind whipped across his path, but David didn't mind. The only sound to be heard was the snow crunching beneath his boots. In the stillness, he meditated on Psalm 23: "Though I walk through the valley of the shadow of death, Thou art with me. Thy rod and Thy staff, they comfort me." The words of the psalmist soothed David's disquieted soul as they brought to mind assurances of God's protecting and abiding love. Once again he sensed the presence of God and felt the freedom to pray. After he had walked to the edge of the college property and back again, David hurried to his room, ready to face anything for the Lord's sake.

A few days later, he suddenly fell ill. It was early in the evening, and he had just left the dining hall to stroll across campus when he felt faint. He ran to his room and leaned over the wash basin, trying to steady himself. Splashing some water on his face and looking into the mirror, he noticed some red spots on his face. He sat down on his bed and pulled a blanket around him. A chill swept through his body, and beads of perspiration formed on his forehead. He wiped them away with his shirt sleeve.

"Oh, no," he moaned. "I've got the measles."

The next day, one of David's professors visited him in his room to see how he was doing. When he saw the red blotches and felt David's high fever, he advised him to go home where friends and family could properly take care of him. That day, David rode on horseback to Haddam to stay with his sister Spenser. While he was traveling, his fever soared, and he felt faint most of the time. Finally, he arrived at his sister's house, nearly falling off his horse from exhaustion. His brother-in-law cradled the young man in his arms and carried him to the guest bedroom where he stayed for the next few days, tossing and turning from the burning fever. He became so ill at one point that his brothers and sisters feared he might die.

But one day, just as his family was about to lose hope, his fever broke. He was then able to sleep soundly and eat a complete meal. After that, he recovered quickly. He rested in bed for about a week, spending the time in meditation, study, and prayer. Even when he was sick, David could not waste his time in idleness. He believed it was his duty before God to be active—and being sick was no excuse.

As he grew stronger, he became anxious to return to his studies. Time was slipping away, and he didn't want to fall behind in his first-year courses. His sister insisted that he remain in bed until he had fully recovered, but David wanted to get back to school. He reassured her and his brothers that he had enough strength to travel. After packing his clothes and books, he saddled his horse, said goodbye to his family, and rode back to New Haven.

For the next few weeks David threw himself into his studies in the same way as he had before he became ill. Determined to make good marks and learn as much as possible, he studied late into the night. In the mornings, he woke up early for devotions, prayer, and meditation, but he still missed being able to spend more time with the Lord. He longed for the days at Mr. Fiske's home when he would spend hours reading the Bible. In just a year, he had read through the Bible twice. David regretted that much of that time was lost on his hardened and self-righteous heart. But God had been gracious and used much of what he had learned to bring him to a conviction of his self-righteousness and hypocrisy. But now that he had a heart and mind that were able to know God, he didn't spend the time with Him as he once had. Even though many of his classes were biblical studies of one sort or another, it was not the same as engaging in personal, quiet, reflective communion with the Lord.

Burdened with regrets concerning the little time he spent in prayer and meditation, but spurred on by ambition to perform well in his collegiate studies, David continued an exhaustive pace until the following August. Then, while listening to a lecture one summer afternoon, he began to lose focus. He squinted and rubbed his eyes but couldn't shake the light-headed feeling that had overcome him. Even though he hadn't felt well the previous day, he had spent most of the night studying. Tired and weak from so little rest, he barely had the strength to sit in his chair and concentrate on the professor's lecture. He was about to leave to get a drink of water when he started coughing. David grabbed a handkerchief and put it to his mouth. He tasted blood.

The professor paused in the middle of his lecture.

"Mr. Brainerd, are you all right?" the professor asked.

David shook his head. He didn't have the strength to respond. A student sitting next to him took him by the shoulders and helped him out of the room. The professor followed. Once out in the hallway, the student ran to fetch David some water while the professor helped him outside to get some fresh air.

"I think you have been pushing yourself too hard, Mr. Brainerd," his teacher gently chided as he helped the pale young man sit down on the steps. "I think you need to put away your books and go home for awhile. Get your strength back. You can return to college later in the fall."

David reluctantly took his advice and, with the help of some other students, made arrangements to return home once again. He spent the next few months recovering not only physically, but spiritually. He prayed, took quiet walks in the woods, and enjoyed the worship of God on Sundays. As the weeks flew by, the pressures of school faded from his mind, and he was able to focus on his relationship with the Lord. His sickness had driven him away from his studies, but it drew him closer to God. It allowed him to put away the pressures of college to seek God in prayer, to delight in the study of His Word, and to fellowship with Him throughout the day.

As the weeks passed, David regained his strength, but he did not look forward to returning to school as he had previously. When he had gone home earlier that year, deathly ill and in need of much rest, he couldn't wait to get back to school. But this time, he was not so eager to face the hectic schedule that sapped his time with God and tempted him to place his own ambitions over the practical necessity of caring for his health. But despite his misgivings, he needed to return. So, in early November as the morning frost covered the road to New Haven, he set off from home to enter his second year at Yale College.

4

Revival

Shortly after David's return to Yale, a spiritual revival swept across New England, catching the college in its path. People who formerly had been strangers to Christianity suddenly became concerned for their souls. Men, women, and children from all walks of life flooded the churches to hear how they might be saved. Everywhere one went—in the markets, in the fields, in the schools—people were excitedly talking about Jesus Christ. Sunday worship services were packed. As preachers thundered from the pulpits, warning sinners of the coming wrath and proclaiming the Good News of redemption, the congregations would cry out praising God for the forgiveness they had found in Jesus Christ.

David found himself deeply affected by the revival as he took great joy in seeing more people become serious about religion. Whenever an evangelist would come to town, David would go to hear him preach. He was drawn to those men who appeared to be so devoted to the Lord, so filled with a desire for others to come to know Christ in a saving way—men like Gilbert Tennent and George Whitefield, both preachers whose names have become synonymous with the Great Awakening. David basked in their presence, as did many of the other students.

This fervor, however, caused some problems at the college. Many of the students, inflamed with excitement about the revival, became judgmental of their professors. The students compared them to the evangelists and found them lacking in the religious zeal that so greatly characterized the guest preachers. In the students' minds, some of the professors seemed empty of spiritual life; they were all show but no substance. As a result, many of the students began to question the religious sincerity of the professors and even went so far as to call them hypocrites. To deal with the mounting tension between the students and the faculty, the trustees of Yale issued an edict that any student who called a professor a hypocrite would be expelled from the college. The rector thought the best way to deal with the situation was to keep the students away from the evangelists. To obtain that end, he announced that any student who left New Haven to attend the services of a traveling preacher would be fined.

These prohibitions caused quite a stir among the students—including David, who was very supportive of the visiting evangelists. He simply could not contain his excitement over the changes he witnessed among the students and the townspeople. Everywhere he went in the college and in the town, he heard religious conversation: students and townspeople talking about the holiness of God; merchants and farmers talking about the grace they had found in Christ. Almost everyone appeared serious about religion, and David praised God for the outpouring of His grace on New Haven.

He was also thankful for witnessing firsthand the

changes in students' lives. Of particular concern to David was a student who had always lacked godly devotion in the past. But one day, after hearing a powerful sermon by Mr. Tennent, the student's attitude toward God changed dramatically.

"Did you hear the sermon Sunday morning?" the student asked David at meal time. "When the preacher described how Christ died on the cross to save me from my sins, I started crying and couldn't stop! I couldn't help myself."

David was delighted to hear such a confession from his schoolmate, who previously had not cared about religious matters. David had actually heard him snoring during the preacher's sermon one Sunday. The student commonly slept through church services and never mentioned anything about Christianity during the week. Seeing him excited about a sermon was a surprise to everyone, especially David.

"Why did you feel the need to cry during the sermon?" David asked, wanting to gain a better understanding of the young man's experience.

"I realized for the first time how sinful I was," he replied thoughtfully. "And I suddenly saw the love and mercy of Christ like I never had before. He gave up His life for people who didn't deserve it. He died for me! The only thing I deserve is eternal punishment, but God chose to save me, not because of anything I had done, but because of His love and compassion."

The student smiled and thought for a moment. His eyes filled with tears. He looked at David and said, "That's why I cried. For the first time, I loved God for who He is, not for who I wanted Him to be. For

the first time, I realized not only how holy God is, but
how merciful."

David reached across the table and handed the
young man a handkerchief to wipe away his tears. "It's
just as Micah 7:18 says, 'Who is a God like unto Thee,
who pardoneth iniquity, and passeth by the transgression of the remnant of His heritage? He retaineth
not His anger forever, because He delighteth to show
mercy.'"

More tears fell onto the young man's cheeks as he
listened to David quote the Old Testament verse.

"Listen," David said, "two other students and I
are getting together in the evenings for prayer and
fellowship. Would you like to join us?"

"I'd love to," he replied.

The following Sunday, David's new friend joined
him at services. The chapel was bursting with students, all excited to see what God would do among
them that day. As the congregation began to sing a
psalm, many of the students appeared greatly affected
by the music. They cried and knelt on the floor, their
heads bowed, tears streaming down their cheeks.
Many continued to weep and carry on throughout the
sermon. One student fell into such a fit that he had to
be helped from the meeting room. From the back of
the chapel, David watched the commotion with concern.

"Could all these religious affections be real?" he
asked himself. "Surely, some of these people are just
caught up in the moment, and are letting their
emotions get the better of them. They don't really
appear to be moved by an awareness of the excellency
of God or by their sins, but only by the stirrings of

their own emotions."

David's fears were confirmed when later he talked with the young man who had been carried from the meeting room.

"What happened to you during worship?" David asked the student.

"I don't know," the young man stammered. "I just started crying and couldn't stop."

"Did you have a new realization of your sin or a new understanding of God?" David asked.

"I don't really know what you're talking about," he replied. "It's not about sin or anything like that. I was just overwhelmed by all these feelings about God. They seemed to well up inside of me."

"What things about God made you feel that way?" David asked.

"I don't know," the student said. "Nothing specific."

After talking with the young man, David wondered if some false enthusiasm, stirrings of emotion without a true love of God and His ways, might have crept into the revival at the college. One evening after an assembly meeting of the entire college, David mentioned his concerns to a classmate who appeared to share his view.

"It's not that I'm against showing emotion in public worship," David explained. "I know how emotional spiritual change can be. It should be emotional, and different people will express those emotions according to their experience and their personalities—some might be more expressive than others. I have certainly been just as zealous, if not more so, than any other student during the past few months. But I also know how easy it can be to get caught up in the singing and the passion of the preacher without ever having a change of heart."

"I see what you mean," his friend replied. "I think even some of the faculty members have gotten a little carried away. It seems like Mr. Whittelsey's prayers are more like a performance to excite our emotions than a sincere prayer to the Lord."

David agreed. He had noticed the dramatic prayers of Mr. Chauncey Whittelsey, but the professor seemed untouched by any deep spiritual change. He was a kind man, but, as David saw it, he just didn't have the zeal of the visiting evangelists, which was legitimate grounds for questioning the sincerity of his religion—at least according to the students. And besides that, David had already seen too many examples of people who appeared to be religious but really weren't. Such things caused David to be concerned about the sincerity of Mr. Whittelsey's profession of faith.

As the two young men continued to talk, one of their friends joined them. The three often met to discuss their spiritual struggles, to pray, and to encourage one another in their studies.

"We were just discussing Mr. Whittelsey," David said to his friend.

"What do you think of him?" the student asked hesitantly, realizing that he was treading on dangerous ground, considering the trustees' decree that forbade judgments being made about faculty.

David looked down, gripped the back of a chair, and thought for a moment. "I think he has no more grace than this chair," he replied gravely. He didn't make the comment lightly because he realized how easily people can be deceived into thinking that God has renewed their hearts when He hasn't. Jesus often warned the disciples to watch for hypocrites. He said they would know true believers by their fruit, and as David saw it, Mr. Whittelsey didn't bear any true spiritual fruit—except for exceptionally eloquent prayers.

As the three talked in the meeting room, a first-year student walked by in the hallway. David and his friends didn't hear him and assumed they were alone. When the young man heard them talking, he paused long enough to overhear David's comment. He missed the first part of the conversation so he did not know whom they were talking about, but he recognized David's voice.

The next day, the student told the story to a woman from New Haven, who was well-known for being a busybody and a gossip. When he told her that David Brainerd had made the disrespectful comment about a faculty member, she didn't waste any time reporting it to the rector, Thomas Clap. The rector became livid at the thought of a second-year student daring to make such a judgment about one of the professors at the college, and he wanted to get to the bottom of the matter. When he heard that David Brainerd was the one who made the comment, he became even more angry. He had thought many times during the past few months that David's promotion of personal piety among the students was extreme, that he seemed overly zealous and, in the rector's opinion, self-righteous in his desire to see others take religion seriously. But most of all, the rector believed that David

Brainerd was the type of student who was responsible for conflicts brought on by the revival, for the attitudes of judgment toward the faculty, and for the reckless admiration of visiting evangelists among the students.

Anxious to deal with the problem, Mr. Clap sent for the young man who had overheard the conversation.

"I want you to tell me everything you heard," the rector demanded.

The student cleared his throat. "I was walking by the meeting hall last night when I overheard Mr. Brainerd say, 'He has no more grace than this chair.' I couldn't see Mr. Brainerd, but I did see who was with him," the student said. He fidgeted with the hem of his jacket and looked at the floor in front of him.

"And you think they were talking about one of the professors at the college?" Mr. Clap asked.

"Yes, sir, I think so. But I don't know who," the first-year student replied.

"Very well, tell me the names of the other two students, and then you can go," Mr. Clap said, pointing to the door.

The rector summoned the two students named by the young man, and they arrived at his office that afternoon.

"What do you think he wants?" one of David's friends asked.

The door opened, and Mr. Clap called them inside.

"I have no idea," the other replied. "I guess we're about to find out."

"Gentlemen, please have a seat," the rector said,

motioning them to the two chairs in front of his desk. "I'm going to get right to the point. Someone has informed me that Mr. Brainerd has called one of our professors a hypocrite. I want you to tell me who he was talking about and exactly what he said."

Puzzled, the two students looked at each other.

"We have not heard David speak ill of anyone," one of the students replied as the other nodded in agreement.

"I know for a fact that he said something about one of the professors during a conversation with you in the meeting hall last night," the rector explained.

The students appeared more puzzled than before. How could the rector have known about that conversation, when no one else had been in the room?

"We were having a private conversation, sir," one of the students blurted out. "David did not gossip about anyone."

"Sir, David would never purposely speak ill of anyone," the other added.

"I realize Mr. Brainerd is your friend, but I happen to know for a fact that he did call one of our faculty a hypocrite. Now, I want to know what he said exactly," Mr. Clap demanded, standing up and slamming his fists on the desk. He leaned forward and glared at the two students.

"Don't you think it would be best to ask David what he said, sir?" one of the young men stammered. "If we have a problem with someone, we should always go to them first."

The rector's face turned scarlet. He tightened his fists, the knuckles turning white.

"Don't you presume to lecture me," he bellowed.

"I want you to tell me what happened or you will regret it."

The two looked at each other again.

"We were discussing Mr. Whittelsey when I asked David what he thought of him," one of the young men said, looking up at the rector.

"David said, 'He has no more grace than this chair,' or something to that effect," the other added. "He didn't say it to gossip, sir. He was concerned about false religion that might have crept into the college."

The student's comment didn't seem to help the situation. Appearing angrier than before, Mr. Clap turned around and stared out the window.

"Thank you, gentlemen. You may leave now," he said without turning.

The two young men hurried from the room and quietly shut the door, leaving the rector staring out the window, his hands drawn into clenched fists and his mouth set in a tight grimace.

5

Caught in the Crossfire

After the two second-year students hurried from the administration building, Mr. Clap sent a messenger to David, ordering him to come to his office at once. He was studying in the library when he received the message and had no idea why the rector would want to see him so urgently. Leaving his books on the table, he walked hastily to the administrative office. Softly, he knocked on the rector's door and, finding it partially open, stepped inside.

"Mr. Brainerd, please have a seat," Mr. Clap commanded as he stared out the window, not bothering to turn around. David sat down.

"I hear you have been taking the liberty of making public judgments about members of our faculty."

David was speechless. He didn't know what the rector was talking about.

"Don't play innocent with me. I want to know what you said in the meeting hall last night to your two revival friends," the rector sneered.

"I don't know what you mean," David replied.

"I want to know what you said to them," Mr. Clap repeated as he stood behind the desk, his fists clenched at his hips.

David thought for a moment and then suddenly

realized which part of the conversation the rector was talking about.

"We were having a private conversation," David said. "With all due respect, sir, I don't know what concern that is of yours or anyone else's."

The rector slammed his fist onto the desk.

"You have spoken ill of a leader of this college, and I want to know exactly what you said," he seethed. "Either you tell me or you and your fellow students will face severe consequences."

David tried to sit still and choose his words carefully.

"We were talking about the revival—"

"I don't care about the revival! I want to know specifically what you said about one of our instructors," Mr. Clap snapped.

"All right, sir. One of the students asked me what I thought of Mr. Whittelsey, and I said, 'He has no more grace than this chair.' I was not gossiping, sir—"

"Thank you, Mr. Brainerd, that was all I needed to hear," Mr. Clap said coolly.

"But, sir, don't you want to hear the context?" David pleaded.

"I don't need to hear it. I know what was going on. You have totally disregarded the trustees' edict that no student is to call a professor a hypocrite. It is not your place to make such judgments about your superiors. But you have violated this order from the board because of your holier-than-thou attitude, which has only been encouraged by those visiting evangelists. You think you are such an expert on religious matters," Mr. Clap said, sarcasm biting into his words. Without finishing the sentence, he walked to the window again. "Anyway, it doesn't matter. You publicly defamed the character of one of our faculty members, and you will publicly apologize to the entire college."

"But, sir, I did not publicly defame Mr. Whittelsey," David argued. "It was a private conversation. No one else was in the room."

"Well, someone was in the hallway, and he overheard you," Mr. Clap said, turning to catch David's reaction of unbelief. "I called your two friends in here, and they confirmed what happened."

"Why didn't you come to me first, sir?" David asked. "I was the one accused. You should have dealt with me directly."

"It doesn't matter now," Mr. Clap replied. He turned and walked back to his desk. "First, you will apologize to Mr. Whittelsey this evening. Second, you will stand before the entire college at the meeting hall tomorrow night and confess what you have done."

"But I have plans to go to a revival meeting in town tonight," David said, a little hesitantly.

"I forbid you to go to the meeting. You have obviously attended too many of them already," the rector bellowed. "You will stay in your room, and then you will go and apologize to Mr. Whittelsey."

"I will apologize to Mr. Whittelsey. I realize now that I have shown disrespect to one in authority, that I had no right making judgments about his religious character," David replied, dropping the subject of the meeting. "But because I did not make the comment publicly, I will not confess publicly."

"You had better reconsider," he warned. "If you

do not apologize before the entire college you could face expulsion."

David knew the board would not expel him on such grounds. The edict the trustees had issued stated that a student would be expelled only on his second offense. On the first offense, he would have to make a public apology. But David thought a public apology would be required only if the student made the comment in public. Confident that he was in the right, David resolved then and there not to confess before the college the following night.

"You may leave now," Mr. Clap said. "I expect to see you at the meeting hall tomorrow night."

David left the room, not stopping to shut the door behind him.

That night, several of the students gathered to attend the meeting in New Haven. David went with them despite the rector's order that he stay at the college. Somehow the rector found out about it, and the next day he sent a message to David, telling him that he would have to answer for his blatant disobedience. David read the message and slumped on the edge of his bed. He put his head in his hands and asked himself why he had to go and make things worse by disobeying the rector's orders. He knew he had been wrong to disobey, but he had gone to the meeting anyway. Now he wondered what consequences he would face because of his disobedience.

That evening when the students and faculty gathered at the meeting hall, David arrived with his classmates. As he entered the dimly lit hall, he spotted the rector talking with Mr. Whittelsey near the faculty table. David made his way through the crowd to where the two college leaders were huddled. As he walked up to them, Mr. Whittelsey straightened and cleared his throat.

"Are you ready to make your public confession, Mr. Brainerd?" Mr. Clap asked. "I have already informed Mr. Whittelsey of the situation."

"No, sir," David replied. "I will not publicly apologize for something I said in a private conversation. However, I do want to apologize to Mr. Whittelsey since I didn't do it last night."

David turned to Mr. Whittelsey.

"Mr. Whittelsey, I have sinned against you and against God," David confessed. "I have injured you and for that I humbly ask your forgiveness. I had no right to speak so freely about your character, and my sin is aggravated by the fact that you are my superior. I am obligated to treat you with honor and respect, and it was not my place to say what I did. I must confess that my behavior has not become that of a Christian."

David took a long breath and looked the gray-haired professor in the eye.

"In saying what I did, I took too much upon myself," he continued. "I was presumptuous and did not give you the respect you deserve. For that, I sincerely apologize and beg your forgiveness."

Mr. Whittelsey cleared his throat. "I do forgive you," he told David, "but I do not think that will keep you from facing the judgment of the board. Your comment about the rector will not be kindly received by the trustees."

"What are you talking about, sir?" David asked, bewildered by these new accusations.

The rector stepped between David and Mr.

Whittelsey. "Someone told me that you said, and I quote, that you hoped I would 'drop dead' because I fined some students for going to Milford last week to hear one of those revivalists."

David's mouth hung open. He didn't know what to say. He had heard about the students getting into trouble, but he had never said anything about the rector.

"What is all this about?" David sputtered, now more confused than ever.

"You said that you expected me to 'drop dead,' " Mr. Clap replied, his brow furrowed. "You will pay for this! Now, go up there and publicly confess."

"I will not, sir," David said firmly. "I have already explained why I will not confess. And as for the comment someone claims I said about you, I said no such thing."

"Then prepare to meet the trustees," Mr. Clap said, and, with a nod to Mr. Whittelsey, he stormed out of the room.

Several weeks went by following David's confrontation with the rector as various faculty members, the trustees, and Mr. Clap discussed David's situation. A number of professors who were supportive of the revival and who thought the rector was being unduly harsh spoke on David's behalf. They pointed out that he was at the top of his class and a fine student, but nothing would change the rector's mind. Mr. Clap believed David should be expelled for defaming the character of his superiors on two occasions, refusing to confess publicly, and attending a meeting in New Haven when he had been told not to go. Despite David's repeated claims that he had said nothing disrespectful concerning Mr. Clap, the trustees were inclined to agree with the rector even though it was only his first offense.

In the winter of 1742, David's third year at college, he met with the board. When they questioned him about his comments concerning Mr. Whittelsey, he humbly confessed his transgression and explained how he had apologized to the professor.

"Why would you not confess your crime publicly?" one of the trustees asked him during his examination.

"It was a private conversation," David replied.

"And what about the comment you made concerning the rector?" another trustee asked.

"I do not recall making any statement of the kind," David said calmly. "I know I didn't say it."

"Did you go to a meeting in New Haven despite the rector's order for you not to go?" one of the trustees asked.

"Yes, and I humbly apologize to Mr. Clap for disobeying him," David said, looking at the rector who sat at the far end of the table. "I was wrong. I sinned against him and against God. I should never have gone into town that night."

"Thank you, Mr. Brainerd. I think we have heard enough," Mr. Clap said. "You may wait in the hall."

David settled into a large chair in the dusky hallway outside the meeting room. He gazed up at the high ceiling. The carved figures on the walls stared coldly back at him. They seemed to sneer and laugh as the flickering candlelight danced across their stone faces. David looked down at his feet and prayed that God would be merciful to him and allow him to remain at the college. Other students had tried to encourage him. They had agreed that he had been unfairly treated, but David had given up defending himself. He admitted he had been wrong. The rest was in God's hands.

The door to the conference room swung open, and one of the trustees asked him to step inside. Looking at the floor in front of him, he walked in and sat down in the same chair he had previously occupied. The trustees watched David with grim, serious eyes.

"After examination of the evidence, we have decided that you, David Brainerd, are to be expelled from Yale College," Mr. Clap announced. "Your conduct is not worthy of a student of this college. You may prepare to leave immediately."

David remained in his chair a moment, too stunned to move. He felt as if an arrow had pierced his heart. He couldn't believe all his hard work had ended like this. What would he do? How could he deal with the shame of being expelled? He tried to calm himself. After a few minutes, he stood up, looked each trustee in the eye, then left the room. He shut the conference door quietly behind him and hurried across campus, the cold winter air stinging his cheeks.

Once he arrived at his room, he packed his few belongings and said goodbye to some friends who were grieved to see their classmate leave under such dishonorable circumstances. Many of them complained that the board was using David as an example of what might happen to those who continued to follow after the visiting evangelists. The trustees had done everything in their power to get the revival under control. They had issued another edict forbidding preachers who had not graduated from Harvard or Yale to preach in New Haven. And now they had expelled David Brainerd, one of the most outspoken students in support of the revivalists. The students suspected that there was more going on in David's expulsion than punishment for his comment about Mr. Whittelsey. David brushed all the speculation aside. He had been expelled, and nothing was going to change that.

In the fading afternoon light, he rode north across campus. The formidable halls of the college threw their long shadows across his path as he made his way to the entrance. Passing through the front gate, he glanced over his shoulder. He felt no bitterness, only the pain of a broken heart and the humiliation of an outcast. The doors that had once swung wide open to welcome him to a life of study and scholarship had slammed shut. Only God would be able to pry them open again. With one last glance back at the shadowed halls, David nudged his horse toward the road that led to Haddam.

"God's will be done," he whispered and rounded the bend toward home.

6

The Fire is Lit

David walked around the bark hut, stretching his legs. He hoped the movement would help ease the cramping in his stomach. He reflected on the day the trustees had expelled him from Yale College. It had been one of the worst days of his life. He had left college not knowing where to go or what to do. Dejected but trusting in God, he had gone home, still wanting to be a minister but lacking direction. David had thought it would be a long time before he would discover which direction God wanted him to take, but as it turned out, it was sooner than he had expected.

A few months after his expulsion, he had gone to visit a pastor in a neighboring town to seek advice on making an appeal to be reaccepted into the college. Many pastors throughout New England had heard of David's expulsion, and those who were supportive of the revival wanted to help him. They thought the board's decision to expel David was ultimately an attack on the revivalists. The rector and members of the board were suspicious of the revivalists and claimed that they were introducing false teaching into the churches. But one pastor told David that the rector and others actually envied the success of the revivalists, and in reaction used David's transgression to send a warning: preaching by visiting evangelists would not be allowed in New Haven. Because many of the local pastors believed David had been unjustly treated, they did everything they could to help him in his studies, in his preparations for ministry, and in his effort to be reinstated to Yale College.

It was at the church of one such pastor that David visited a few months after he had been expelled. The warm day whispered of spring, and rocks glistened on the winding path that led him to the front of the Stratford church. He knocked on the thick, oak door, and a woman wearing a quilted shawl answered. When she saw who it was, her face brightened.

"Good afternoon, Mr. Brainerd. Are you here to see Pastor Cooke?" she asked.

"Yes," he replied. "I hope I'm not disturbing him."

"No, of course not," she said with a modest smile. "He is always so pleased to see you. Would you like to wait in the hallway while I fetch him?"

"That's all right. I'll wait here in the garden and enjoy the nice day," he said, looking around at the rainbow of flowers surrounding him.

"Please make yourself comfortable," she said. "I'll tell Mr. Cooke to meet you in the garden."

As the young lady shut the heavy door behind her, David walked down the steps and strolled through the garden that surrounded the Stratford church. Since the day of his expulsion from Yale College, he had been visiting various ministers in Stratford, Southbury, and Bethlehem. He had moved in with Mr. Jedediah Mills of Ripton, who promised to help him finish his college requirements on his own. Mr. Cooke had also been assisting him in his studies and allowing him to preach on occasion.

"Hello, David," Mr. Cooke said from behind him.

David turned around and grasped his mentor's outstretched hand.

"Good afternoon, Mr. Cooke," David said, smiling. "Thank you for visiting with me today. I was on my way home to Ripton and wanted to talk to you about something I've been considering. I'll only keep you for a few minutes. I know you are very busy."

"I'd love to talk with you. But first, how's the Reverend Mills doing these days?" the old minister asked.

"He's doing just fine," David answered. "He has been a great encouragement to me since my expulsion, and I'm so thankful that he is helping me with my studies."

The two walked side by side through the garden, engulfed in the sweet fragrances of flower beds and the rich aromas of upturned soil. Mr. Cooke paused in front of an old wooden bench.

"Have a seat and tell me what's on your mind," he said, motioning for David to sit beside him.

The young man sat down and rested his elbows on his knees. He looked straight ahead, focusing on a row of sun-soaked daffodils that swayed in the breeze.

"I've been thinking about asking the board of governors at Yale to restore me to the college," David explained.

"Well, I think that would be a splendid idea, and it's providential that you would want to make the request now," Mr. Cooke replied, putting his hand on David's shoulder.

David straightened up. "What do you mean?"

"A number of local ministers have discussed speaking to the rector and the trustees on your behalf. What would you think about that?"

David thought for a moment.

"Well, I don't know," he said a little hesitantly, not wanting to get his hopes up but unable to forego an opportunity to return to college. "When could I meet with them to talk about it?"

"A council of ministers meets at Hartford next month. You could go there and tell them your side of the story. I'm sure that after hearing what you have to say, they will do everything they can to see you reinstated."

"I know a number of pastors in the Hartford area," David replied with growing excitement. "I'll take your advice and go there next month and give them an account of the whole situation."

"Wonderful," Mr. Cooke said, slapping David gently on the back. He stood up, grunting as his old knees cracked. "I will pray that God's will be done in this matter. Until then, give my best to Mr. Mills upon your return to Ripton."

"I will, and thank you for your help, sir," David said, picking up his hat from the bench.

"Oh, before you go, there's something you need to know," Mr. Cooke said. His expression suddenly turned gravely serious. "The board of trustees at Yale has issued another edict. No visiting preachers are allowed to preach in New Haven. I know that you have preached there recently, and I just wanted you to be aware of the risk. The board has stated that anyone who is caught preaching there will be jailed."

"Thank you for informing me," David replied

sadly. "I wonder whether this conflict will ever be put to rest. It grieves me to see the church so divided."

"It grieves me as well, my friend," Mr. Cooke said grimly. "Well, you must be on your way. It was good to see you again, Mr. Brainerd. Do take care of yourself."

David waved goodbye and strode from the garden. He barely noticed the countryside around him as he left Stratford behind. Thoughts of the conflicts surrounding the revival and concerns about the restrictions placed on preachers raced through his mind. He had developed a fierce aversion to senseless arguments in the church, and he longed for peace to come between the revivalists and those who opposed them. But, as was evidenced by the new edict, the war continued, and David felt as if he were caught in the crossfire. Any hope of the board reaccepting him into Yale College seemed lost.

The sun had dropped below the horizon by the time he arrived in Ripton. Before heading to Mr. Mills's farmhouse, he stopped at a trading post to buy some syrup. The tavern buzzed with activity as travelers stocked up for their various journeys. David pulled the reins of his horse and jumped to the ground. The night was cool so he fastened his jacket near his neck and hurried to the entrance, anxious to make his purchase and get home.

As he walked up the creaking steps to the trading post, a rowdy group of Indians burst through the front doors. They jostled their way down the steps beside him, none of them seeming to notice David as he leaned against the rail to keep from getting trampled.

David stared after them. Their dark hair shimmered in the moonlight and their ruddy skin seemed to absorb the darkness of the night. One of the Indians, holding a large jug at his side, swayed behind the others, his buckskins swishing against his legs. From the light of the trading post, David could see that his arms were covered with purple and red paint, and a multicolored headband drooped on his forehead, nearly covering his right eye. From up the road, one of his companions grunted something back to him as he continued to stumble down the narrow street. The drunken Indian growled something in reply, picked up his pace, and joined the others. Then, as suddenly as they had made their boisterous appearance, they disappeared into the forest, leaving the road quiet and desolate.

David gazed thoughtfully after them as they faded into the night. How wild and untamed the Indians were! "They live more like the beasts of the forests than like civilized men," he said to himself.

Many white people considered the Indians to be less than human. David, however, attributed their savage nature not to a lack of humanity, but to their idolatrous religions. They refused to glorify the one true God and, instead, worshiped false idols, their gods of nature made in the images of birds, reptiles, and other animals. But David knew that worship of the true God, who has revealed Himself in nature and in Scripture, will raise humanity to the dignity and nobility for which it was made. Instead, the Indians had foolishly turned their backs on God. They honored the creation instead of the Creator and even imagined that they were one with nature, equal in value to the birds, reptiles, and brute beasts of the fields.

"God created man to rule over the creation and subdue it in wisdom and to be in communion with God," David thought. "Until the Indians understand that, they will continue to bear the savage scars of idolatry."

David sighed as he thought about the Indians' desperate need of salvation. He turned his eyes from the misty road and headed into the trading post. Quickly, he made his purchase, then rode home. During his brief ride to the house, David thought about how wonderful it would be if the Indians knew Jesus as their Savior. Right then he began to pray that God would use him to spread the Gospel among the Indian people.

"Oh, that God would bring great numbers of them to Jesus Christ!" David thought. "I hope I will see that glorious day."

For the next few weeks, he spent his free time praying for the Indians of North America. He would walk deep into the woods until he found a secluded clearing, and there he would kneel and pray for hours, asking God to bring the Indians into His kingdom.

"Dear heavenly Father, use me to enlarge Thy kingdom among the Indians," David would pray, perspiration dripping into his eyes. "I know I am not worthy to be Thy servant, but I pray that Thou wilt prepare me for this great work. I don't know when or where or how Thou wilt use me. I don't know what kind of trials I will have to face; but I am willing."

In early May, David's thoughts turned from the Indians to matters concerning his expulsion. He rode on horseback to Hartford to visit with some Christian friends and to meet with Mr. Cooke and the council of ministers. Humbly, he told the council about the events that led up to his expulsion from college.

"I blame myself for being so disrespectful to one of the tutors at the college," he explained. "I have apologized to Mr. Whittelsey. I don't know what more I can do. If you can help me in any way, I would be very appreciative. I want very much to continue my studies at the college."

Once the council saw how repentant David was over the wrong he had done, some of the pastors promised to speak to the trustees, which they did soon after David left Hartford. Later, he received a letter from one gentleman who had interceded on his behalf. The minister wasted no time getting to the point of the letter and bluntly told him that the trustees of the college would not change their minds. No matter what the council had said, they would not listen. Under no circumstances would David be accepted as a student at Yale College.

David folded the letter, put it in his pocket and took a long walk, thinking about what God had planned for him now that he would not be returning to college. He stopped beside an old oak tree and lay on the ground, prostrating himself before God. Despite his situation with the college, his thoughts kept turning to the Indians.

"Father, I am a sinful and wicked creature," he prayed. "I am not worthy of Thy mercy. I sometimes wonder if I have the power to remain in a dark world such as this. But I know I can do anything if Thou givest me the strength. I want so much to see the poor

Indians come to know Thee. I can't do anything without Thee, Lord. Please give me more grace so I can serve Thee with my life. Let me see Thy glory ever before me, and I can do anything—even travel into the deepest wilderness to bring the light of Thy Word to the Indians."

From that point on, David knew God's will for his life, that he was not meant to hide away in the halls of scholarship or even minister among his own people in Haddam or any other town in Connecticut. God had given him a desire to proclaim the Gospel to the Indians, to the scattered tribes that inhabited the vast wilderness of North America. When and how he would carry out his mission David did not know, but he did know that if preaching to the Indians was what God wanted him to do, the day would come when he would leave the familiar behind to forge a trail of Christian love through the American wilderness.

7

A Growing Vision

David spent the summer and fall of 1742 traveling to various towns in Connecticut on a preaching tour. Families in every town would welcome him into their homes and listen attentively as he explained passages from Scripture. Young and old alike would go to church any day of the week to hear him preach. His kind disposition, zeal for the Lord, and knowledge of the Scriptures reminded many of evangelistic preachers such as Whitefield and Tennent.

David didn't know how to respond to all the attention. He was honored by the praise and encouragement of others, but in his heart he felt unworthy to teach about Jesus Christ. Humbled by his sin and by the solemn responsibility of being a minister of the Gospel, he didn't want to be put on a pedestal or singled out because of any special ability he might have. No matter how much praise he received, he remembered that he was a minister dependent on the power of the Spirit, and that he, like everyone else, was a sinner in need of God's grace. If anything, he thought he was more sinful than others. Every prideful reflection on his abilities, every wandering thought in prayer or worship hung heavily on David's heart and caused him to think lowly of himself.

"If only they knew my heart, if only they could

see that I am counted among the worst of sinners," he would say to himself, "if only they could see inside of me, they wouldn't be so willing to show me respect."

David would step into the pulpit plagued with thoughts of his own sinfulness, and he would often fear that he would be unable to preach. But God would strengthen him and enable him to proclaim the message with sincerity, zeal, and compassion. As he would stand with the Word of God spread before him, he would become emboldened with the knowledge that the authority and power of the Gospel did not come from his meager efforts, but from the Spirit of Christ who alone opens the eyes of the blind and causes the deaf to hear. David was simply an instrument in the hand of God, and throughout his brief life he would never forget that. He realized that if a person's conversion depended on anything he did, no one would ever be saved. As he had learned from the Bible, and as he had come to accept on that day in the woods when God changed his heart, salvation was all of God. David longed for others to come to know Christ, and he was faithful in obeying God's command to tell the nations about the Good News, but he remained dependent on the grace of God and always gave Him the glory.

That longing for others to know Christ was never more evident than when David preached to the Indians, which was something he did not always have the opportunity to do as he traveled mostly among the white settlements. One time, however, when he was preaching near Kent along the western borders of Connecticut, some Indians attended the service. David saw them standing in the back of the room.

Their long dark braids fell across their shoulders and colorful strands of beads hung from their necks. Buckskins gripped their legs and scuffed moccasins covered their feet. The young women sat on the floor with their beaded dresses tucked under their knees.

Compassion overwhelmed the young preacher as he longed for the Indians to enter the kingdom of heaven. Silently, he prayed that God would open their hearts and minds to the truth. Then he took a deep breath, opened the Bible, and began to preach. As he spoke on a passage from the book of Job, his voice quivered with emotion as he urged his listeners to consider the state of their souls and to confess their need of Christ's forgiveness.

"The Bible tells us that all men are destined to die," he proclaimed. "Where will you go when that day comes? Will you go to heaven or to hell? If you do not know Jesus Christ as your Savior, you will go to hell. But if you confess your sins and put your faith in Jesus Christ as your only hope for salvation, you will be freed from your sins, and you will live forever in the presence of God. And no other place is more beautiful, more peaceful, more glorious than the presence of the one, true God."

The Indians in the back of the room appeared greatly affected by David's words. With tears streaming down their faces, they fell to their knees and cried out as they grasped for the first time how sinful they were. Like a candle illuminating a darkened room, the preacher's words pierced their hearts, and they began to realize how much they needed Christ.

After the service, David and some others from the town talked with the Indians late into the night. They explained how God had originally made mankind perfect and innocent, but man rebelled against God, just as children rebel against their parents. The Indians nodded in understanding. Their children were no different from the white people's. They could not deny that their children were naturally disobedient. Encouraged by the Indians' quick grasp of his teaching, David went on to explain that the only way people could be restored was through the work of the Holy Spirit. He comes into their hearts and changes them, enabling them to have faith in Christ. The Indians responded by asking the Holy Spirit to change their hearts, to give them faith, and to save them from their sins.

The next day, David arranged for a school to be set up in the town to help teach the Indians more about Christianity. With the help of local ministers, the townspeople hired a schoolmaster to teach English to the Indians who lived along the borders of Connecticut. Some of the Indians who had been hostile to Christianity accused David and the others of turning the Indians into Englishmen, of stripping them of their distinctive Indian culture, of conquering the Indian people under the guise of Christianity. David refused to dispute with those who had no understanding of the ways of God. He simply reassured the Indians who wanted to learn more about Christianity that his goal was the salvation of their souls, not the advancement of the English domain. The purpose behind teaching them English was so they could read the Bible themselves, at least until it had been translated into their own tongue. All David wanted was for the Indians to be conformed to the image of

Christ. Wherever that goal conflicted with the culture of the Indians, he hoped the Indians would choose Christ's ways over the darkened, pagan traditions of their own people.

Leaving the Indians in the capable hands of the townspeople, David traveled to Bethlehem, Southbury, and Eastbury to preach. He visited Christian friends and heard other ministers preach, such as Mr. Cooke of Stratford and Joseph Bellamy of Bethlehem. The Rev. Bellamy was well-known throughout New England as a powerful preacher, and he was David's good friend. Many of David's friends had graciously provided opportunities for him to preach after he had been expelled from Yale. The dishonor, however, still hung over his head like a threatening storm. Sometimes, it seemed as if he would never be totally free from it.

One day in early September, as he rode to preach in New Haven, a friend intercepted him.

"David, you must not preach tonight," the young man warned as he tried to catch his breath.

"But why not?" David asked, surprised to see his friend so upset.

"The board of governors from the college has issued an edict that no visiting pastors are allowed to preach in New Haven. They intend to jail anyone who violates the order."

David felt overwhelmed with disappointment. Mr. Cooke of Stratford had told him of the edict, but he had hoped it had been repealed or that it was not being enforced. His friend's news proved otherwise.

"I'm going to preach anyway," David quickly decided. He nudged his horse forward, but his friend grabbed hold of the reins to stop him.

"They will not hesitate to put you in prison, David," his friend warned. "Please, do not go. The board is on the lookout for you because they heard that you planned to preach in town tonight. Instead, hide in the woods along the road. Then ride to my house tomorrow. People from town will be less likely to notice your arrival because everyone will be busy at the commencement ceremony. "

David did not like giving in to unjust threats by those in New Haven, but he didn't want to upset his fretful friend. Shaking his head in frustration, he agreed to stay away from New Haven that night.

"I'll do as you say, but only for tonight," David said, glancing back down the road and thinking about where he should set up camp.

"Until tomorrow, then," his friend said, relieved.

"Until tomorrow," David echoed.

Waving to his friend, he turned his horse around and headed back down the trail. He came to a spot that opened into the woods, paused, then rode onto a narrow path until the forest swallowed him up in darkness. Pushing his way into a small clearing protected by gnarled oak trees and twisted underbrush, he pulled his horse to a stop, slid to the ground, and took some supplies from his saddle bag. The night was cool, so he built a small fire and ate some fruit, nuts, and bread he had packed that morning. After he finished his sparse dinner, he spent the rest of the evening in prayer.

"I know that I deserve much worse than this, Lord," David prayed. "What I did at college was wrong, and now I am suffering the consequences. But,

Father, I deserve judgment from Thy hand, not from these men who seek to keep me from preaching. Please protect me from those who have hardened their hearts against me. Thou art my refuge and my strength. 'The Lord is my light and my salvation; whom shall I fear? The Lord is the strength of my life; of whom shall I be afraid? When the wicked, even mine enemies and my foes, came upon me to eat up my flesh, they stumbled and fell. Though an host encamp against me, my heart shall not fear; though war should rise against me, in this will I be confident. One thing have I desired of the Lord, that will I seek after: that I may dwell in the house of the Lord all the days of my life, to behold the beauty of the Lord, and to inquire in His temple.' Amen."

The next day, David arrived safely at his friend's house. He wanted to attend the college commencement, but his friends advised him against it. David was greatly disappointed by the turn of events because he wanted to see many of his friends from school. But that would have to wait until another day.

As the others attended the commencement, he decided to take a walk in the woods and pray. He couldn't bear the thought of being cooped up inside all day like a common criminal. So, early that morning, he headed toward the forest where he could be alone with God. Later in the day, when he didn't think he would be seen by anyone who would report him to the college board, he emerged again, comforted by God's presence. The time he had spent alone with the Lord left him less attached to things of the world than ever before. It did not bother him as much as it had in the past that he could not always do the things his friends did, that he could not attend classes at college or even preach where he wanted. God had replaced his desires for such things with a desire to serve and please Him, to live for His glory, even if it meant sacrificing his own wants and needs.

A couple of months after David's perilous trip to New Haven, he received word that his older brother, Nehemiah, had died of consumption at the age of 30. This latest tragedy hit David hard because he had greatly loved and respected his brother. After he received the news, he spent many days alone in prayer and meditation. His retreat to solitude, however, was soon interrupted when he received an important letter from New York. The Scottish Missionary Society for the Propagation of the Gospel in America had heard of the young preacher and wanted him to be a missionary to the North American Indians. The letter was from Mr. Ebenezer Pemberton, a minister from New York City, who asked David to visit him and others in the Missionary Society about setting up a ministry among the Indians.

David could hardly believe his eyes. He reread the letter to make sure he didn't miss anything. Flushed with excitement—an emotion that had been lost to him for many days—he made plans to meet with friends in Haddam to tell them the good news. Once they read David's letter, they encouraged him to seek advice from some trusted ministers. He immediately thought of Mr. Mills in Ripton so he decided to go there the next day and talk to him.

Mr. Mills knew something was up as soon as he saw David. A wide smile brightened his face, and his eyes sparkled with excitement as he jumped from his horse. Anxious to tell his friend the good news, David quickly pulled the letter from his pocket and showed it to Mr. Mills. The older minister sat down on the front steps of his farmhouse to read it.

"What do you think?" David asked as he sat on the edge of the bottom step.

"I think it's an answer to prayer," Mr. Mills said, placing his hand on David's shoulder and handing back the letter.

"I think so, too, but it's such a big responsibility. I don't know if I'm ready."

"I don't think anyone could ever be completely ready for something like this," Mr. Mills said. "But if this is what God wants you to do, He will strengthen you for the task. Think of King David. He was able to endure many things because he was called by God. He had confidence to lead armies and to suffer at the hands of enemies because God had called him. God is calling you, David. He's calling you to a hard task. You will face many dangers and be deprived of friendship, food, and protection in the wilderness. But God will be with you and give you strength."

David smiled and shook his friend's hand. Taking a deep breath, he stood up.

"I'd better get ready to go to New York," David said as he climbed onto his horse. "Thank you for your advice, and please remember me in prayer."

David spent the next few days praying and preparing for his meeting with the association in New York. In late November, he set out for the bustle of New York City, heavily burdened with the importance of his business. He rode to Mr. Pemberton's, praying all the way for God to give him peace and direction in the many decisions he would have to make.

As he rode through the streets of New York, he was overcome by the noise and confusion of the city. People were yelling, merchants were peddling on the corners, dogs were barking, children were scurrying underfoot. Tired from his journey and startled by the city's chaos, David longed for his secluded haven in the woods.

After settling in at Mr. Pemberton's, he spent some time alone in his room, hidden away from the clamor of New York's busy streets. He prayed and read Scripture. Then a knock came at his door.

"Mr. Brainerd, it's time to meet with the Society," he heard Mr. Pemberton say.

David and the older minister wrapped themselves in their coats and walked to the meeting where members of the Scottish Missionary Society would examine the young preacher. The men on the examination panel served as representatives in New York, New Jersey, and Pennsylvania, and their goal was to spread the message of Christianity in America. The devout Christians of Scotland kept a vigilant eye on the progress of their America brethren, and were always willing to assist them, especially in spiritual matters.

The members of the Society spent most of the afternoon interviewing David. They asked him about his Christian studies, his personal experiences, and his desire to minister to the Indians. Throughout the examination, David struggled with miserable thoughts about himself.

"I am the worst wretch who ever lived," he thought. "I know that I am a sinner, but do they realize it? How can these honorable men show me respect? They would be so disappointed if they could see inside my heart."

The Society had no way of knowing David's doubts about himself. Like others who had met him, they saw only a humble, pleasant young man who was willing to deny himself for the sake of others. They knew he was not perfect, that he was a sinner just as they were, but they saw that he loved the Lord and longed for others to be brought into His kingdom.

After questioning him, they asked him to preach a sermon just as men do when they are ordained for the ministry. Flooded with self-condemning thoughts, David stepped into the pulpit to preach to other ministers and to members of the Society. At one point, he thought he would not be able to continue because he felt so unworthy to proclaim the holy Word of God, but the Lord gave him the grace to preach with confidence. Still, he could not completely shake the melancholy that had settled over him, and as soon as he was finished, he returned to his room where he spent the rest of the evening alone.

The following day, the Society informed him that he had passed the examination and that he had been selected to be a missionary to the Indians of Pennsylvania. Mr. Pemberton advised him to leave for his mission in the spring, after the weather improved.

David left New York excited about his future but concerned about the responsibility he had been given. He had a lot of doubts about himself, but he remembered what Mr. Mills had told him. God would be with him and help him as he ministered to the Indians of Pennsylvania. If he relied on his own

strength, he would never be able to do it; but if he
relied on the strength and grace of the Lord, he could
endure the many dangers and spiritual darkness that
waited for him in the North American wilderness.

As soon as he arrived back home, he made arrangements to sell the estate he had inherited from his
father. He would not be able to take his worldly pos-
sessions to the mission field with him. Wanting to put
his money to good use, he thought it would be best to
sell his land and give the money to a dear friend
named Nehemiah Greenman who needed financial
help to remain in school. The young man planned to
become a Presbyterian minister, but his family did
not have the money to allow him to complete his college training at Yale. David couldn't think of a better
way to use his money than to support a friend who
wanted to be a minister. So he encouraged Mr.
Greenman to follow his heart's desire in serving the
Lord and provided him with the means to do so.

After a seemingly long winter, the day arrived for
David to leave for the Forks of Delaware. With only a
few supplies and some food for the journey, the young
missionary made his way toward the Indian lands of
Pennsylvania. The many months of planning, prayer,
doubts, and hopes had finally come to an end. And
with that ending came a new beginning, an exciting
but frightening opportunity to serve the Lord among
the natives of North America. As David traveled the
long and treacherous path to the Indian lands, he
prayed that God would give him strength to live in
the lonely wilderness, love for the Indian people, and
faithfulness to preach Christ and Him crucified with
courage and compassion.

8

Among the Wigwams

Still unable to sleep, David paced up and down the damp and musty hut. Outside the storm had eased its violent assault, leaving behind the patter of a steady drizzle. From the other side of the hut, Moses shifted in the darkness.

"Are you still awake?" he groaned, barely awake.

"I'm sorry if I woke you," David replied with a yawn. "I'm tired, but I can't seem to sleep."

"You need your rest if you are going to have the strength to keep traveling tomorrow," Moses said.

"I know," David said wearily. "I've tried to sleep, but I can't get comfortable because of the pain in my head and stomach."

"Have you just been lying there all this time?" Moses asked.

"Yes. But the night hasn't been totally wasted. I've spent the last few hours thinking about my past, about the many ways God has blessed my life," David replied thoughtfully. "I'm constantly reminded of how God has helped me through all the trials I have faced: the death of my parents, expulsion from college, all the difficulties of ministering to the Indians. He's always been with me."

"Expulsion from college?" Moses asked. He had never heard the word "expulsion," so he didn't know what it meant.

"Never mind," David said, not wanting to talk about it. "You had better go back to sleep. At least one of us needs to be rested tomorrow."

Moses didn't press him. Instead, he rolled over and instantly fell back to sleep.

David lay down again on the dirt floor and cradled his head in his arm. He remembered the day he had first set out for the Indian territory. His head had ached then much as it did now. But the pain had passed quickly as the excitement of seeing the Indians took over.

It was early spring in 1743, just before his twenty-fifth birthday, when David and his first interpreter had set out early from Stockbridge, Massachusetts, not far from the New York border. David's original plans to go to Pennsylvania were changed at the last minute because conflicts between whites and Indians in the region had escalated. His new orders from the Missionary Society were to travel into the mountainous region of New York. There he would preach to the Mohegan Indians at Kaunaumeek.

On his way to the Indian lands, he stopped by Stockbridge to visit Mr. John Sergeant, a minister who had been preaching to the Indians along the Massachusetts border for years. He knew the customs and language of the Indians and was willing to assist David as he embarked on his mission to the Indians in New York. Mr. Sergeant made arrangements for him to lodge with a Scottish couple near the Indian lands and provided him with an interpreter—a brilliant, young Indian named John Wauwaumpequunnaunt. John had been converted to Christianity through the preaching of Mr. Sergeant and had been well trained in the English language. Because of the young Indian's exceptional qualifications, the Missionary Society requested that he work with David by starting a school for the Kaunaumeek Indians.

Once all the arrangements had been made, David had saddled his horse and began the hard ride toward the mountains of Kaunaumeek. He and John would travel nearly twenty miles before reaching the bark huts, or wigwams, of the Indians. Besides a few Dutch settlements within six or seven miles, the Indian lands remained fairly isolated within a tangled web of forests and mountains.

As the two young men weaved their way through the untamed landscape, David's head began to ache. He tried to keep his head up, but every time he lifted his eyes, pain would shoot through his temples. Closing his eyes, he vigorously rubbed his head with the palms of his hands, trying to ease the pain.

"The white man's house is over that ridge," John said, pointing to the north as they broke free from the thick forest onto a vast meadowland.

David squinted in the direction of the ridge. The Scottish family he planned to stay with had settled a couple of miles from Kaunaumeek. Mr. Sergeant had reassured him that the Scots would be helpful, but he warned him that they did not have access to many supplies. Sometimes the food might be no more than bare essentials—corn, water, and bread—if that much.

Finally, after riding a good part of the day, David could see a log cabin through the trees. As they rode closer, the front door opened, and a stocky man with red hair strutted out.

"Hello," he said with a thick Scottish accent. Puffs of smoke engulfed him as he blew from a pipe gripped between yellow teeth.

David nodded but could barely hold up his head because of the pain.

They stopped in front of the cottage where David unsaddled his horse. He and John introduced themselves to the husky pioneer.

"Whenever you're ready, you can eat dinner," the Scotsman said after they had rubbed down the horses.

"Thank you very much," David replied as he walked through the front door of the cottage. He entered a large dark room with a fireplace to the right. A table and some rickety chairs stood in the center of the room, and a middle-aged woman leaned over a bed of hot ashes where a loaf of bread was baking. Smoke filled the cottage, burning David's eyes. Drab quilts hung from the ceiling, dividing the room into two private quarters. The Scotsman pulled back the quilt on the left, revealing a doorway that opened into a tiny room where logs were stacked for the fire. David looked into the room, and the cold, hard ground stared unmercifully back at him. There were no boards on the floor, only trampled dirt and scattered wood chips from the logs. The room smelled stale and moldy.

"This is where you will sleep," he told David.

David dropped his bags on the dirt floor. Rubbing his head, he stared for a moment at a pile of straw that would serve as his bed. The straw had been stacked on some logs to give him protection from the harsh ground, and a bowl of water had been set out for him on a roughly carved table. The water was brown, but he washed his hands anyway and dried them on a rough cloth.

His interpreter walked through the door behind him and dropped his supplies beside David's.

"We need to rest if we are to travel before the sun rises," he said. "You will be able to meet with more of the Indians when the sun is still low. Any later and most of the men will be gone hunting in the forests. We will go to the chief tomorrow morning."

David nodded in agreement.

Once he finished a meal of bread and boiled corn, David thanked his host and hostess for their hospitality, then retired to his room where he collapsed onto the pile of stiff straw. Before drifting off to sleep, he prayed silently in the dank, chilling darkness.

"Lord, take all fear and self-dependency from me," he prayed. "Strengthen me for this task, and open the hearts of the poor Indians."

After quietly quoting one of his favorite psalms, he fell asleep almost immediately and dreamed of Indians falling on their knees, crying, "What must we do to be saved?"

The next morning, David woke long before sunrise. Smoke filled the cottage like a gray mist, barely perceptible in the dark. David's joints ached from sleeping on the hard boards. Quietly, so as not to wake up the rest of the house, he stretched his legs and walked outside. There he was greeted by a chorus of crickets and grasshoppers, vibrantly singing the final movement of their nocturnal performance. David took a deep breath and walked a few paces from the house. The forest rose up before him like the entrance to a dark cave, full of whispers. Stepping into the misty shadows, he knelt beside a gnarled, moss-covered tree. He remained there for half an hour and prayed that God would give him strength and deepen his love for the Indian people.

After he finished his prayers and ate some wild berries for breakfast, David tucked his worn Bible under his arm and set out for Kaunaumeek with John. The way was too treacherous to ride on horseback, so the two men walked. Carefully, John led his horse through the thick brush. As they dodged ditches and jagged rocks, he explained that the Indians of Kaunaumeek did not live together in one place. Their homes were scattered throughout the forests. David wondered how he would ever gather them together, but John reassured him that many were willing to come and hear the white people talk about Christianity. They had listened to Mr. Sergeant on a number of occasions and were open to learning, though they found it difficult to understand even the most simple doctrines of Scripture.

It was mid-morning by the time David and John arrived at the wigwam where the chief of the Kaunaumeek Indians lived. The little village that surrounded the chief's hut was bustling with activity. A couple of young men building a bark-covered hut glanced at the strangers before returning to their work. They had twisted a number of saplings to form a dome-shaped frame for the hut. One young man was tying the trees together with tough bark fibers while another fastened slabs of bark to the frame to form the hut's walls. John told David that once they finished the exterior, they would build platforms inside for beds and tables.

Nearby, a group of children was throwing long,

sharp sticks through rolling hoops. Each time one of the wooden darts passed through its target, the children jumped up and squealed with delight. The women, dressed in wrap-around dresses with one shoulder bare, were busy with their chores. Two were scraping excess skin off a deer hide. They would scrape it until it was smooth, then they would wash the hide and stretch it. Some of the hides had been drawn tight between tall poles, and an old Indian woman with deep, dark wrinkles was spreading a yellow mixture onto the skin, rubbing it vigorously. John explained that the concoction was a type of soap made from roots, which would clean the hide and keep it from spoiling.

A group of young women with babies strapped to their backs was grinding corn in wooden bowls. John explained that they were making hominy—a type of corn meal similar to grits. Once in a while a baby would cry, and the mother would quickly strap the wailing infant to her front and let it nurse while she continued to work.

Some young men with tattered buckskins wrapped around their waists were sharpening their arrows for the day's hunt. Most of them had shaved their heads, leaving one scalp lock in the back. Some of the locks were braided and decorated with feathers. The Indians stared at David as he and John approached the long house where the chief lived. Many of the huts were small, with enough room for just one family. But a few, like the chief's, were large and wide. Two or three families would often live in one long house, sharing meals and watching over one another's children. David thought the long houses would be a good place to hold meetings. As they approached the entrance of the chief's hut, he became anxious to begin his work.

John asked David to wait outside while he talked to the tribe's leader. Not wanting to barge in on the chief unexpectedly, the young missionary stood beside the entrance. He surveyed the busy village and noticed a group of men preparing for the day's hunt. They were tightening their bows and painting their faces. By their hand motions, David assumed they were discussing their hunting strategy. He tried to distinguish their words, but everything they said seemed to stream together. As he listened to the garbled but rhythmical language, he was thankful to have an interpreter.

Just as the hunting party disappeared into the forest, John pulled back the flap to the chief's hut, squinting in the bright morning sun. Behind him stooped an old Indian decorated in a headdress of yellow and red feathers. His weathered face bore no expression as he looked David over from head to foot. A deep, white scar in the shape of a crescent moon ran from the left corner of his mouth to the temple. And his eyes, black as midnight, remained fixed like stones as he motioned the missionary to come inside.

"He has agreed to meet with you," John said.

David stepped into the hut. Smoke from the night's fire hung like a dull haze throughout the wigwam; furs and skins covered the floor of the room. The old Indian sat in the center of the hut, picked up a knife, and began to sharpen it. David nodded his head in greeting and glanced at John, who motioned for him to sit down across from the chief. The old man said something to John in abrupt, guttural tones.

"He welcomes you to Kaunaumeek," John said.

"Tell him I am pleased to be here and am looking forward to getting to know his people and serving in whatever way I am able," David replied, looking at the chief as he spoke.

David spent the next half an hour talking to the Indian chief about why he had come to Kaunaumeek. The chief told him that he knew Mr. Sergeant and had been pleased with the results of his teaching among some of the tribe's members. David did not know what results those might be, but he knew he would find out soon enough. Just as David was about to ask the chief to tell him more about the tribe, the old Indian stood up, signaling that their conversation was over. David had wanted more time to tell the man about Jesus Christ, but before he had the opportunity, the chief motioned for them to leave.

John and David spent the rest of the day traveling to the various pockets of Indian camps within the Kaunaumeek territory. Most of the men were either hunting or visiting taverns and trading posts along the river. The Indians would often trade with white settlers, exchanging furs and weapons for liquor instead of more essential supplies. Many of the Indians had become addicted to the strong drink that the white people had brought from overseas. During the months to come, David would become increasingly concerned about this particular vice. He did not approve of the way the white people took advantage of the Indians in this manner, but he did not excuse the Indians for continuing to buy liquor instead of purchasing tools and farming materials. Confronting the Indians, however, was not always easy. Most of the time when David would preach, only the women would gather to hear him. The men, especially the young men who were more likely to visit the taverns, disappeared into the woods.

One cool afternoon, however, a young man with long, jet-black braids wrapped in red feathers stayed behind and quarreled with David about the influence of Christianity on the Indians.

"You have come to take advantage of our people just like all the other English," the young man scoffed. "You want to make slaves out of us and put us in chains like the black man. You want to make us drunk and steal our lands."

The Indian beat the ground with his fist. "You do not care about us. You only want to steal from us like all the other Christians." His face twisted into a sneer as John finished translating.

David decided not to challenge the young man on the assumption that the Indian habit of drinking was all the white man's fault. Certainly, the strong drink was introduced by many English and used to exploit the natives, but it was the Indians themselves who continued to frequent the taverns. Instead, he focused on the Indian's complaint about the hypocrisy of the white settlers. David had met many English who did not care about the Indians. They took advantage of them and stole their lands just as the young man said. Many of the Indians thought all white people were the same, and, considering how many of the white people behaved, David understood the anger and fear of the young Indian.

With John's help, he explained that not all white

people were alike. Just because someone claimed to be a Christian did not mean he was one. Those who continued to get drunk and to steal from the Indians were not Christians, even though they professed to be. David tried to reassure the Indian that he did not come to enslave his people or to take their lands. He came to tell them about Christ for the salvation of their souls.

"The Christian God is the God of the white people, not the Indian people," the young man snapped.

"The God of the Bible is the Creator of all people," David replied. "And everyone, even the white men at the taverns, need to be saved through Jesus Christ. All people have sinned. Those who continue to sin and do not believe in Jesus Christ are not Christians, and, unless they repent of their sins, they will not be saved."

Angry and frustrated, the Indian didn't respond. Instead, he turned around and stomped off into the woods. Staring after him, David prayed that God would open the young man's heart to the message of the Bible and that the Indian would learn to trust him. That trust would be difficult to earn, but he knew it was necessary if he wanted to make any progress. David's life would have to be a shining example so the Indians would see that he was different from those "Christians" who professed faith in Christ but lived worse than heathens.

He would also have to do as much as he could to help the Indians in their conflicts with the white people. David defended the Indians when they deserved it, but if they had brought trouble on themselves either through stealing or drunkenness, David would confront the Indians about their sin. Stealing and drunkenness were common sins among the Indians—sins that caused fights, tore apart families, and embittered friends against one another.

The tribe at Kaunaumeek, however, proved to be less immoral than other tribes in the region. Adultery, which was common among many Indian groups, was rarely practiced. The people of Kaunaumeek seemed to hold the family in high esteem, and commitment between husband and wife was encouraged. John attributed their faithfulness to Mr. Sergeant's teaching, one of the "results" the Indian chief had referred to when David first met him. The people of Kaunaumeek also refused to participate in the idolatrous festivals that were so common in the Indian culture. Many of the tribes in New York and Pennsylvania were famous for their wild dancing and bloody sacrifices to the Great Spirit, or to the gods of the wind, water, and earth.

Because of their exposure to Christianity and God's mercy in restraining the evil of their own hearts, many of the Indians seemed to bear the marks of true religion. They remained faithful to their wives, disciplined their children, refrained from idolatry, and prayed before meals. But, to David's disappointment, their religion did not seem to go much deeper. There did not seem to be an awareness of their sin, or a recognition of their dependence upon God, or a deep love for Christ. David was afraid that these Indians had moved from one trap to another, from idolatry to formalism, and only by God's grace would he be able to free them from that most deceptive and dangerous snare.

9

Kaunaumeek

After living with the Scottish family for three months, David decided to build a log cabin closer to the Indians. The two-mile trek every day had taken its toll on his already frail health. He fought illness and fatigue throughout the spring, and the lack of nourishing food at the home of the Scots in addition to his long hours of labor among the Indians only aggravated his condition. So whenever he had a free morning or afternoon, he would do a little work on the cabin, cutting wood and piling logs.

That spring and summer in Kaunaumeek were lonely times for David. Because the Scotsman was gone hunting most of the time and his wife barely spoke a word, David had no one to talk to except his interpreter. The young missionary never imagined how much he would miss his Christian friends and his family back in Haddam. The harsh wilderness brought little comfort as he labored among the Indians, trying to instruct them in the ways of God and to impress upon them their need of salvation.

His difficult ministry, the scarcity of good food, and the loneliness were compounded by his frequent illnesses. Many a long night would pass as David lay in his straw cot, burning with a fever. Times such as these were bearable as long as he felt close to God.

But sometimes doubt, that old enemy which brought him down so often in the past, would once again bar his way to the glorious presence of God. During such times, he felt dejected, miserable, and alone, adrift on the currents of a dark and hostile wilderness. But just as he was about to be swallowed up in doubt and hopelessness, the Lord would draw him close once again, bringing him comfort and assurance, chasing away the melancholy, and soothing his lonely and disquieted soul.

Periodically, the solitary days at Kaunaumeek would be interrupted by calls from the outside world. David would be summoned to attend meetings in distant towns concerning his ministry. In the middle of May, he traveled to New Jersey to make arrangements for setting up a school among the Indians and to seek final approval from the Missionary Society for his interpreter to serve as the schoolmaster. At other times, he would travel to visit friends, preach at churches to tell them of his work among the Indians, and attend presbytery meetings.

Such trips gave David a break from the loneliness of Kaunaumeek, but the journeys were long and hazardous, draining him of his strength. He would often be forced to ride in fierce storms, and, more than once, he became hopelessly lost in the vast forest that surrounded the Indian territory. One Saturday evening he took a wrong turn as he returned from business in New Jersey. He had taken a different route than usual because he had made arrangements to stay with an Indian family until his cottage was finished. After hours of wandering in the dense forest, he lost all sense of direction and finally decided to set up camp for the night. This frustrated David because he wanted to be in Kaunaumeek the next morning to preach.

That night he had to sleep under the clear mountain sky with dew settling over him like a wet blanket. The smell of pine filled the night air and the scurrying of animals through the underbrush kept David awake into the early hours of morning. The night was cool and the breeze damp, aggravating his poor health, but God protected him from the weather and the dangers of the wilderness until morning. Following a restless night's sleep, he set out to find a familiar path and, after riding through the forest maze for most of the morning, found his way back to the Indians.

He arrived in Kaunaumeek just in time to preach his Sunday message. Dirty and rumpled from sleeping outside in the forest, David overcame his fatigue and immediately put out of his mind any thoughts of his weary wanderings the previous night. All that mattered was preaching the Good News to the Indians. He was driven, as only a man indwelt by God's Spirit could be, to tell the Indians about God's mercy in sending His only Son. David longed to see a hint, just a spark, of understanding, of sincere love for Christ, of heartfelt repentance. But no signs of lasting change could be found. Like a farmer who had faithfully cleared his lands, tilled the soil, and planted choice seed, all David could do was patiently wait and see if God would bring forth a harvest of new life.

That summer David finished building his new home—a sturdy, one-room log cabin with a fireplace and a thick oak table where he would spend many nights huddled, studying and writing by the light of a single candle. The cottage was sparse, but it gave him much-needed privacy. Because food was scarce, he bought his bread at the nearest town, but it would often spoil before he arrived back at Kaunaumeek, leaving him to scour the forests for berries and roots.

The night he moved into his cabin, he sat at his table and began translating psalms and hymns into the Indian tongue. He had been traveling back and forth to Stockbridge to study the Indian language under the guidance of Mr. Sergeant. The traveling was difficult for him because he had to ride so many miles, often in inclement weather. The lessons helped a little, but David found the Indian language difficult to learn. Often English words could not be translated because there were not any Indian words that meant the same thing. For example, he could find no adequate translation for *Lord, Savior, salvation, sinner, justice, condemnation, faith, repentance, glory, heaven*, and many other words that are essential to Christianity. To communicate, David's interpreter would have to take a great deal of time explaining what these words meant in ways that an Indian would understand. Despite his training in the native tongue, the young missionary still relied mostly on John in communicating with the Indians. But he knew how much it meant to the Indians to be able to worship and praise God in their own language; so he worked on the translations late into the night, long after everyone else had gone to sleep.

David did most of his teaching in the evenings when he would go from house to house and meet with the families as they gathered for dinner around flickering campfires. An Indian family would often invite him to teach at their wigwam, and other families would join them. Because their own religions and traditions emphasized the miraculous, the Indians were especially interested in the miracles of Jesus, and they asked many questions about the work of the Holy Spirit. David patiently answered their questions. Some of the Indians were eager to learn, but they found it difficult to accept the Christian teaching that they could not be saved by good works and that they were totally dependent on the grace of God. David understood their focus on works all too well, so he pressed on in his teaching, emphasizing the mercy and grace of Christ in giving up His life as a ransom for many.

Early in September, David's instruction of the Indians was briefly interrupted by another call to the outside world. This time the occasion was graduation at Yale College. As he rode to New Haven, David was afraid that he would be depressed because he would not be receiving a degree with his former classmates. He had written to the board of governors at the college the previous spring, asking them once again to grant him his degree, but they had refused. David accepted their decision. "The will of God be done," he had said to himself as he had read the rejection letter. Knowing that God was in control of everything that happened to him gave him peace about the board's decision. God had a plan for his life, and He evidently thought it best that David did not receive a degree from Yale College.

Still, David was not quite sure that he had exhausted all the means necessary to be accepted back at Yale. He wanted to be sure that he had done everything humanly possible to be reconciled to the board and, in turn, be reinstated as a student. With this on his mind, it was providential that he would receive yet another opportunity to appeal to the board during his visit to Connecticut. But the source from which this opportunity arose was, as David was about to discover upon his arrival in New Haven, very unexpected.

Present at the graduation ceremony was a famous pastor by the name of Jonathan Edwards. He was a man David had always respected and admired. Mr. Edwards ministered to a congregation in Northampton, Massachusetts, and was well-known throughout America and England for his various writings and his powerful preaching—preaching that played a major role in the great awakenings and spiritual revivals in America. This, of course, made Mr. Edwards sympathetic to the revivalists, and anyone else, who had been opposed by the trustees at Yale College.

Mr. Edwards was a tall man with serious eyes and a kind face, and David liked him from the first moment they met.

"Hello, Mr. Edwards," David said, extending his hand in greeting. "I've heard so much about you, and it is truly a privilege to meet you."

Returning his handshake with a firm grip and a warm, modest smile, Mr. Edwards, who had heard of David from other ministers, praised him for the work he was doing among the Indians.

"I have heard about your ministry to the Indians in Kau-nau-meek—am I pronouncing it right?" Mr. Edwards asked. David nodded. "I hope you will visit me and my family in Northampton and tell us about your work. I know my congregation would be very excited to hear how God is using you among the Indians."

"I would love to visit you," David replied, red-faced because of the unexpected invitation. "It would be my honor to tell your people about God's work at Kaunaumeek. I must admit, it has definitely been a challenge."

The two talked for the rest of the afternoon about ministry, books they had read, and about Yale College. The more David talked with Mr. Edwards, the more he knew he could confide in him; so he told the older minister about his expulsion from Yale. To David's surprise, Mr. Edwards offered to help him by talking to the board of trustees on his behalf. David, of course, could not refuse the offer, and he began to hope that the board would listen to someone as famous and respected as Jonathan Edwards.

Mr. Edwards was not the only minister who interceded for David. The Rev. Aaron Burr of Newark, one of the correspondents of the Society in Scotland that sent David to be a missionary to the Indians, also asked the board to grant his request for reinstatement. With both Mr. Burr and Mr. Edwards applying pressure, the board finally agreed. But there was a catch. David would have to return to the college for a year; only then could he receive his degree. Unwilling to leave his mission, he tried to convince them that he had completed most of the necessary requirements on his own and that any additional studies could be done by correspondence, but the board stated that he needed to return to college anyway. Both the Society and David agreed that this would be impossible because he still had much work to do among the Indians. David wanted his degree so that it might help him in his ministry, not hinder him. When he saw that it would keep him from his calling to the Indians, he informed the board that he would not return. Not willing to bend its conditions, the board refused to work with him by way of correspondence. The decision was final; there would be no possibility of David receiving his degree from Yale College.

David felt no disappointment or bitterness when he heard the news because he had already accepted God's will in the matter. He had done everything possible to receive his degree, but time and again his efforts failed. All he could do was thank the ministers who helped him, especially Mr. Edwards, and put the matter behind him once and for all.

The night before his journey back to Kaunaumeek, he talked briefly with Mr. Edwards one last time. The older minister had observed David's poor health and guessed that he had not been taking care of himself. Gently, he advised the younger man not to push himself too hard. David thanked him for the counsel but did not seem convinced that his health was that much of a concern. He believed that his mission to the Indians was worth the inconvenience of poor health. Little did he know that what appeared to be merely an inconvenience would eventually threaten his very life.

Before saying goodbye, Mr. Edwards put his arm around the younger man, and the two prayed together, thanking Christ for His mercies and asking for continued physical and spiritual protection in both their ministries. Feeling much refreshed and encouraged by the prayers and friendship of the famous pastor from Northampton, David prepared to return home.

His journey back to Kaunaumeek, however, did not go as expected. With Mr. Edwards's warning about his health still ringing in his ears, David fell victim to a violent fever while visiting friends in Bethlehem. His head throbbed with pain, his teeth ached, and he shivered from the fever all night, making his whole body ache with pain. His friends tried to make him comfortable, but nothing they did seemed to help. All they could do was pray and wait until the sickness passed.

In the midst of the pain and sleepless nights, David longed to die and be with the Lord, but as he fixed his eyes on heaven, his heart grew heavy with thoughts of the Indians. He wanted to live if for no other purpose than to see God graciously bring the Indian people into His kingdom. Too sick to move, he remained bedridden for nearly a week until the pain eased and his fever broke. Once again, illness could not keep him from his duties for long. After just a few days of rest, he struggled to climb onto his horse and then headed back to the lonely mountains of Kaunaumeek.

David spent that winter fighting fevers, preaching at the English settlements, visiting the Indians night and day, and traveling to Mr. Sergeant's to study the Indian language. The weeks clicked by with no exceptional change among the Indians, and David often became discouraged. To battle the melancholy that threatened to overwhelm him, he spent many hours in prayer, asking God for strength to continue.

Finally, the following April, after he had been

with the Indians for about a year, David decided that it might be best if the Missionary Society sent him elsewhere. Those Indians in Kaunaumeek who wanted to learn more about Christianity could continue to learn under the instruction of David's interpreter, John. Once David told them that he would be leaving, some of the Indians asked to move closer to Mr. Sergeant at Stockbridge so they could continue to hear the preaching of the Word through his ministry.

Despite the Indians' requests that he remain with them, David believed he could be more useful elsewhere, and the Missionary Society of Scotland agreed. After receiving David's request to relocate, the Society asked him to consider going to the Forks of Delaware in Pennsylvania. The conflicts in that region had died down and it would be safe for David to travel there. The Indians of the Forks of Delaware had never received any instruction in the Christian religion, and David would be able to spread the Gospel among a people who had not adopted the external morality of Christianity. The Indians of Pennsylvania might be hostile to Christianity, but one thing David could be sure of, they would not be lukewarm like those of Kaunaumeek.

As soon as David's decision to leave Kaunaumeek became public, a church in East Hampton sent a letter asking him to be their pastor. David had visited East Hampton before and found it to be a beautiful town— nothing like the lonely wilderness of Kaunaumeek. He would be surrounded by Christians, by people who spoke the same language, something he had missed terribly as he had labored among the Indians. How wonderful it would be to live among English-speaking people again, to eat fresh, hot bread, to drink cool, creamy milk, to sleep in a comfortable bed, to live in a warm house! It was very tempting, but as David thought about all the wonderful benefits, his heart turned to the Indians. He knew where God wanted him to be, and he also knew that he would not be happy anywhere else, no matter how beautiful and comfortable it might be.

The journey to the Delaware River would be a difficult one. A harsh wilderness stood between him and the Indians, and he would have to travel through rough terrain, sometimes on foot. Part of his journey would be on the river, where he would be exposed to the dangers of traveling in the open. But David looked beyond the dangers and into the souls of the Indian people. There he saw emptiness, an emptiness that could only be filled by Jesus Christ. In David's mind no obstacle was too difficult, too hazardous to overcome for the sake of the Indians who lived in darkness beyond the mountains.

Before leaving for those distant regions, he helped some of the Kaunaumeek Indians from his congregation move closer to Mr. Sergeant in Stockbridge. Sad to see him go, many pleaded with him to stay, but the young missionary shook his head and reassured them that God would always be with them. God wanted him to travel elsewhere to tell other Indians about Jesus Christ.

With his thoughts fixed on the mission before him, David waved to the Indians who stood along the rocky trail and turned his horse south toward the Delaware River. He didn't know what kind of life would be waiting for him there, but he knew that God would be with him to strengthen him, to encourage him, and to guide him. All that mattered to David was that God's glory be displayed among the Indian nations like the sun at noonday.

Slowly, the chatter of the Kaunaumeek Indians faded behind him. Before him, the road stretched like a ribbon of stone, as unbreakable and resolute as his commitment to serve his blessed Lord. In the pale morning light, he lifted his eyes toward the distant mountains and silently prayed, "All for Your glory." That was his purpose, and no matter what sacrifices he would have to make, no matter what hardships he would have to endure, that purpose would never change.

10

Forks of Delaware

The fierce storm moved on, but the weary missionary could still hear its pounding echo through the Pennsylvania mountains. Moses was sleeping again, but David remained wide awake, his mind spinning with memories of when he first arrived at the Forks of Delaware. As he listened to the distant drone of thunder, he was reminded of a time during his first weeks in Pennsylvania when the beating of Indian drums had thundered through the earth just like the faraway storm.

He had been studying in his room when the ominous boom of Indian drums began to rumble through the mountains. David remembered the feel of the distant beat as it pulsated through the earth beneath his feet. The Indian camp was three miles away, but the chorus of drums could be heard all the way to the English village where David was staying.

A man from the nearby Irish settlement who had stopped by the house with food supplies told David that the Indians were preparing for an idolatrous feast. The drums would continue all day Saturday and throughout the night until the Indians gathered on Sunday to worship the Great Spirit. David's heart sank, grieved by the Indians' idolatry. He had heard rumors about the pagan rituals among the Delaware

Indians, but he had never seen one.

David had soon discovered that the Indians of the Forks of Delaware were very different from any he had ever encountered. They seemed wilder and more hostile to Christianity. And unlike the Indians of Kaunaumeek, these were fearfully attached to their powwows, or religious leaders, and their idolatrous ceremonies. Many of the Indians were frightened by the power of the powwows, and some refused to listen to David because they were afraid the powwows would put a curse on them. He tried to reassure them that they had no such power, and that the Christian God was more powerful than the religious leaders of the Indians. But, despite his efforts, they were not convinced. They remained suspicious and watched the missionary closely to see if he fell victim to any of the powwows' curses.

On the evening that David first heard the rumble of drums in the distance, he sat in his room quietly listening to their relentless cadence. With each boom, his burden over the forthcoming festival grew heavier. The hours passed, and still the drums droned on and on. David thought about all the ways he could try to stop the festival, but he decided that, for now, the best thing he could do was pray.

Evening had just draped its dusky veil over the village when he walked outside and stepped into the shelter of trees. Kneeling on the warm ground with mosquitoes buzzing around his ears, the young missionary began to pray. With the star-studded sky spread above him like a majestic cathedral, David spoke to the Lord with tears streaming down his face. He could not contain the grief that overwhelmed him.

Just a few miles away fellow human beings were preparing to commit a most grievous sin—idolatry. In their sin and their shame, the heathen of the wilderness refused to honor the one true God. Just as Paul wrote in the book of Romans, they exchanged the glory of the Creator for images of created things, for snakes, rocks, birds, and bears. Instead of bowing down and worshiping the God who gave them life, clothed them, and nourished them with food, they worshiped creatures that had no power. A rock could not save them from their sins. A snake could not cause the rain to fall on their crops. A bear could not heal a sick child. A bird had no power to raise the dead or give sight to the blind. Only the true God could do those things.

David's tears mingled with perspiration as he continued to pray, pleading with the Lord to break the chains that Satan had wrapped around the minds and hearts of the Indian people. He had heard many stories of spirits who visited the Indian people, who showed them where to hunt, who led them to water. The spirits did many things to gain the trust of the Indians, but eventually their true evil nature would show. They would cause some of the Indians to wound themselves with knives in the midst of a trance, or they would tell a witch doctor to drive a stake through the temple of a sick child to drive away the fever. The horror stories were well-known. David grimaced, hating Satan's schemes and the thought of devils being honored by the Indians when they should be honoring God.

"Help me, Father, to break up this idolatrous meeting," David prayed. "Stop this evil by the power of Thy Word. I can do nothing against Satan on my own. I am totally dependent on Thee. Please, Lord, bring glory to Thyself, and save the Indians from their slavery to evil."

As he prayed, every earthly concern faded into the darkness about him. He thought only of God. Even the hum of the insects seemed to grow silent. All his fears, all his desires, all his cares drifted away like a puff of smoke. The only thing David wanted was to see God glorified in the salvation of the Indians. Nothing else mattered. He wanted them to know the peace and joy that can only come from bowing in humble submission to the Lord, experiencing the mercy of Christ, and showing that mercy to others.

Growing weary, David drifted in and out of sleep beneath the night sky. Occasionally, he would awake and continue praying. When he would fall back asleep, he would dream of the salvation of the Indian people, hundreds of them bowing down in humble repentance and professing faith in Christ. Sometime during the night, he returned to his bed and slept till morning, still dreaming of the Indians. When he awoke to the rumble of beating drums, he could not get out of bed until he prayed again for strength and courage. Once he climbed from his bed, encouraged and strengthened by his prayers, he quickly washed and dressed. He grabbed some berries to eat as he hurried out the door, then returned to his place in the woods to pray once again.

"Dear Father, I know that Thou canst bow the heavens and come down and do some marvelous work among the heathen today," David prayed.

Continuing to pray, he mounted his horse and rode the three miles to the Indian village, barely noticing the tangled wilderness about him, the briars that scraped against his legs and the humidity that clung to his clothes and hair. All he noticed was the drums, steadily growing louder. Like Paul before the pagans in Athens, David's heart stirred within him as he prayed for the Indians. Suddenly, just as he reached the edge of the Indian camp, the drums stopped. A loud shrill shattered the silence like a thunderclap, sending chills down David's back. The scream echoed through the forest and was suddenly joined with shrieks from every direction, converging at the center of the camp. David headed in that direction. As he rode among the empty wigwams, the drums started again—this time faster. The unrelenting beat bore into David's head, his temples throbbing with every boom.

Billows of smoke climbed from a mass of trees in front of him. Cautiously, David dismounted and tied his horse near a cluster of thick bushes, then pushed his way through the underbrush. As he peered between two large maples into a vast clearing, he caught his breath sharply. The Indians were dancing wildly around an immense bonfire, their bodies and faces grotesquely painted, their features twisted into expressions that looked barely human.

The overcast day caused the clearing to grow dim and the fires to cast eerie shadows in every direction. At the far end of the glade, a group of women was fanning the smoke into rhythmical patterns. Older Indians lined the edge of the clearing with painted drums set before them. Sitting cross-legged and staring into the fire glassy-eyed, they struck the drums fiercely. Before them, the dancers pounded the ground to the steady, ominous beat. Some of the dancers wore masks of bears; others wore antlers or covered themselves with snake skins. Shadows from the fire distorted their faces, causing them to look more like the devils they worshiped than the men they actually were. All of them moved as if in a trance. Sometimes they would beat the ground; other times they would strike themselves, drawing blood on their backs and shoulders.

David trembled, terrified by the display of human depravity before him. The evil within the clearing seemed almost tangible, as if it possessed a life of its own. David recoiled at the thought, his hands shaking. He wasn't afraid of the Indians, only the evil they ignorantly danced with, the shadows that seemed to flitter at the edge of the firelight. The frightened missionary shook his head; no matter how afraid he was, he knew he had to do something. Before making a move, he knelt in the cover of the trees and prayed that God would give him the courage to break up the wild frenzy that brought God so much dishonor. As he focused his thoughts on God, he was comforted and encouraged by the truth that God was greater than all the evil in the world and that, as a child of God, he had nothing to fear from the forces of darkness that controlled the Indian ritual before him.

With newly found courage, David pushed his way into the clearing and walked steadily into the midst of the riotous dancing, barely escaping the thrashing arms of the dancers. Some of the drums stopped as Indians at the edge of the clearing noticed the lone figure walking toward the fire. Once he reached the edge of the scorching blaze, David stretched his hands high over his head, perspiration streaming down his face.

"Friends, I come in peace," David declared in a broken Indian dialect. "Listen to me."

The drums fell silent, and the dancers stopped and stared. The Indians knew who he was because David had been preaching in their villages for the past couple of weeks. One of the leaders took off his bear headdress and stood before the pale-faced missionary. To David's surprise, the tall Indian wasn't angry, merely perplexed.

"What do you want?" he asked.

"I want you to stop this . . . ," David stammered, trying to find the words to describe the idolatrous revelry he had just witnessed. Giving up on searching for an appropriate description that the Indians would understand, he went on. "The one true God is not honored by what you are doing. You are worshiping created things, things that have no power. You must, instead, honor the true God."

Murmurs scattered among the Indians. The chief looked around him and suddenly motioned the others to take off their masks and headdresses. One by one they removed their costumes. The beastly apparitions that had been dancing around the bonfire disappeared, leaving behind a group of men in their right minds and curious to hear the words of the white man.

"If your God is as powerful as you say, we will listen to you," the chief said, sitting down in front of the dying fire. The others sat behind him. David could feel himself begin to tremble, overwhelmed by such an immediate manifestation of God's grace.

"This is what God Himself proclaimed to the

prophet Habakkuk in ancient times," David boldly declared. "'What profiteth the carved image that its maker hath engraved it; the melted image, and a teacher of lies, that the maker of his work trusteth in it, to make dumb idols? Woe unto him that saith to the wood, Awake; to the dumb stone, Arise, it shall teach! Behold, it is laid over with gold and silver, and there is no breath at all within it. But the Lord is in His holy temple; let all the earth keep silence before Him.' "

As the fires died and the clouds disappeared, David preached, captivating the Indians with every word. An Indian who spoke a little English volunteered to translate for him. So, with his help, he told the Indians about God, how He created the world and how He made all men in His image. He described the first man, Adam, and his close relationship with God. Boldly, but with compassion, he explained that all people—the black man, the white man, and the Indian—were descendants from that one man. Without seeming to tire, he told them about man's disobedience and how a serpent had tempted the first woman to disobey God. Those Indians wearing snake skins shifted uncomfortably, but David preached on, telling them that the rocks, the animals, the wind, the waters were all created things and should not take the place of honor reserved only for God Himself; and the only way they could worship God in sincerity and truth was through Jesus Christ, God's only Son, who came to save them from their sins and to bring peace between the sons of Adam and God.

"Those who have faith in Christ," David preached, "will one day see the face of God. They

will walk with Him in the beautiful gardens as Adam
once did. They will live forever in peace. No harm
will come to them. They will never grow old or sick.
Their bodies will be raised from the dead and transformed into glory. Never again will they die. They
will live forever worshiping the one true God. That
worship can begin among you right now. Do not worship things that God has made—not the spirits or the
creatures of the earth. Worship God through the only
One who can bring you into His presence, Jesus
Christ our Lord."

The Indians listened intently, but despite their
willingness to hear about Christ, there did not seem to
be any remarkable change among them, no deep realization of their need of Christ or confession of their
sin, and no love for the beauty and glory of Christ.
They appeared to be more serious than they had been
on previous occasions when David talked with them,
but no one was ready to turn from their Indian traditions and put their faith in Christ.

Once David finished preaching, the Indians dispersed, returning to their villages in the forest. The
tired missionary returned to where his horse was
tethered and, after getting some water for the animal
and himself, headed for home. As he rode alone
through the dark forest, David was overcome with
fearful thoughts that God would never convert the
Indians. Satan tempted him to despair, to give up,
taunting him with doubts that God would never
change the hearts of these tribal people. David pushed
the thoughts from his mind by thinking about the
power of God. The God who raised Jesus Christ from
the grave by the power of His Spirit could change the

hearts of the Indians, no matter how hard they might be. Though there had not been the great response from the Indians that David had hoped for, that he had prayed for, the young missionary could praise God for His powerful work in stopping the Indians from continuing their pagan ritual. A day that had begun in worship of idols ended with the message of Christ ringing through the still forest. A single voice, ignorant of the Indian language but armed with the powerful Word of God, broke the savage spell of Satan's servants and brought the Gospel to bear on the consciences of those Indians who had gathered that day.

11

Along the Susquehanna

Throughout the long, sweltering summer, David preached to the Indians of the Six Nation Confederacy— an alliance of Indian tribes that began in the sixteenth century. At first there were only five tribes: the Seneca, Mohawk, Cayuga, Onondaga, and Oneida. But in 1710, the group admitted another tribe into its alliance, the Tuscaroras. This tribe lived along the southern borders of the confederacy territory. The Six Nations dominated the lands that stretched from Lake Erie to the Hudson Valley and all the way south to North Carolina. This confederacy was very powerful and conquered many other vast regions before its tribes were forced to move elsewhere (John Thornbury, *David Brainerd, Pioneer Missionary to the American Indians* (Durham, England: Evangelical Press, 1996, pp. 145, 146).

Just as he had done while at Kaunaumeek, David lived with white settlers until he completed a cabin of his own closer to the Six Nations Indians. His living arrangements gave him many opportunities to preach to the white settlers as well as the Indians. But because of the distance between the various Indian lands and his home at the English settlement, he would often ride for many miles every day. In the morning, he would travel to the English and nearby

Irish settlements; then, soon after he finished his message, he would ride fifteen to twenty miles to the Indians of Sakauwotung and preach in the evening. Such journeys were not only long, they were dangerous. Fierce wolves, hazardous trails, and deadly Indians remained a constant threat for anyone who traveled in the wilderness. As David had soon learned from other settlers, not all the Indians were friendly. Some would stalk travelers in the woods, kill them in their sleep, and cut off their scalps—a trophy that symbolized the Indians' power over the "pale face." David had much to fear, but God kept him safe during his long journeys.

Eventually the traveling began to wear on him. He became sick more frequently and would sometimes be confined to his bed for days. David found it very difficult to stay inside when he was ill because he felt as if he were wasting precious time—time that could be spent preaching and ministering to the Indians. One Sunday he refused to remain idle for another minute and dragged himself to the Indian camp, where he preached his sermon sitting down. To the surprise of the Indians, he proclaimed the Word of God with a fervency and zeal that belied his weak condition.

That evening when he returned home, he was too sick to read or meditate or pray—spiritual duties that gave David great delight. As he lay in his bed, tossing and turning from a high fever, he thought about how he felt like a small boat adrift on a swift torrent with the owner of the boat standing on the shore, helpless to recover his loss. He wondered if he would ever recover, if he would ever regain his strength so he could spread the Gospel among the tribes of Pennsylvania.

One day, just as David thought there was no hope of recovery, his imaginary boat veered toward the riverbank and grounded on shore. He had finally recovered. Even though he was tempted to remain in bed to regain his strength, he wasted no time preparing to preach to the Indians. The day after his fever broke, he traveled through the wilderness to visit them, and he was not disappointed by his efforts. The Indians listened to his preaching and seemed more interested than ever before. For the first time, the young missionary saw some of the Indians become genuinely and radically concerned about the state of their souls. Many, however, refused to listen to him preach for long because they were afraid of the pow-wows, but David did not give up on them. He continually reassured them that God would protect them.

"I am a Christian," David would often say to them. "Why have the powwows not bewitched or poisoned me?"

After many weeks of watching and waiting, they could see that he had escaped the curses of the pow-wows, and it gave them confidence to listen. Their acceptance and willingness to learn, despite their fears, encouraged David to take the message of the Gospel to other Indian tribes that lived along the Susquehanna River in Pennsylvania.

In early October, he prepared for a missionary tour that would take him four-hundred and twenty miles into the wilderness. His only companions would be his interpreter, whom he had hired that summer; a fellow minister by the name of James Byram from a nearby settlement; and two Indian chiefs from the Forks of Delaware. Mr. Byram would not remain with him after their return from the river, but David was delighted to have the young pastor along for the journey anyway. As he had faced the many difficulties of ministering among the natives, David had often regretted not having help on the mission field. He had asked the Missionary Society many times to send him an assistant, but, to his disappointment, it was not able to find a suitable helper.

David and his traveling companions loaded their horses and began their trip on a Tuesday morning in early October. They rode twenty-five miles until they came to a house along the border of the Indian settlement. The secluded cabin was not very large, but they decided it would be a good place to spend the night, protected from the clinging dew and roaming wolves. That night, as they slept in the musty cabin, the constant howl of the wolves invaded their dreams. David expected one of the hairy beasts to crash down the cabin door any minute and tear them to pieces. But as the dawn approached, the howling subsided, and the small company shook the sleep from their eyes, ready to begin another day's ride through the mountains.

Anxious to get to the river country, the five travelers headed up the mountain trail just after the sun peered over the horizon. Huge mountains dressed in a dense maze of tangled underbrush, jagged rocks, steep cliffs, and deep valleys towered before them. The men secured their belongings on the backs of their horses and set out, prepared to face the challenges that waited for them along the trail.

The day proved to be uneventful until just before dark. As David was winding through a maze of mossy rocks, his horse jerked under him. She caught her leg between two twisted roots and lurched forward. He tried to hold onto the horse's neck to keep from being thrown, but he slid off its back. The others stopped when they heard him yell from behind them. Mr. Byram jumped from his horse and ran back down the trail to help him. To everyone's surprise, David wasn't hurt. But the same could not be said for the horse. The new interpreter, Moses Tinda Tautamy, checked the horse's leg.

"She's broken it," he said.

"Is there anything you can do?" David asked.

Moses shook his head. "The break is too bad. We will have to kill her. She can't be moved, and we can't leave her here to be mauled by the wolves."

David said he would do it. Taking out a small pistol that he carried on his journeys, he walked behind her and pulled the trigger. The gun blast echoed eerily through the mountains.

That night the little company was forced to sleep outside in the howling forest because they were nearly 30 miles from the nearest lodging. They cut some branches for shelter and built a small fire for protection from the frost. After eating a sparse dinner of dried meat and nuts, they asked God to protect them during the rest of their journey. As the others drifted off to sleep, David listened to the crackling of the fire mingled with the distant howling of wolves. Rubbing his bruised leg, he thanked God for protecting him from serious injury when his horse fell. God had been good to him, enabling him to continue his mission to tell the Indians of the Susquehanna about Christ.

Two days later, they arrived at the Susquehanna River at a place called Opeholhaupung, a village of about seventy people. According to his own custom of meeting the chief of any tribe he visited, David went directly to the chief's hut, greeting him kindly and informing him of his desire to teach the Indians about Christianity. The king, as the Indians called him, hesitated at first; but finally, if not a little reluctantly, the old Indian gave him permission to preach.

As soon as they left the chief's hut, the missionary stood in the midst of the camp, introduced himself, and began to tell the tribe about Jesus Christ. The Indians became so interested in what David had to say that the men put off their hunting trip, which would normally last for three or four days, just to hear him preach. This was unusual because nothing ever came between a tribe and its hunting. But, by God's grace, this tribe was so captivated by the new teaching about religion that they remained to listen.

Most of the Indians from the camp appeared willing to learn, but as soon as they realized that the missionary and his friends did not embrace their own religious beliefs along with the Christian teaching, they became angry and began to argue.

"Why do you say there is only one God?" an aged Indian asked after David had finished preaching. "Our fathers have always told us that there are many great invisible powers, many spirits that speak to us through the trees, the water, and the animals. One time when I was young, a bird spoke to me, warning me of danger on the road. Ever since, I have been guided by the spirit of the bird. Does your God speak in such a way?"

"Not usually," David replied. "There is a record in the Bible of God speaking to the prophet Balaam through a donkey, and He has spoken from the whirlwind and from fire. But since the completion of the Scriptures, He no longer speaks in such a manner." After Moses interpreted what he said, snickers rippled through the crowd. "God has revealed Himself through writing, through the Bible. In ancient times, He spoke in dreams and visions, and through prophets. Now He speaks only through His Word. In it, we learn everything we need to know about God, about creation, about salvation through Jesus Christ, and about God's will for our lives."

"Your God does not seem very powerful if He can only speak through a book," the old Indian scoffed.

David felt as if a knife had ripped through his heart when he heard the Indian speak so dishonorably of God. If only he could open the Indian's eyes to see the truth, but he knew only God was able to open the eyes of sinful men. Silently, he prayed that God would give the Indians ears to hear and eyes to see the truth.

"Why do you consider it a weakness for God to reveal Himself through the writings of His servants?" David asked. "Do not even men write down their laws and agreements so there can be no dispute about the truth? As for spirits revealing themselves through animals, the demons can deceive us in many ways. Satan himself used a snake to tempt the mother of all races to rebel against God. Yet he is surely not as powerful as God. No matter what you have always believed, there is only one God."

"We have many gods," a young brave shouted.

"It is impossible to have many gods," David exclaimed. "If God is all-powerful, then there can't be anyone equal to or more powerful than God. If there were many gods, each one would have to be all-powerful in order to be God. But that cannot be."

David paused for a moment, trying to think of a way to explain why there is only one God in a way they could understand.

"Do you have a champion brave among you? One who hunts better than anyone else?" David asked. Moses translated, and the Indians nodded, pointing to a strongly built youth standing near the back.

"Is it possible to have more than one champion?" David asked.

"No," they replied. "If he is the champion, and someone else defeats him, then that brave would become the champion."

"That is how it is with God," David said. "He is the best, the greatest, the only champion. And unlike our friend here," David continued as he pointed to the young brave, "no one can ever defeat Him or share in His glory. He is the greatest and always will be. That will never change because God never changes."

He waited as they thought about what he had said.

"Our fathers have spoken of one Great Spirit, who reveals himself in different ways," the old Indian replied thoughtfully. "It might seem to us that there are many spirits when there is one in many—many spirits speaking in the trees and the animals, but coming all from the one."

"That's not what I have always been taught," one of the Indians said in a gruff voice. "There are four gods that guide us through life, not one."

As the Indians began to debate among themselves about their own traditions, David found it difficult to talk to them any more about Christianity. He grew increasingly frustrated because it was pointless to argue with them when they didn't even know what they believed. They seemed confused about the nature of God. Who was He? Was He one or many? Did He live in the animals and trees or simply speak through them? They didn't have the answers. Some of the Indians continued to quarrel among themselves while others argued with David until dark, but when he saw that he wasn't getting anywhere with them, he decided to return to his camp.

Early the next morning, he and his companions set out on the river to visit the scattered Indian tribes north of that region. Whenever they arrived at a village, David met with the chief and asked permission to speak with the Indians about Christianity. Every tribe he visited seemed willing to listen, but many of them made the same objections he had heard from other tribes: Christians could not be trusted because they wanted to steal their lands; the "pale faces" were plotting to enslave them and drag them from their homes; the white men did not want Christians but English subjects to extend the English empire; the Christians had no right to tell them anything about God when they were getting drunk and stealing worse than the Indians; Christianity would bring the curses of the powwows; and the Christian God is not the only God because their forefathers had taught them that many spirits guided them through life.

On and on it went. David thought he would never hear the end of it. The Indians wouldn't, or couldn't, listen to the truth because they were too busy making so many excuses. The constant arguments from the Indians and the difficult traveling, most of it on foot, began to show their wear on the company. They were tired, sore, and ready to return to the Forks of Delaware. One cold morning, David looked at the weary faces of his fellow sojourners and decided it was time to go home. After gathering their supplies and saying farewell to the Indians, they made their way to the Susquehanna and piled onto a sturdy boat loaded with traders.

As David sat near the front of the boat, he watched the wilderness along the far banks speed by. "All this time and effort and not one convert," David thought to himself. "Sometimes I think I am just wasting the Missionary Society's money and time. If I don't see any fruit from my ministry by next year, I will send my resignation to the Society. I don't want to be a burden to them."

"Hey mister! What'cha reading?" a tall burly trapper, draped with skins and furs, bellowed. David's thoughts scattered with the sudden interruption.

"Excuse me," David replied. "What did you ask?"

"I asked, what is that you're reading?" the trapper barked.

David looked down at the Bible on his lap. "I'm reading the Bible," David said, holding it up so the man could see.

"Are you some kind of holy man?" the trapper asked with a laugh. Two other husky hunters joined him. They had scruffy beards, their clothes were filthy, and they smelled as if they hadn't bathed in months. They probably haven't, David thought to himself.

"No, I'm just a missionary from Connecticut," David replied. "I've come to tell the Indians about Jesus Christ."

"The Indians!" one of the trappers scoffed. "Don't waste your breath. They're good for nothing. Wasted flesh, that's what I say."

The others nodded in agreement, laughing. The first trapper spat a wad of tobacco over the side of the boat. "Why would you waste your time with those worthless savages?" he scowled.

"All men are made in the image of God," David replied boldly. "They need to hear the message of salvation just as much as the English, Irish, or Scottish. They are humans, just like you and me. God created them and gave them a soul. They are not animals, and yet you speak of them as if they were lower than the game you hunt."

"They are!" the trapper growled. "You may think they're made in the image of God, or whatever, but I know different. I've seen them ravage and kill innocent women and children for no reason. They don't deserve to drink from the same river as us civilized people. If you want to play holy man to those savages, then you had better steer clear of the likes of us. We don't take kindly to folks like you pandering to the Indians, as if they're something special. Dirt under my feet. That's what they are, and don't you forget it."

With that, he and the other trappers stalked off to the other side of the boat. David sighed. Those were the kind of white people who prejudiced the Indians against his preaching. Fear and hatred had driven a wedge so far between the white man and the Indian that only God's grace could remove it. David saw sin, sin on both sides, as the heart of the problem, and until the hearts of both the whites and the Indians were changed, the bitterness would only grow deeper. Only in Christ could there be unity and peace. He sighed again and yearned for the quiet solitude of his room back near the Forks of Delaware.

On a Friday afternoon in mid-October, David arrived at his lodgings near the Irish settlement. Throwing his bags into a corner, he walked to the center of the room and knelt in a pool of sunlight that spilled through an open window.

"I thank Thee, Lord, for bringing me home safely and for protecting my companions during our journey," David prayed. "I know I am not worthy of the kindness Thou showest me. I thank Thee for keeping all sickness from me during this journey. My good health enabled me to travel farther and tell more people about Christ. I pray, Father, that Thou wilt cause the seeds that I have sown among the Indians to bear fruit. I also pray specifically for my interpreter. Change his heart, Father, and open his eyes to behold Thy glory and grace. I fear his lack of spiritual understanding inhibits him from translating what I am teaching with the fervency and zeal with which I speak. I know, Lord, that if Thou wouldst bring him to Thyself, he would be an invaluable testimony and help in my work. As in all things, may Thy will be done. Blessed be the Lord who continually preserves me in all my ways. Amen."

12

Crossweeksung

Memories of that first trip to the Susquehanna faded as David finally drifted off to sleep. Just a few hours later, the spring sun peeked over the western horizon, its golden rays scattering into millions of fiery fragments as they skipped across the rain-drenched mountains. A steady dripping from a leak in the hut's roof interrupted David's dreams, stirring him from his brief night's sleep. He opened his eyes and gazed up at the sunlight streaming through a maze of cracks in the roof. Rainwater glimmered as it fell like tiny drops of melted gold onto the cold floor. David sat up and looked around the room. He grimaced as pain shot through his back.

"At least the pain in my head is gone," David groaned to himself. Slowly, he stood up and walked outside, still tired from the treacherous journey the day before and the long night of tossing and turning. Even though he had been exhausted when he and Moses had finally found the hut, it had taken him hours to fall asleep as he thought about all the events that preceded this second trip to the Susquehanna. Stretching his arms and legs, he looked around for his interpreter but couldn't find him. Then he heard one of the horses snort from behind the hut. David guessed Moses might be getting the animals ready for the day's ride. As the drenched soil sank beneath his boots, he sloshed through the mud to where the horses were secured. There he found Moses busily rubbing them down.

"Good morning," Moses said, looking up from his work. "Beautiful day, isn't it? I can hardly believe a storm passed through these mountains last night."

David nodded. They had barely made it through the narrow passes the previous night without being swept off one of the craggy cliffs. The storm had come upon them so suddenly. But God had provided a dry place for them to sleep, and now they would be able to continue their journey to the Susquehanna River without any delays.

"How are you feeling?" Moses asked. "Are you coughing up any more blood?"

"No, I feel much better, thank you," David replied, not really wanting to talk about his health. "I think we had better get moving as soon as possible."

After rubbing down the horses, the two ate some dried fruit for breakfast, packed their supplies, and set off down the mountain toward the Susquehanna.

Once they arrived at the river, they found a place to house their animals and booked passage on a boat heading to the Indian territory. There they would visit many of the tribes they had met on their first missionary tour, and David hoped they would have the opportunity to visit several others as well.

One night after they had spent the day preaching to a group of Indians who were fishing along the river, Moses joined David near the back of the boat where he was reading the Bible by candlelight.

"Where do your people, your family, come from?"

Moses asked, curious to know about this white man who had left his own people to tell the Indians about Christianity.

"My great-grandfather was a minister in England," David answered, putting the Bible in his lap and staring out across the dark river. "He ministered to a congregation at a place called Hingham, Norfolk. There was a time when the Protestant ministers preached freely in England, but that soon changed. The monarchy demanded that the ministers preach doctrines that were contrary to Scripture, so many of the ministers left. If they had stayed, they would have been put in prison or killed. Some fled to Europe. Others came to America. My great-grandfather was one of them."

"Did he preach when he came to America?" Moses asked, fascinated by David's story.

"Yes, he would not have been happy doing anything else," David replied. "He raised his family here and never returned to England. He had a son named Jeremiah who was also a preacher, and Jeremiah had a daughter named Dorothy, my mother."

Moses leaned against some bundles that were piled in the back of the rickety boat. As the distant shoreline washed away into the darkness, the Indian grew quiet, relaxed by the steady rhythm of the silent river. David was about to ask him if he wanted to talk about something in particular when Moses suddenly cleared his throat.

"Uh-um . . . I've been thinking," Moses said as he twisted and untwisted a strap of leather around his finger. "I've been thinking about your sermons. I know that I have been a bad person. For most of my life I have been a drunk. I must confess, I have had a drink or two since I started interpreting for you."

David tried to keep his face free from expression. His interpreter's drinking habits were no secret to him. Avoiding the missionary's gaze, the Indian looked down and cleared his throat again.

"Anyway, I want to know this God of yours, but every time I try to come to Him, to pray, it seems like mountains are standing in my way," Moses said sadly. Pulling his gaze from the river, he looked over at David. "What can I do?"

"The Bible tells us that salvation is a gift of God," David told his interpreter. "You can't earn it, you can't buy it, you can't do anything to make yourself worthy of it. God has to change your heart."

"Why hasn't He, then?" Moses asked, his face lined with frustration.

"I don't know why," David replied. "I do know that you must continue to seek Him, listen to His Word, ask Him to change your heart and to give you faith. Jesus said, 'Ask, and it shall be given you; seek, and ye shall find; knock, and it shall be opened unto you.' Do not put off what you must do today, Moses. Jesus commanded all who heard Him to 'repent or perish,' to turn from their sins and follow Him. That is our responsibility. Of course, we cannot do it unless God changes our hearts, but we cannot read the mind of God. We do not know when or how He will give us new life; we are simply called to turn and follow. His Spirit works like the wind; we do not see where it has come from or where it is going. We only see its effects as it moves the trees and blows through the grass. Do not wait, Moses. Seek Him while He may be found. Seek Him today. Put sin behind you and trust in Christ for your salvation. Do not trust in yourself. Do not put your faith in anything you have done, but trust in Him alone who can give you eternal life."

After David finished speaking, the two sat beside each other for a few minutes, not saying anything, just listening to the gentle beating of the waves. From the front of the boat, the muffled voices of fellow travelers drifted back on the night breeze. Deep in thought over what David had said, Moses leaned against the railing and breathed deeply, soothed somewhat by a scent of pine that had strayed from the now invisible shore. The faint candlelight flickered across his face, exposing deep lines that creased his wide forehead. Tired from the long day, David blew out the candle and spread his blanket on the deck. Following his companion's lead, Moses nestled into a pile of soft hides and furs. As the boat rocked back and forth, they drifted off to sleep.

The two travelers spent the rest of their journey speaking to Indians who lived on both sides of the river as well as on one of the islands farther north. The Indians, even those living close to one another, spoke in different dialects, so David was forced to use other interpreters because Moses was not familiar with all the languages. The Indians were willing to listen, but, like so many others, they did not evidence any change of heart. They seemed curious but not convicted of the truth.

David and Moses traveled nearly a hundred long and weary miles up the river. Their journey was a difficult one as they slept out in the woods every night with no protection from the rain and wind. Hampered by his usual frail health, David eventually grew too ill to travel. At one point as they were riding through the wilderness, he spit up blood, ran a high fever, and was stricken with extreme pain in his head. Moses found a trader's hut where David remained for nearly a week. When he was finally strong enough to ride, they returned to the Forks of Delaware. Exhausted and discouraged, they arrived home in late May after having traveled nearly three-hundred and forty miles.

"And no converts," David said. Frustrated, he sat at a table with his Bible spread open before him and a plate of cold, boiled corn pushed to the side. "I don't know how much longer I can keep this up. I have been working among the Indians for two years now. Will God ever bring these people into His kingdom?"

A couple of weeks after David's return to the Forks of Delaware, he spoke with Moses about visiting Indians at a place called Crossweeksung. A trapper had told him that the Indian village was located about eighty miles southeast.

"I don't seem to be making any progress here," David told Moses in early June. "Maybe there will be more interest among the Indians at Crossweeksung."

In mid-June, David said goodbye to the Indians of the Forks of Delaware and promised to return to them in a few weeks. Moses kissed his wife and children goodbye, and the two travelers set off through the woods toward New Jersey where Crossweeksung was located. They arrived at the Indian territory the next day. At first David wondered if they were in the correct region. He saw only a few Indian huts along the path. When he asked a young woman for directions, she informed him that the Indians of Crossweeksung lived scattered throughout the forest in isolated camps. She told him he would find no more than two or three families in one place. The rest of the camps were six, ten, fifteen, twenty, and even thirty miles from the camp he had first encountered. David sighed and prayed that God would bring the Indians to hear him preach. He could not possibly gather them together himself.

Undaunted by the sparse number of Indians, David decided to return to the first camp. He invited the few people he saw along the road to come hear him preach, and they agreed to listen. Most of those who gathered that day were women and children. The men were either trading at the white settlements or hunting in the forests. David looked out across the small group of expectant faces and reminded himself not to forsake the little things. Children with large brown eyes and feathers in their hair sat on the ground in front of him, listening as Moses interpreted. The women, old and young alike, dressed in wrap-around buckskins and beads, stood at a distance or sat with the children.

As the sun rose high in the sky, David told the little assembly about how God created the world in six days and that there was only one God, not many as the Indians believed. Just as he always did when he preached to a new tribe, he told them how sin entered the world because the first man and woman did not keep God's law. To David's surprise and delight, the Indians reacted in a way he had never seen before among the natives. As he described the consequences

of sin, how death and disease came into the world, and
how the hearts of all people were filled with wickedness and idolatry, tears rolled down their cheeks.
David went on to explain that they did not have to
remain in bondage to sin, but there was hope in Jesus
Christ. He had died to reconcile sinners to God, had
lived a life free from sin, and had given up His own
life as a payment for many.

When David finished preaching, he promised that
he would return the next day. The Indians were very
excited and told him they would bring others to hear
him preach. That evening, David took a short stroll
through the woods. He was tired and weak, still feeling the effects of his arduous trip to the Susquehanna.
Stopping to pray, he asked God to use the words he
had preached that day to bring others to hear about
Christ. He had been greatly encouraged when a young
woman had told him that she was going to travel fifteen miles that evening to tell some friends about his
preaching. She had been confident that they would
return with her the next day so they too could hear
about Jesus Christ.

The woman kept her word, as did the others.
When David arrived at camp the next morning, the
little assembly from the day before had doubled in
size. Finding a place in front of the wigwams where
he could be seen by everyone, he introduced himself
to the newcomers and began preaching. David was
surprised by the calm that seemed to settle over the
Indians. The group sat quietly and listened, not
yelling out any objections as Indians had done elsewhere. Whenever David had preached to other
tribes, the Indians allowed the children to run around

and play games. The men would talk among themselves, and the women would walk to and fro as if he weren't even preaching. Sometimes it had been difficult for David to concentrate on what he was saying because of all the noise. But these Indians were different. They seemed genuinely interested in hearing about Jesus Christ.

A few days later, David preached again, and the number of Indians increased from about seven to nearly thirty. As before, they remained quiet and attentive while he preached, and many had tears in their eyes as they listened to Moses translating. As David told them about the misery of sin and the offer of eternal life through faith in Jesus Christ, some of them began to tremble and cry quietly. After David finished preaching, a few of them pulled him aside and confessed that they realized for the first time how sinful they were, how wrong they had been for worshiping idols instead of the one true God.

Excited to hear more about the God of the Bible, the Indians continued to ask David to come back every day to preach. Sometimes they asked him to preach twice a day. They never seemed to grow tired of hearing the Word of God. Every day the numbers increased. After David would finish preaching, he would spend time with some of them in private so he could answer their questions and tell them more about Christ. Although the long hours began to wear on him, he was spurred on by the Indians' excitement and desire to know God.

One morning, a young woman told David that the men would have to miss his preaching to go hunting the next day. They would probably be gone several days to gather enough meat to satisfy the needs of the entire village. Despite the absence of the men, David preached the next day as usual. When evening came, he saddled his horse and started toward the path that would take him to his camp. Suddenly, he heard a shout behind him. The men had returned from their hunt. To everyone's amazement, they had caught enough deer in one day to supply the village with what it needed. David praised God for making it possible to keep the men at the camp so they could hear the Good News of Christ.

Tired from the many hours of preaching, but encouraged by the Indians' faithful attendance, David continued to preach and meet with the people of Crossweeksung every day. He would preach a sermon and then ask them questions concerning the things he had taught. David was very surprised to see how much they remembered in just a few days. Whenever they were not clear about something the missionary had taught, the Indians would keep him up late into the night, asking him question after question. They wanted to know how God created the earth, how He made the white people and the Indians, how God had become man in the person of Jesus Christ. They wanted to know how the Holy Spirit changed men's hearts. Some of them talked to David about their sins. Some were thieves, others had committed adultery, others were drunkards. David assured each of them that God could forgive even the worst sinner. Often, after all the questions had been answered and the doubts had been chased away, many confessed their sins to Christ, relieved to be finally freed of their burden of sin.

David praised God for opening the hearts of the people of Crossweeksung. After years of serving the Lord in the North American wilderness, burdened by the taunts of skeptical Indians and strained by the onslaught of illness and discouragement, David began to witness the budding fruit of his ministry. He had not made any changes in his preaching or the message of the Gospel. He had simply and faithfully proclaimed the Word of God, the Good News of Christ, to anyone who would listen. Now, after more than two years of labor, the scales seemed to be falling from the eyes of the Indians. Excited by this change among the people of Crossweeksung, David looked forward to the days ahead, to days when the Indian camps would be filled with praises to God.

13

Reaping the Harvest

"Must you to leave?" asked a young woman in broken English. Tiny feathers tucked in her shiny braids fluttered in the warm breeze.

"Yes, I need to see how my friends at the Forks of Delaware are doing," David replied with a smile as he packed his supplies. "Besides, I promised them that I would return as soon as possible."

The Indians of Crossweeksung gathered around the young missionary as he saddled his horse and prepared to leave their camp for a brief visit to the Forks of Delaware. Because he had not known how his preaching would be received at Crossweeksung, he had not made plans to stay very long. But now that he had discovered how receptive these Indians were to the Gospel, he wanted to return to the Forks of Delaware to tell the Indians there that he would be moving to the Crossweeksung territory before the end of summer. So, in early July of 1745, not long after he had arrived in Crossweeksung, he packed his bags as the Indians, earnest and sincere in their quest for truth, pleaded with him to return quickly.

"We promise to meet with you when you come back to us," the woman said. Other Indians who were standing nearby nodded in agreement. "We will go to the distant villages and tell others there to come hear you speak of Jesus."

"That would be wonderful," David replied, delighted by the young woman's enthusiasm. "I promise I will return as soon as I can."

After saying their goodbyes, the Indians drifted off to their homes, but the young woman lingered.

"Is there something I can do for you?" David asked as he fastened the harness on his horse. The young woman sobbed quietly. He stopped what he was doing and walked over beside her. "What is it?"

"I wish . . ." She sobbed louder and tears streamed down her face. "I wish God would change me, make my heart new."

An older woman who had been standing nearby walked over and put her arm around the girl's thin shoulders. Looking at David, the older woman said in a soft voice, "I also want to find Christ. Will you please hurry back so you can help us?"

"Yes, I will," David promised. "Remember, seek the Lord while He may be found. Jesus said, 'Knock and the door will be opened to you, seek and you will find.' Think about what I have taught you during the last few days. Most of all, seek God in prayer, ask Christ to forgive you of your sins, and trust only in Him for your salvation."

As he and Moses led their horses toward the path that led to the Forks of Delaware, one of the chiefs of Crossweeksung stopped him. His headdress of feathers hung limp in his grasp, his cheeks wet with tears.

"I know I am lost," he cried. Moses quickly translated. "I have sinned greatly against God. I know if I were to die today, I would be lost forever. But I am not yet ready to believe in this Jesus Christ of yours."

"Please think about everything I have taught you and your people," David said. He put his hand on the old man's shoulder. "Jesus Christ can save even the most hardened sinner. Put your hope and faith in Him. We will talk some more when I return."

As David rode with Moses through the forest to the Forks of Delaware, he wondered if he should stay and talk more with the two women and the old man. But the more he considered it, the more he knew that he needed to get back to the Forks of Delaware just as he had promised. If the spiritual concerns expressed by the Indians at Crossweeksung were the work of God's Spirit, they would not disappear simply because he was not with them. If God had purposed to renew their hearts and bring them under conviction of their sin, that conviction would only increase over time. In a way, it would be better if David left them alone for a while; then they would not feel pressured by his presence but would come to a profession of faith on their own because it was truly the desire of their hearts.

Shortly after David arrived back at Sakhauwatung in the Forks of Delaware, the Indians and a few white people from a nearby settlement gathered to hear him preach. The Indians sat in front of their huts as the tall missionary stood in the middle of the camp with his Bible in hand. Near the front of the crowd sat Moses' wife. She had listened to David preach many times before and had been one of the few who seemed genuinely concerned about learning the truth. She sat cross-legged on the grass with her three children sitting quietly beside her.

The day was hot, so David took off his brass-buttoned jacket. He kept his white undershirt tied at the neck but rolled up the sleeves. The Indian men wore light, pale buckskins wrapped around their waists. Their feet were either bare or covered in smooth skins. The women wore short dresses with a strap over one shoulder, their long hair pulled back in a bouquet of braids and feathers. Standing off to the side, the white visitors found shelter from the summer sun under the shade of the massive oaks that lined the forest.

As perspiration rolled down his face, David told the small assembly about Jesus' last night with His disciples. He described how He prayed so hard that drops of blood dripped from his forehead, how the soldiers came under the cover of darkness to arrest Jesus, and how Judas, His own disciple, betrayed his Lord with a kiss.

The Indians fixed their eyes on David as he spoke. Even when a bird would screech loudly from the forest, the Indians didn't seem to notice but kept focused on the missionary who stood before them. Many wept as David described Jesus' painful death on the cross. Some of the women sobbed when he said that Jesus gave up His life for people of all races, the Jews, the blacks, the whites, and the Indians—that God had chosen people from every tribe and every nation to be a part of His family.

At some point during the sermon, David noticed that Moses seemed to interpret his words with more zeal than he ever had before. The Indian's voice cracked, and tears welled up in his eyes as his native speech rolled off his tongue. David glanced at the older man and wondered if he would be able to continue to interpret. Moses didn't return the glance but kept explaining what had been said even after David had finished. As the young preacher read a verse from the Gospel of John, Moses' wife stood up and walked over to her husband. She put her hand on his arm and smiled through a veil of tears.

As soon as David finished his message, Moses and his wife asked him if they could speak with him privately. The three walked a short way into the woods and stopped at a small clearing. Birds chattered with the squirrels in the trees overhead. Sunlight shifted through the branches, shining rays of light in every direction. It was cooler in the glade than at the Indian camp, and the three sat down on the thick grass. No one said anything for a few minutes. Sniffling, Moses could barely keep back the tears. David let him take his time.

"We both have come to realize how much we have offended God," Moses finally said in a strained voice. "I have struggled for many months to find peace with God. Until today, it had escaped me."

Sobs overwhelmed the interpreter. He tried to get himself under control by taking deep breaths. His wife held his hand and put her chin on his shoulder.

"For many months now I have wanted to know what I could do to be saved. I haven't been able to sleep or eat. My family and friends could see that something was going on inside of me—as I know you have noticed—but I still did not want to turn my life entirely over to God."

"But that has changed?" David asked.

"Yes," Moses sighed, relieved from the burden he had been carrying. "For so long I have felt like I have been surrounded by a hedge of thorns on all sides. If I moved even an inch, I would be pricked by the thorns. But now, it is as if God has cleared away that hedge of thorns. I do not need to fear their sharp needles, for I know now that Christ has already borne them in my place."

He looked at David. A tear strayed onto the Indian's cheek. Moses brushed it away and smiled. His wife smiled too. She did not understand much English, but she knew what her husband was saying. God had been opening her eyes even as He opened her husband's.

"I realize now that I cannot save myself. I am totally dependent on God. I *want* to be dependent on Him. I know that if God left me to myself I would perish. I have never done one good thing in my life. I know others have done worse things on the outside, but I know that there is no good thing inside of me. It is the same with everyone in the world—my people and yours. The world is lost. My people are lost. Even though they believe they are good, they are not. They offend God by worshiping idols, but they do not even realize it. Unless they turn to Christ and put their faith in Him, they will certainly perish."

Moses took his wife's hand. "My wife knows this to be true as well," he said gently. "It is as if I have awakened from a sleep or as if a cloud has been removed from my eyes. I used to think I knew what happiness was, but I really had no idea. Until now I had been living without any hope, but that has all changed. Today, it is as if I heard God say, 'There is hope. There is hope.' I cannot say I fully understand everything about Christ, but I know I need Him. I know He is the only one who can save me. He is my only hope."

David's heart stirred within him as he listened to Moses tell him of God's work in his life. Tears fell from his eyes when the Indian said that he wanted his people to know the one true God. "How glorious is the grace of God!" David thought. "Here sits a man who at one time had no concern about Christ and the Gospel. He drank his liquor and earned his keep as an interpreter. Little else mattered. But now he sits here, crying like a little child, with joy in his eyes and humility in his voice. Praise be to God!"

"Well, there is something we need to do," David said to Moses and his wife after he had asked them a few questions concerning their understanding of sin and salvation in Christ.

"What?" Moses asked.

"You and your children need to be baptized," David said, smiling. "We can go to the river right now."

The three walked from the woods, gathered up the children, and headed toward the river that ran beside the Indian camp. A number of Indians followed them, curious to see where they were going in such a hurry. When they reached the river, David and the Indians waded into the cool, clear water. Whispering, a group of Indians gathered along the shore to watch the strange event.

"Could you please translate?" David asked Moses. The older man nodded.

"The sacrament of baptism was instituted by our Lord Jesus Christ as a seal of the covenant of grace, of our union with Him, of the cleansing of our sins, and of eternal life," David said, loud enough for the Indians on the shore to hear. "The water represents and signifies both the blood of Christ, which takes away the guilt of our sin, and the work of the Holy Spirit, which sanctifies us. The sprinkling of the water is not magic; it signifies the cleansing of sin and our rising unto a new life by the death and resurrection of Christ."

Turning to Moses and his wife, David asked, "Do you both confess and repent of your sins?"

"We do," they replied.

"Do you confess your dependence on the grace of God for salvation?"

"We do."

"Do you put your faith in Jesus Christ who is the Way, the Truth, and the Life?"

"We do."

"Do you promise, in humble reliance upon the grace of God, to live as becomes followers of Christ?"

"We do."

The river swirled around them, and the sunlight danced on the gentle waves, shining like stars in the night sky. David cupped his hands and dipped them into the sparkling river. Moses, his wife, and their small children knelt in the shallow water and bowed their heads. Turning to face the shore, David sprinkled the water over the Indians' dark hair and proclaimed, "I baptize you in the name of the Father, and of the Son, and of the Holy Spirit. Amen."

Rising from the waters, Moses wrapped his arms around the young missionary. Both of them wept and held each other, basking in their common love for Christ. The Indians on the shore glanced uncomfortably at one another. They had never seen an Indian and a white man embrace each other as if they were brothers.

"We must listen more to what this preacher has to say," an old chief said to one of the tribe's braves. The young warrior watched curiously as the missionary embraced the Indian.

"Yes, maybe we should listen," the brave echoed thoughtfully.

14

The Fire Spreads

The camp at Crossweeksung scurried with activity as the Indians prepared to gather for another day of mid-week worship. Children washed in the stream, mothers cleaned up from the noon meal, and fathers gathered the little ones who had wandered off to pick clover behind the wigwams. Some of the older people had already assembled near the center of camp, anxious to hear the lesson for that day. Since the missionary's return a few weeks earlier, the Indians had listened to him nearly every day as he taught from the Bible about Christ and salvation. The sparse crowd that had first gathered to hear him speak had grown to more than forty people. Those who had wanted to know more about Christianity before he left for the Forks of Delaware were just as interested when he came back to stay.

Just outside the borders of the bustling village, a young Indian woman made her way through the dense forest toward the Crossweeksung territory. She had heard rumors of a white missionary who brought a strange teaching about God to her people. Offended by the white man's presumption that he could come and teach the Indians foreign ideas about religion, she decided to confront him.

As the August sun baked the dry forest, she

pushed her way through the branches that blocked the tangled path in front of her. Perspiration glistened on her forehead and her chestnut hair trailed behind her. Her face, smooth and delicate, was marred by a haughty grimace. The light buckskin dress that draped across her slender frame swished loudly against her legs as she stomped down the path.

Suddenly, the trail opened into a grassy field where children were playing as their mothers gathered twigs. Not knowing which direction to take, she stopped a boy who was heading for one of the forest trails with a slender bow in his hand.

"Where does the white preacher camp?" she asked.

"In the house through those trees," the boy replied, pointing to his right.

The young woman hesitated for a moment, her hands on her hips. She looked around to see if anyone was watching her. The only people nearby were some women grinding corn and twisting saplings they had gathered at the edge of the field. They worked quickly as if anxious to be done so they could be off doing something else, and they seemed too preoccupied with their work to notice the young woman. Slapping dust off her buckskin dress and glancing at the women who were hard at work, she hurried across the clearing to the house that was partially hidden in the shadow of the trees.

Inside, David was putting the last touches on his sermon for that day. As he jotted down notes on waxen paper, he sipped some stale water from a tin cup. Just as he was about to set the cup down, someone banged on his door. Startled, he jumped at the noise, spilling some of the water onto his notes. He quickly dried the paper with the edge of his shirt and hurried to the rattling door.

Opening the door, he found a young woman standing before him, her hands drawn into tight fists at her side and her pretty face twisted with a scowl.

"Good afternoon," David said pleasantly. "Can I help you?"

The girl said something in broken English, but David could barely understand her, although he could tell from her hand movements and expressions that she was angry. He was about to ask her to repeat what she had said when Moses walked up the steps behind her.

"Moses!" David exclaimed with a sigh of relief. "I'm so glad you are here. Could you please ask this young lady what I can do for her?"

Moses nodded.

"I want to know what this pale face is doing here," she said angrily after Moses finished translating David's question.

"I am here to tell these people about Jesus Christ, about the one true God," David replied gently. He had grown accustomed to hostility from some of the Indians and had learned to speak softly and directly to them about why he had come to live among them.

"Why would you try to change our own traditions, our own beliefs that are just as sacred as yours?" she asked.

"For the salvation of your soul," David explained. "I realize that your own beliefs are very important to you and your people, but that does not make them right. The truth about God is the same for all people. I cannot simply believe what I want, and you cannot simply believe what you want without any regard to the truth."

"The truth, as you call it, is for the white man," she scoffed. "We have our own truth. I have my own truth."

"First of all, Christianity is not the white man's religion," David said patiently. "Our Savior, Jesus Christ, was not an Englishman, but a Jew, from a distant land, a land more distant than even England where the settlers come from. Second, we do not create our own truth. Truth is not like a shifting shadow that changes from culture to culture. There is one truth, and it is revealed in the person of Jesus Christ. He has spoken to us through His Word, the Holy Scriptures, and has commanded that the Good News of salvation be proclaimed throughout the world. That is what I am doing here."

"The Indian people do not need salvation," she scoffed again, but seeming to be less sure of herself than she had been. "We don't even have souls. When we die, we return to the earth."

David found her comment perplexing because most of the Indians he had met believed they possessed a soul. This woman certainly had her own ideas about things, ideas that conformed neither to the truth of God's Word nor to her own Indian traditions.

"The Bible says that when animals die they return to the earth, but the spirit of man goes upward to stand before the judgment of God," David replied.

"How do you know that?" the girl laughed. "Do you think it is true just because a book told you so?"

"And how do you know what is true?" David

asked. "Do you have any standard for truth other than yourself?"

"No, I can know what is true for myself by figuring it out on my own," she retorted.

"And are you so sure that what you think is really the truth, especially when it contradicts what other people believe?" David asked.

"I know what I know," she said, glancing away from the fixed gaze of the missionary. She shuffled her feet and rubbed her hands anxiously.

"And what if it is true, or right, for me to steal from you, is that acceptable?" David asked. "What happens when something that is right for me conflicts with something that is wrong for you?"

The girl didn't answer but simply looked up at the trees that swayed back and forth in the gentle summer breeze.

"Well, while you think about it, why don't you come hear me preach today? I will be talking about Jesus Christ, who proclaimed that He alone is the Way, the Truth, and the Life. Now, if you will excuse me, I am supposed to be at the main camp in just a few minutes."

The girl laughed nervously. "I don't want to listen to you tell foolish stories."

"The choice is yours," David replied, deciding that he had argued with the girl long enough. "But I hope you will come. For now, I really must go."

After gathering his Bible and notes from inside, he and Moses walked into the woods toward the camp. They left the girl lingering indecisively outside his house, her face scarlet with anger. She waited a few minutes as the two men disappeared into the woods, and then, when they were just out of sight, she followed them down the path. Cautiously, she kept her distance so they would not notice her.

When David arrived at the camp, a large crowd of Indians had already gathered. Some of the children ran over to him and clung to his legs as he hurried to the center of camp. The crowd hushed, and David asked the children to sit down with their parents. Once everyone was settled, he opened his Bible and, with Moses standing at his side, began to preach.

Peering from behind the trees, the Indian woman peeked over the shoulders of some young people who stood near the back of the crowd. As David preached, she looked for an opportunity to expose his foolish ideas in front of the other Indians. But instead of disagreeing with him, she suddenly found that what he said made sense. "Maybe I do have a soul," she thought. "And if I do, that means I will live forever. But where will I live? Will I fly southward like the Indian legends taught, or will I go somewhere else?"

The young missionary read from the Book of God and declared that everyone would go before the Creator and be judged for the things they did. The girl thought about her life. "Haven't I been a good person?" she asked herself. But even as she asked the question, the preacher described how no one in the world is good, that everyone has broken God's holy commandments. Somehow she knew what he said was true. She was a sinner just as the white man said.

"If God is going to judge me for what I have done, then there is no hope for me," she thought. "I am guilty, and that means I will be punished."

She glanced around at the other Indians. Some

were crying, others were smiling. Nervously, she began to pace up and down near the edge of the forest. The more she paced, the more upset she became. Then, as if drawn against her will, she made her way to the front of the crowd.

"The Lord is merciful and gracious, slow to anger, and plenteous in mercy," David said, quoting from Psalm 103. "He will not always chide; neither will He keep His anger forever. He hath not dealt with us according to our sins, nor rewarded us according to our iniquities."

As the young woman listened to the beautiful words of God's mercy, she began to cry. Her hands shook, and her body trembled. Overcome by feelings and convictions that she could not fully understand, she leaned over, barely able to sit up. She cried out, sobbing uncontrollably. David looked over at the young woman who had fallen back onto the ground, crying and mumbling. Once he completed his sermon, he walked over to where the Indians had surrounded her. An old woman tried to help her stand up, but the girl pulled away from her, wailing and crying.

"Guttummaukalummeh wechaumeh kmeleh Ndah," the girl cried over and over again.

"What is she saying?" David asked Moses as he leaned over and helped the girl to her feet.

"She says, 'Have mercy on me, and help me to give You my heart,' " Moses replied as he helped David carry the girl to one of the bark huts. They set her down near the entrance and someone brought her some water. When an old woman put the cup to the girl's lips, she refused to drink and kept repeating the same prayer again and again.

"There's nothing we can do now," David said. "I think it would be best if we just leave her alone to pray to God."

The girl remained there for the rest of the day. Finally, that evening, she stood up, calm and in control of herself. One of the older women asked her if she was all right.

"Today I have seen God's mercy, and somehow it has changed me," the girl replied with a faraway look in her eyes. "Now I am at peace."

The old woman sent a message to David, informing him that the girl had come to her senses and appeared calm and peaceful. The young missionary had been eating dinner with one of the families and quickly excused himself when he received the message. He walked through the camp under the clear night sky and found the girl sitting calmly in front of a small fire, eating a bowl of corn. She looked up when she heard him approach. The scorn and unbelief that had marred her features just a few hours earlier had disappeared, replaced by a humility and contentment that could only come from the Spirit of God.

David sat beside her, not saying a word. From the darkness behind him, Moses walked up and sat across from the girl. She glanced over at him, then back at the fire.

"I was wrong," she whispered. "I don't know how I understand the things that I do, but I know that what you said today is true."

Moses translated, and David listened intently. He looked directly into the young girl's eyes, now bright with an inner joy.

"I realize now that I do have a soul, that I am accountable to God for my actions," she said. "I understand that His way of doing things, His standard for our lives, is the same for everyone, no matter what our own traditions tell us, no matter what I might think. I don't really understand everything about who Christ is and what He did, but I know that I need Him to save me because I cannot change myself. I know I need His Spirit to make me into the kind of person God wants me to be."

David was stunned by the insights the girl had gained in such a short time. For someone who had been so angry, so hostile to the truth, she had turned completely around, changed from the root, made alive in Christ. As the fire crackled and the girl continued to explain the many things God had shown her through the missionary's preaching, those things that He had enabled her to understand about herself and about Him, David prayed that more Indians would be changed just as she had been. In silent devotion, he prayed that more would come to know the richness of God's grace, His compassion, and His glory.

15

Birth of a Church

One evening, as David walked along a shadowy trail that led from one Indian camp in the Crossweeksung territory to another, he heard rustling behind him. He paused and glanced over his shoulder but saw only the silent boughs bending like a grand archway over the narrow path. Shaking his head, he kept walking as dirt and pebbles crunched beneath his tired feet. The day had been filled with teaching and preaching and David was exhausted. His shoulders hung limp, and his head drooped as he walked through the lonely woods. He took a deep breath, but it was suddenly cut short as a cough ripped through his congested lungs. David paused in the middle of the path, coughing until his chest burned with pain. Finally, just when he thought the pain too great to bear, the coughing eased and he was able to continue his walk down the path.

Just as he passed through the shadows of a thick pillar of trees, David heard the sound of light footsteps on the pebble-strewn path behind him. He jerked his head around just in time to catch a glimpse of a young Indian boy, about the age of thirteen, dash behind a moss-covered tree. David grinned to himself, then cleared his throat.

"I know you are there," David said gently in the

language of the Crossweeksung Indians. "Come out so I can see you."

David knew his grasp of the Indian language was meager, but he hoped the young boy would understand and trust him.

The boy's round, dirty face peered out from behind the trees, his eyes wide and curious. David recognized the youngster from the camp meetings.

"Come here," David urged in English. "Don't be afraid."

The boy walked forward, looking David up and down. "He has probably never been this close to a white man," the missionary thought to himself. David smiled, trying to reassure the boy that he would come to no harm. The boy seemed to relax as he edged up to David.

"Walk by you?" the boy asked in his own language.

"You want to walk with me?" David said, pointing down the path in the direction he had been heading. The boy nodded.

"Very well," David told him. "I would love the company."

Always careful not to get too close but constantly watching the missionary out of the corner of his eye, the boy walked beside David until they reached the Crossweeksung camp less than a mile away. Once the first wigwam was in sight, the boy ran ahead. As David made his way to the long house where the chief and his family lived, the boy returned. Grabbing the missionary's hand, he pulled him toward the chief's wigwam. The boy had somehow known where David was heading, and he seemed excited that he could help the missionary in some small way. Once they reached the wigwam, David thanked the boy, who held back the flap on the entrance so the tired missionary could enter. Once David was inside the boy scurried away into the darkness, too afraid to be any closer to the white preacher than he had already dared.

Inside, the chief and his wife were preparing their evening meal. The chief nodded to David and motioned for him to sit down. The wife, who busied herself by the fire, smiled and handed him a bowl of boiled corn. Just as David was about to take a bite, Moses entered the wigwam and sat down next to the chief. The interpreter had returned to the main camp earlier in the day and had been summoned by the Indian chief to translate as he spoke to the missionary.

"I have heard your teaching and am curious," the chief said through a mouthful of steamed roots. "You say when a man dies he goes to be with God. What happens to his body? Does it just rot in the ground?"

"God has promised that after we die, not only will our souls be transformed into perfection, but our bodies will be reunited with our souls in glory," David explained as Moses translated. "That means our bodies will be resurrected, brought to life, but not in the same form as they are in now, but in perfection. We will never hunger or thirst. We will never get sick or grow old. We will live forever with our Lord. We will be changed even as Jesus Christ was changed when He rose from the dead. We must never forget that Christ rose again physically. If He had not, He would not have conquered death. But He did; and because He did, we too will be brought to life just as He was."

David continued to talk with the chief late into the night. They covered every topic from Adam's sin in the garden to David's personal testimony of how God had changed his heart. The chief seemed unable to tire, but the late hour weighed heavily on David; as the night deepened he knew he had to get some rest. After thanking the chief for the dinner and promising to return to teach again the following day, he left the wigwam with Moses beside him.

As he and Moses walked back down the path to their lodgings, David suddenly coughed violently.

"Are you all right?" Moses asked, putting his hand on David's shoulder.

"I'm fine," David replied, irritated that he could not get rid of the congestion in his lungs.

He coughed again and kept walking. Moses stared after him with a skeptical look on his face. The Indian waited a moment, then hurried to catch up. Neither said anything else on the way back to the cabin.

Later that week, while David was helping some of the Indians negotiate a trade of furs and knives with some white men, one of the Indians asked him if he could speak with him privately. David agreed and took his leave of the other Indians.

"Some time ago I put my wife away and took another woman," the man confessed to David without looking at him. "I've been listening to your preaching and to your warnings against drunkenness and adultery. I listened the other day as you taught about God's design for marriage, that a man and a woman should be joined together until they are parted by death. I have not been able to stop thinking about how wrong I was to take another woman. I realize it is common among my people to do such a thing, but that does not make it right."

"Did your wife give you any reason to put her away?" David asked. "Did you find her with another man?"

"No, no, it was nothing like that," the man said. "She did nothing wrong. It was me. I was the one who was wrong. What should I do?"

"Have you talked with your wife?" David asked. "Is she willing to forgive you and take you back?"

"Yes, she told me so just this morning," the man said. "She is a very kind woman and did not deserve to be treated in such a cruel way." He stopped walking and looked up at David, his eyes brimming with tears. "You said that Christians cannot continue to live in sin. I know I must do something because I am living in sin right now. Tell me what I must do."

"You must end the relationship you have with this other woman, confess your sin, and return to your wife," David said, his expression grave but gentle.

The man stared at the ground and thought for a moment. He looked at Moses, then at David.

"That is what I will do," the man said eagerly. He then thanked David for his help and hurried back up the path to the camp.

"I hope the other Indians will not be hardened against Christianity when they see how difficult it is to live as children of God," David said to Moses. "The cost of following Jesus is great, but those who are truly changed will give up their former ways and follow Him."

Just as he had promised, the man publicly confessed his sin of adultery. He ended his adulterous relationship, returned to his wife, and promised to live with her, to be kind to her, and to remain faithful to her. The other Indians supported him in what he did. They did not appear hardened in the least by what happened. Quite the contrary—they took the matter seriously and agreed that the laws of Christ concerning marriage were good and right. No longer would it be so easy for the Indians to put away their wives whenever they wanted. From that point on, they would live by a higher rule, one that required them to love their wives, to honor them, to protect them, and to remain faithful to them all their days.

During the following weeks, Indians came from miles around to hear the young missionary preach about Jesus Christ. Some came out of curiosity. Some came because friends urged them to. Others just happened to be passing through the area when they saw crowds gather around the wigwams. Sometimes white people from nearby settlements would drop by to see what was happening among the Indians. It had not gone unnoticed that fewer Indians were visiting the taverns and trading their furs and knives for liquor.

One Sunday afternoon David baptized twenty-five people—fifteen adults and ten children. Following the service, David met with the new converts, reminding them of their commitment to the Lord and their responsibility to live in a worthy manner. It was very important for the Indians to remain faithful to God's commandments because so many people were waiting for the opportunity to call them hypocrites. David advised them to go to the Lord often in prayer, to rely on His grace to keep them from sin, and to guard their hearts against temptation.

"You will need to encourage one another every day," David said. "It will be difficult to remain faithful to Christ while your friends and neighbors continue to worship false gods and ridicule you for worshiping the Christian God. They will accuse you of selling out to the English, of turning your backs on your own people, but remember that God's ways are above the English and the Indian traditions. It is Him you must follow and His commandments that you must obey."

"We will meet together and pray," an older woman said as she put her arm around one of the young women. "God will protect us."

By the end of the summer, the crowd that had first come to hear David preach had grown to about ninety-five people. The development of a congregation in Crossweeksung changed David's role from an evangelist to a pastor. He met with his people, trained them in the ways of Christianity, and counseled them when they had disputes with one another or conflicts within their families. He even helped them with their everyday business affairs. Once they became Christians, the Indians were very concerned about their testimony before others. They immediately wanted to pay their debts and work hard to earn a living for their families. Those who had a problem with drinking quit going to the taverns. Husbands cared for their wives and children as they had never done before, and children obeyed their parents. Everyone honored the Sabbath by not working and playing. Instead, they spent the day praying, enjoying Christian fellowship, and caring for the sick.

As David watched his little congregation grow, his thoughts turned to the Indians along the Susquehanna.

He asked himself whether he should make another trip to those tribes. The fall season would be the best time to make the journey because most of the Indians would be at home. After praying about the journey, David decided he would inform his people that he would be leaving them for a short time so he could go and tell others about Christ. While it was tempting to remain in the comfort of Crossweeksung, surrounded by eager Indians who wanted to know Christ intimately and to follow His ways, his heart yearned for the Indians of the Susquehanna who still lived under the darkness of idolatry.

After speaking to his congregation one evening in late August 1745, David told the Indians that he would be traveling to the Susquehanna in a few days.

"I must go see more of your people who live far away from here," David explained to them. "Please pray that the Spirit of God would go with me because, without Him, I will not be able to do any good among the Indians. If you can, please spend the rest of the day in prayer for me, that God would be with me and that many would be brought to Christ through the preaching of His Word."

Excited murmurs spread throughout the congregation as the Indians agreed to pray for him.

"We will pray all night if we have to," said an old man with deep wrinkles around his eyes.

About an hour before dusk, the Indians began to pray. David needed to make preparations for the journey so he returned to his cabin just outside the village. Faithful to their word, the Indians prayed until the morning, and Moses told David later that they did not seem to notice the time. The Indians only realized how long they had been praying when the sun came up, announcing the beginning of a new day.

David returned to the Crossweeksung camp early the next morning where all the Indians had gathered to meet him. As the missionary said his goodbyes, a very old Indian shuffled over to where David stood. The crowd hushed. Everyone knew the man. He had been a powwow for many years and was well known for his commitment to the Indian traditions. With uncommon zeal, he had worshiped the "great spirit" and had refused to hear about Christianity when David first arrived at Crossweeksung.

Without looking up, the bent old man reached for David's hand and opened it before him. Slowly, he placed two snake rattles in the missionary's hand. The rattles were used in the idolatrous dances to call on the spirits. David closed his hand around them and handed them to Moses. The man looked into David's face. Tears fell from the Indian's eyes, washing his wrinkled skin. Gently, David took his hands and held them. The man was trembling. Moses gave the rattles to one of the Indians who took them and set them on a flat rock. Grabbing a large stone, he smashed the rattles into pieces. The old Indian never said a word. He didn't need to. David understood the significance of giving up the rattles. Without reservation, he had turned his back on Indian superstitions and embraced the teaching of Christ.

After praying for the man and thanking God for opening his eyes, David and Moses checked the supplies on their horses and climbed into their saddles.

"Remember us in your prayers," David said.

"We will," the Indians replied. "Christ be with you."

With a wave of his hand, David turned his horse toward the narrow trail that led to the Susquehanna River. Behind him, the Indians of Crossweeksung embraced the old man, welcoming another lost sheep into the fold and praising Christ for bringing home one who had been lost for so many years. As his thoughts turned toward the journey ahead, David prayed that the tribes he would preach to along the Susquehanna would find the same freedom in Christ that the old man and other Indians at Crossweeksung had found.

16

Shamokin

The night before David set off to the Susquehanna River from the Forks of Delaware, he spent the evening with Moses and his family. The interpreter's wife prepared a meal of roasted deer meat and vegetables, which David and Moses ate heartily. Pleased to see them well fed, Moses' wife smiled as they finished off the last helping of corn bread and leaned back to sip hot herb tea and discuss their upcoming journey.

"I think it will be best to take the same route as before," David commented. "I want to see whether my preaching from our previous trip had any effect on the Indians. Once we have visited all of those tribes, then we will go farther up river to find Indians who have never heard the Gospel."

As the two men talked, Moses' children gathered nuts, berries, and roots to store away in traveling bags. They scurried to and fro, excited that they could help their father in his work. They stuffed the food into dry packs to keep it fresh for the journey and stacked them by the wigwam. Once the supplies had been packed, two of the older boys brushed down the horses, and the younger children ran off to fill water skins from a nearby stream. Back at the wigwam, Moses sharpened his knives, and David made notes on a map that recorded the locations of various tribes along the river.

The two men worked in silence until Moses let out a long sigh.

"What is it?" David asked.

"I realize that the money I earn from working for the Missionary Society is necessary, but I regret not spending more time with my family," Moses said. "Not that I'm complaining. I want to go with you and know it is the right thing to do for now, but I will miss being with my wife these many weeks."

As David scratched his ink-stained pen across the parchment, he looked up at Moses. Surprise sparkled in the missionary's eyes. He was pleased to see the interpreter growing in his love for his wife and children. David smiled and put down his pen.

"Well, we shouldn't be gone too long," he said, patting Moses on the shoulder. "Before you know it, you'll be back helping your children strip buckskins."

Moses nodded and silently watched his wife as she cleaned up from the evening meal. Then he glanced back at David.

"Have you ever considered taking a wife?" Moses asked a little hesitantly. He didn't want to overstep his bounds and intrude where he was not wanted. Moses had already observed that the missionary kept his private life very much to himself. But David didn't seem to mind the question. He simply sighed and looked up into the trees whose branches danced in the evening breeze.

"Once during a visit to Yale College a couple of years ago, I met a godly young woman, the daughter of a minister whom I greatly admire, the Rev. Jonathan Edwards. She had accompanied her father to a commencement ceremony at the college," David said. "I only spoke with her briefly, but I remember how her reverence for God struck me during our conversation. If there were any woman in the world for me, it would be her. But it is not to be."

David grew silent. Thinking about Jerusha Edwards made him realize how much he missed the companionship of Christian friends as he labored in the lonely wilderness. But then he looked back at Moses, at the first man who had been converted under his ministry, and he realized that his life in the untamed forests was not as lonely as it had been. Even though David had left friends and family to travel into the Indian territories, God had not left him alone. He had given him a new family, new friends, who shared his love for Christ and longed for others to come into His kingdom. David could pay the price of not having a wife because he was content. He possessed a peace that truly "passes understanding" as he traveled to the distant tribes, to those Indians who one day might become brothers and sisters in the family of God just as Moses had.

"Anyway," David said, pulling himself from his thoughts, "I have thought, on occasion, of marrying and settling down, but I know it is not what the Lord wants me to do. I cannot do the missionary work I need to do, face the hardships that I must, and still care for a wife. No, that privilege is not for me. At least I don't think so right now."

David said no more after that, and Moses did not pursue the matter. Without another word, the two continued to work until they were finished with the final preparations for their trip. Once everything was packed, David said good night to Moses and his family, then returned to the cabin he had built when he had first arrived in the Forks of Delaware. The cabin was drafty and barren. Most other men would have preferred to sleep·back among the lively wigwams, but this was the closest thing David had to a home. He preferred its solitude to the chatter of the village. Here he could think more clearly, pray more fervently, and sleep more peaceably. Yawning, he lit a candle and threw a blanket onto the cot. Then, before turning in for the night, he knelt beside his bed and prayed, asking God to give him spiritual and physical strength, to have mercy on the Indians, and to use his preaching to bring them into the kingdom of Christ.

The next morning, after eating a breakfast of hominy, berries, nuts, and wild roots, David and Moses set out from the Forks of Delaware to the Susquehanna. Three days later, they arrived at Shamokin, a large Indian town on the river. Like so many other native camps, this one was spread out on both sides of the vast river. But unlike the others, Shamokin included a small island in the middle. About half of the Indians who lived in the village were Delawares, and the others were called the Senakes and Tutelas. Each group spoke its own language, which often created conflicts among the Indians as they quarreled over hunting zones and trading deals. Altogether, the village comprised about fifty houses. The Indians claimed that nearly three-hundred people lived there, but David had never seen more than half that many.

Some of the Delawares whom David had preached

to during his previous trip recognized him as soon as he entered the main camp. A middle-aged Indian with bags of herbs hanging from his neck invited David to sleep in his wigwam. Since it was nearly dark, and after three nights of sleeping outside in the cool air, David welcomed the invitation. Not minding the night air, Moses said he would sleep outside at the edge of the forest. They ate dinner together, then two husky Indians led David to a spacious hut on the west bank. Lifting the flap that hung over the entrance, they motioned him inside. The room was spacious with furs draped over low-set platforms that lined the walls of the hut. In the middle of the wigwam, a small fire burned brightly. Sitting in a circle around the fire was a group of Indians with red paint on their faces. Some beat on buckskin drums while others shook rattles similar to those David had seen other Indians use in their idolatrous festivals.

As he made his way to the back of the room, David heard a moan in one of the dark corners. He glanced back at the two husky Indians who had joined the others around the fire, but no one looked at him. They seemed preoccupied with the preparations for a dance. David moved to the far corner and noticed a man about his own age lying on some skins. The young man moaned again. Perspiration covered his face and chest. David carefully draped a discarded fur over him, then set his bags down. He was about to walk over to the fire when one of the other Indians brought him a bowl of leafy greens, a common meal among Indians of that region. David pointed toward the sick Indian, asking what was wrong with him. In broken English, the man explained that he had taken a fever while fishing along the river. David asked whether he could do anything for him, but the Indian simply said no and returned to the group around the fire.

David decided not to press the matter. He was too exhausted from his travels to try to reason with the Indians. So he slumped down near the sick Indian and ate the food he had been given. He wasn't very hungry, having just eaten a meal with Moses, but he ate the tasteless greens anyway because he didn't want to offend his host. The man who had invited him to sleep in his wigwam peered in David's direction. David nodded in greeting. The man grinned back—a slanted grin that made him look mischievous. David remained seated, but the Indian didn't come over to greet him. The Indian simply grinned again and turned his attention to the dance, beating the drum that balanced between his knees.

Around him, the other Indians danced wildly, spreading smoke throughout the room. David could hardly breathe. He wondered why the Indians had invited him to stay with them, but as soon as he asked himself the question, he knew the answer. They considered him to be a spiritual man, and they wanted him to see that they too were spiritual, that they were really no different from Christians. David shook his head. There were so many differences, but the Indians couldn't see them. Unlike the Indian religion, a redeemer was central to the Christian faith. Jesus Christ, the God-man, came into the world to save sinners. He lived, died, and rose again to bring redemption to a lost race. Mankind is corrupted by sin and under the condemnation of God, but by the grace of God and through the mediation of Jesus Christ, fallen

man can be saved—if only he puts his faith in Christ.
This primary difference between the pagan religions
and Christianity could not be denied. But the only
thing these Indians saw when David came to preach
was a "religious" man who seemed to share their interest in "spiritual" matters.

As David thought about the differences between
Christianity and the Indian traditions, the sick Indian
next to him began to toss and turn, moaning louder and
more frequently. After a few minutes, David couldn't
take it any more. "Can't these people see they are
disturbing their sick friend?" he thought to himself.
Putting down his bowl, he walked over to one of the
Indians who was sitting at the edge of the firelight. As
best he could, David asked him to stop the dancing.
He pointed to the sick Indian and tried to explain that
the noise and smoke were upsetting him. Glancing
past David into the dark corner where the young man
lay groaning and writhing, the Indian shrugged and
continued to beat the drums.

David was about to get the attention of another
Indian when Moses lifted the entrance flap and
walked in.

"I'm so glad you're here," David said, hurrying
over to Moses. "Could you please explain to these
men that the noise is making their friend over there
very sick? They really should stop their dancing."

Moses spoke to one of the Indians, but David
could tell that he didn't make any progress. The
Indians kept banging, yelling, and dancing. Through it
all, the sick man in the back of the room continued to
moan.

"I wish I could leave," David complained. "I

would rather sleep another night in the damp air than put up with this."

"I know," Moses said. "But you know as well as I that they would be very offended if you did that."

David nodded and plopped down on a pile of skins, trying to ignore the drums and rattles. As he watched the Indians twist their bodies and distort their faces, he found comfort in knowing that God has the power to change even those who worship the devil himself. David prayed for the Indians and for the young man who continued to burn with a raging fever.

"His temperature is high," Moses said as he removed the fur from the sleeping Indian. "There's really nothing we can do for him except continue to give him some water. Watch him, and try to keep him cool. For now I must go. I need to arrange for interpreters to assist us as we visit the many camps in this area. Try to get some sleep, and I will see you in the morning."

David leaned back onto the furs and closed his eyes. His head pounded with the beating of the drums, and his breathing grew shallow as smoke filled the hut. Before he fell asleep, he got up and held a water bottle to the sick Indian's cracked lips. The young man drank deeply and then sank back into a fitful sleep. David set the bottle beside him, then crawled toward the wall where a pallet of soft buckskins had been laid out for him. As he lay in the smoking, throbbing confines of the hut, he struggled to sleep. Trying to be helpful, he would give the sick Indian water from his bottle whenever he woke up during the night. Oblivious to the white man's con-

stant care of their sick companion, the Indians continued their relentless ritual into the early morning
hours.

Some time during the night David had drifted off
to sleep. He awoke to an uncanny silence. Sitting up
on his knees, he glanced around the hut. The first
light of dawn pierced the edges of the hut's entrance
where a flap hung loosely around the door frame.
Ashes from the fire blanketed the floor. The Indians
from the night before were gone, and the sick man
beside him lay still. Gray wisps of smoke drifted in
and out of the streams of golden sunlight like fog at the
beginning of a new day.

David stood up, stretched, then hurried over to
the young man who lay silently beside him. He felt
his forehead with the back of his hand. It was damp,
but cool. The raging fever had subsided during the
night. David let out a sigh of relief. Lifting the
Indian's head, he put the water bottle to his lips, urg-
ing the young man to drink. The Indian moaned and
opened his eyes, squinting in the early morning light.
A quizzical look crossed his face as he stared at the
strange, white man who held his head in his hand.
The Indian drank the water David had offered then
laid back down onto the skins. He grunted something,
but David could not understand him. Just then,
Moses stuck his head into the hut and pulled back the
flap, letting the fresh, morning breeze chase away the
smoke that had been trapped inside the hut.

"Good morning," Moses said cheerfully.

"Good morning," David replied. "I think our
friend is better. I gave him water throughout the
night, but that was all I could do to help."

Moses leaned down beside the young man and felt his head. He said something to him, after which the young man gave a surprised glance in David's direction.

"What did you tell him?" David asked.

"I told him that you helped to heal him," Moses said.

"I think you are exaggerating," David replied. "All I did was give him water."

"Without it, his fever would have gone unchecked, and he might have become worse," Moses said. "So, as far as we can tell, you did heal him."

"Well, God healed him, not me," David said. "It is Him that he should thank, not me."

"I'll be back soon to bring you both breakfast," Moses said. After saying something else to the Indian, he turned and left the hut. While he was gone, David climbed from the stuffy wigwam and walked around outside, breathing in the clean, mountain air. After just a few minutes, Moses returned with a pot of steaming hominy and three bowls. They went inside and helped the sick Indian sit up so he could eat some food. The young man was weak but seemed to gain strength with every bite. As they ate, David and Moses shared the Gospel with the young man, who was curious to know why the white man had visited their village and spent the night tending to the needs of someone he did not know. David explained why they had come, and the man listened quietly. He appeared to be quite overwhelmed by the message the white man proclaimed so earnestly. His eyes grew wide and a look of hope came over his ashen face.

"If you turn from your life of sin and put your

faith in Jesus Christ, you will be given the gift of eternal life," David said.

"I will think about what you have said," the Indian replied. "You have shown me kindness. I have never known nor seen anyone like you before, but you have a light in your eyes that makes me want to believe that you speak the truth. But I must have time to think about Jesus Christ and what it means to have faith in Him. There is much that I will have to give up, beliefs that I have held since childhood. It will not be easy for me to turn my back on those teachings. But I will think about it."

David did not press him. He knew it would take time, and faith would only come by the power of God's Spirit. There was nothing else for David to say. The young man had much to consider, and he was right that becoming a Christian would cost him a great deal. Yet he could not ignore the words of the white man, not after the care he had received from him. God had healed his body, this he knew. But he was yet to be convinced of how much he needed Christ to heal his soul.

After saying goodbye to the young man, David and Moses left the hut to begin a new day of preaching to the Indians. As they walked to the village, David glanced back. He paused, not able to go a step further until he prayed to God for the salvation of the young Indian. Then, without a second glance, David hurried to catch up to Moses. The fields along the Susquehanna River were barren, and they had much work to do.

17

Hearts of Darkness

The Indians at the front of the rickety passenger boat glanced curiously at David as he sat near the back watching the distant shore speed by. He was traveling to a village called Juncauta, an isolated collection of tribes he had visited the previous year. Just below the village, where the Susquehanna flowed through towering cliffs, was an island called Duncan's Island. Many tribes lived on this island, but the one that held David's particular interest was the Nanticoke Indians. These Indians were some of the most pagan and hostile of all the Indians he had encountered. Even the other tribes were afraid of them. They were deeply committed to their superstitions, distrustful of other tribes, and very devoted to the power-hungry powwows. Even their burial rites were unusual. They did not bury their dead as other tribes did, but they left the bodies to decay above ground in closed cribs. At the end of the year, they would then take the bones, wash and scrape them, and bury them. A great ceremony would always accompany the burial.

When David and his interpreter had visited the island the previous spring, he had been distressed by their pagan ways. He had determined then that he would return to preach the Gospel again. This time he went alone. Moses did not know the language of the

Nanticokes, so he took care of business up river while David traveled to the island by himself.

The forest that bordered the vast river looked dark and wild. Gnarled and slender trees massed together in a tangled tapestry, forming a dense barrier along the shore. Some of the trees leaned so far over the water that they looked as if they would fall into the swift currents at any moment. David's eyes followed the line of trees along their massive trunks to where their tips touched the sky. Not a cloud could be seen. He was thankful that the rains, which were so common at that time of year, had held off. The weather remained clear during his boat ride, but the air whispered of fall, cool and restless. Some of the trees displayed hints of the forthcoming season as patches of red, brown, and gold leaves peered out from the blanket of green.

Just as the sun settled behind the mountains, David could see Duncan's Island in the distance. His heart pounded as he anticipated seeing the Indians. Steadily, the island drew closer. Anxious and excited, he gathered his Bible, food pack, and water skin. He disembarked with a couple of his fellow passengers, then hurried up the path to the main camp where the Indians would be preparing their evening meal. As he approached the village, he could hear a great bustle of activity. Indians were running to and fro, gathering wood and digging stakes in the ground between the wigwams. David asked one of them as best he could in their tongue if anyone in the village spoke English. The man directed him to a large hut near the outskirts of the camp. David hurried there and asked a woman who was painting a large mask if he could meet with the man who spoke English. She nodded, put down the mask, and disappeared into the hut. After a few minutes, she returned with a middle-aged man who wore English-styled pants and an Indian tunic, hanging loosely to his knees. David introduced himself and asked the Indian if he would translate for him as he taught the people in the village about Christianity. Without hesitation, the man agreed to work for the missionary.

The two walked through the camp and announced that the missionary had come to speak to any who would listen. Some of the Indians they spoke to remembered David from the year before, but they were so busy preparing for one of their ceremonies that they hardly gave him time to explain why he had come. Unable to gather the Indians together, all David could do was stand by and watch nearly a hundred Indians scurry around a huge bonfire preparing to worship the great spirits.

As evening passed into night, the Indians scraped and cleaned deer hides for a sacrifice to their gods. They took the fat and burned it in the fire as they danced wildly around the leaping flames. The fire coiled higher and higher, casting a ghostly glow on the distant cliffs and across the still river. Frantically, they continued their dancing and screaming all night. Throughout the ritual, David paced back and forth along the edge of the woods that surrounded the frightul display. Anxiety and grief over the idolatry of the Indians swept over him, beating in his mind like the blood that rushed through his veins. He walked back and forth, sat down, then immediately stood up and began pacing again. Just a few yards away, the dancers continued their dance and the drummers beat on.

David was alone, having dismissed the interpreter hours before because his services were not needed. At a time like this, he was thankful to be alone. Isolated in the darkness, he could pour out his heart to God. He could unburden his cares and his longings that the Indians be turned from their idolatry and find freedom in Christ. As the hours passed, his prayers grew more fervent and persistent, but his body could not keep pace with his spirit. His legs began to cramp and his weary back ached. Eventually, he grew so tired that he could barely stand. Hunched over like a defeated warrior, he turned his back on the dancing shadows and stumbled through the vines and branches that blocked his path to the river. He soon arrived at the village but could find no one at home. Too exhausted to take another step, he decided his only refuge would be a small crate where the Indians stored their corn. He crawled on top and, groaning from the ache in his back, stretched out on the cold, coarse rods and instantly fell asleep.

Early the next morning after he prayed to the Lord, David met with the interpreter. The man explained that the Indians would probably not want to hear him that day because they had planned a meeting with the powwows. Many of the Indians had been sick, and they wanted to find out how they could appease the angry spirits. The interpreter seemed convinced that seeking the powers of the religious leaders was the best thing to do. David disagreed, but no matter how many Indians he approached, none wanted to talk with him.

Near noon, the tribe gathered together all the powwows. About half a dozen of them, dressed in costumes of bear and deer skins, began calling to the spirits. They performed juggling tricks and twisted their bodies into frightening positions. As the other Indians watched, the powwows continued their wild antics for hours, dancing around the fires, making all kinds of distorted motions with their arms and hands. Sometimes they would sing. Other times they would howl like animals. They danced to the beat of drums, stretching their arms and spreading apart all their fingers as if they were trying to push something away or keep it at arm's length. Some of the powwows would stroke their faces with their quivering hands and spit water in a fine mist. When the howls and drums would reach a feverish pitch, the powwows would fall to the ground and rub their faces into the dirt. As they snorted in the earth, the Indians would wring their hands at their sides as if they were in anguish, howling, grunting, and squealing. Then they would jump up again and continue dancing.

As David watched from the cover of the forest, one of the powwows turned in his direction, but he could not see the distressed missionary crouching in the shadows. The Indian's painted face twisted, and his eyes turned up into his head. He grunted and puffed until he fell flat on the ground. David looked away, unable to bear the horrible sight any longer. His heart ached as he witnessed how human beings made in the image of God degraded themselves to a state worse than animals. He had to do something, so he sat down in the shadow of the trees not more than thirty feet from the powwows, held his Bible in hand, and prayed that God would keep the forces of darkness from giving the Indians an answer to their cries for spiritual guidance. He knew all too well how the devil would give a sign to keep the Indians chained to his wicked ways. David did not want any signs given that day. So he prayed, and the hours crept by.

The Indians continued to yell out their charms and mutter their incantations throughout the afternoon, but the frustration level was growing. They hadn't received any sign. Finally, they refused to go on. Some of them drifted into the woods. Others pounded the ground, exasperated that they had not been given a sign. Through it all, David had continued to pray. It wasn't until after they all had given up and gone home that he returned to the village. He invited everyone he met along the way to come hear about the God who has the power to heal their diseases, who answers prayer, and who can save them from their sins. But to his disappointment, no one wanted to hear what he had to say. They wanted a sign, not words, not promises from a book. Like the crowds who heard Jesus preach, they demanded a miracle. But a sign would not be given. The power of redemption was in the Word of Christ, not in a supernatural event that could be imitated by the enemy.

Near the end of the day, David had given up all hope of anyone on the island coming to know Christ. Disheartened and weary, he walked alone through the woods to the massive river where he paused for a moment, listening to its gentle beat against the shore. His heart sank as he considered how the Indians refused to hear the Word of God. They were too trapped by their own superstitions to find freedom in the truth. Lost in thought, he passed by one of the camps and almost failed to notice a large crowd that had gathered around an elevated crate until he was shaken from his thoughts by a powwow's rattle. Pausing, David tried to see what was going on in the wooded clearing.

An aged powwow was walking up and down next to the crate, muttering and shaking wet feathers with one hand and a rattle with the other. Moving closer, David squinted. Then he saw what he had missed before. A dead body was stretched out on top of the crate—a victim of the latest disease that had spread through the village. The powwow stroked the body, howled, then clapped his hands over the dead Indian and spurted water from his lips. David sighed heavily and kept walking; he had given up trying to turn the Juncauta Indians from their superstitions. Dejected and longing to be home with his Crossweeksung Indians, he walked toward the crib of corn shucks on which he had slept the previous night. Like an old man climbing into bed, he crawled on top and fell asleep to the distant chant of the Nanticoke powwow.

Having awakened early to pray, David spied a large group of Indians heading down a path toward the woods. Curious to find out what was happening, he followed cautiously. When he reached the edge of a clearing, he immediately discovered the source of all the activity. In the center of a wooded glade danced a large man dressed from head to foot in bear skins. He looked more like an undersized grizzly than a human being. Covering his face was a great wooden mask. One half of the mask was painted black, the other reddish-brown, the color of an Indian's skin. The mouth was set in a deep and twisted grimace, giving the creature a distorted and gruesome appearance. David watched, wide-eyed, as the huge creature stomped around a fire. Moving closer, he peered through the crowd to get a better look.

As soon as David stepped from the trees, the beast immediately turned and faced him. Advancing toward the now trembling missionary, he raised a dry tortoise shell in his hand. Inside the shell was dried corn, and the creature shook it like a rattle. He continued to move forward, dancing with all his might, but he did not allow any part of his body to be revealed. Shaking the rattle frantically, he moved within inches of where David stood. The thing towered over him, and, without meaning to, David flinched back. The creature paused for a moment as if pleased by the reaction, then, in a flash, scampered away to the other side of the clearing.

Some Indians from the village kept their distance in the forest. One walked over to where David stood.

"Crazy, isn't he?" the Indian scoffed in surprisingly good English.

David, still a little shaken, looked at the Indian in surprise.

"Who is he?" David asked, clearing his throat and trying not to look as startled as he felt.

"He is one who represents the ancient Indian religions," the young man said slowly, trying to find the correct words in English. "We call him 'The Prophet.' He has a house through the woods with images carved into it. He says the Indian people have lost their heritage, that they drink too much of the white man's fire water, and that they must return to the old ways. The powwows leave him alone, but he is very zealous for us to follow his traditions. Sometimes he comes into the village and tries to get us to stop drinking. If we do not, he runs away into the woods, howling and crying."

David had seen enough Indian rituals to recognize that the man was indeed very religious in his own way. But regardless of how religious he might be, he was just as lost as the other Indians. He needed to hear the Gospel just as the others did. David's concern for the man's soul soon dispelled his fear, and he decided to talk to him. So he waited, and when the man finished his dance, David hurried across the clearing to introduce himself.

"Excuse me," David said, no longer frightened by the man's beastly appearance. "Do you speak English?"

"Yes, I do," the man said, slightly out of breath from all the dancing. He took off his mask and looked David over from head to foot. Without his costume, the man looked like any other average Indian: brown eyes, dark skin, high cheekbones, wide mouth, his hair dusted with just a touch of gray. David introduced himself and explained why he had come to the island. To David's surprise, the man said he would be curious to hear about Christian teaching and invited the missionary to his home. They walked a short distance through the woods until they came to a house with images carved into the poles, just as the Indian from the village had described. Inside, the floor was beaten smooth from countless nights of dancing.

The man sat down and lit a long pipe, the same kind that David had seen many Indian chiefs use. As smoke curled around his lips, the strange Indian began to tell David how his god had taught him everything he needed to know about religion and how to live a good life. He admitted that he did not think there was anything David could teach him, but he was still willing to listen.

"My people have grown very degenerate and corrupt," the man said. "They get drunk and forget the old ways. Many years ago I left my family and friends and traveled a great distance. I grew tired of the way my people were living. I left them and lived alone in the forest for many months. During that time, my god revealed himself. He told me that I must serve him. He told me everything I need to know."

"I too believe in God, and He has revealed His will for our lives through a book," David said. "It is called the Bible. In it, we learn everything we need to know about God and about how we should live."

"And how should you live?" the Indian asked. "Perhaps our gods have something in common."

"The Bible tells us that we should love one another and put away all immorality, idolatry, and drunkenness," David replied.

"Now, that I like," he said with an arrogant tone. "I too love every man."

"But God has told us that we cannot earn His favor through good works," David replied. "We can only be saved through faith in Jesus Christ. Unless we are liberated by His Spirit, we remain slaves to the devil."

"That I do not like. I have heard of this foreign teaching about the devil. But I do not believe there is any such being. None of our forefathers taught about such a creature. God told me to walk in the way of my fathers. This is not their way."

"But God's Word tells us that Satan is real, and unless God changes our hearts and gives us faith in Jesus Christ, we will remain in bondage to him and perish in eternal punishment," David replied.

"This is what you think happens when you die? That is not true. All departed souls fly southward. The good spirits are admitted into a beautiful city with spiritual walls. They do not need a Jesus Christ to get in, but they must live good lives and carry on the traditions. If they do not, they are bad. And the bad spirits are left outside to hover around those walls. No matter how they try, they cannot get in."

David talked with the Indian until the sun began to set, but he would not turn from his own religious ideas. He accepted those aspects of Christianity that resembled what he already believed, but if anything contradicted his own notions, he refused to listen or to be persuaded differently. Finally, David said good-bye to the man and returned to the village. He needed to prepare to leave the following day for the Forks of Delaware.

The young missionary woke up the next morning sore and a little sick. He climbed onto the passenger boat dejected and depressed. His journey to Juncauta seemed to be a failure, and David longed to be back among his people at Crossweeksung.

Later that day, he rejoined Moses, and they turned toward home. After a long and difficult journey of several days, they arrived at the Forks of Delaware on the first day of October 1745. While there, David invited any of the Indians who were interested in learning more about Christianity to follow him home to Crossweeksung; there they would be surrounded by other Indians who would encourage them to turn away from their Indian superstitions and embrace the truth of the Gospel.

A small group of Indians responded to his invitation and traveled with him to Crossweeksung later that week. As he entered the main camp, one of the women spied him through the trees. She let out a shout of excitement and ran in his direction. Some of the other Indians looked up from their work to see what was going on. When they saw David and the other Indians from the Forks of Delaware, they ran toward him. The heaviness of David's heart immediately lifted as he saw the joyful and expectant faces of his dear friends. He jumped from his horse and welcomed their warm embrace. With squeals of excitement and tears of relief, they praised God for bringing their pastor safely home.

18

Testimonies of Grace

Winter's icy breath blew against David's chapped cheeks as he walked through the woods toward an English settlement near Crossweeksung. Crumpled brown leaves and traces of snow crunched beneath his feet, and the dim, heartless afternoon sky stared down through bare patches in the trees above. Shivering from the cold, he stopped and pulled the collar of his coat close around his neck. He surveyed the terrain around him. Icicles hung from trees that stood like frozen sentinels, silent and still. The wind whistled as it twisted its way through the forest that creaked and groaned from the pains of winter. David shivered again and continued up the trail. Carefully, he led his horse around snow drifts and fallen branches—victims of a winter storm that had plowed through the mountains the night before.

Once he made his way down the path and up a snow-covered hill, he caught sight of smoke rising from chimneys along the river. Not wanting to be late, he quickly made his way to the village where he would meet some of his Indian friends who were already at the trading post buying supplies.

The village was quiet with only a few people scurrying here and there, carrying out their business as quickly as possible before the cold bit too deeply into their cheeks. David led his horse through the town until he came to a large store near the bank of the river. Leaving his horse with the other mounts that stood patiently in the chilly breeze, he hurried inside. The store was warm and stocked with fresh supplies from traders who had just arrived from up river. The missionary spied his Indian friends immediately. They were standing at a counter near the back of the store talking with the proprietor. Bags of supplies were draped over their shoulders. It appeared that they had just finished making their purchases and were ready to return home. David had arrived just in time. Grabbing a few bags of feed, he joined the Indians at the back of the store.

Just as David was about to pay for the supplies, the door of the store burst open. Along with the winter chill, four burly trappers swept into the store. David had seen them at the village on previous visits. The men almost stumbled right over the Indians who were on their way out of the trading post. The Indians stepped aside to let them through, and the trappers were about to pass when one turned toward the Indians and pointed in recognition.

"I know you," the man said to one of the younger Indians. "We used to have quite a few drinks together at the tavern. How about one before you leave?"

The young Indian looked at the red-cheeked trapper and simply shook his head. He recognized the white man, of course. He had taken a few drinks with him when he had visited the English settlement in the past. But that was months ago, and things were different now.

When the Indian shook his head, the trappers

laughed.

"Well, why not?" the man scoffed.

The Indian hesitated. David watched silently from the back of the room. The Indian glanced in his direction, and the trapper followed his gaze.

"Are you afraid you will make that young preacher angry if you have just one drink with us?" the trapper laughed, obviously having heard of David's ministry among the Indians.

"No," the Indian replied, looking the stocky man in the eye. "The only thing I'm afraid of is offending God. He has saved me from that life I used to lead, and I do not intend to turn back to it now."

"What's this talk about God?" the man scolded. "That preacher sure has filled your head with a lot of nonsense. Trust me. You won't be any better off because of the Christian religion. You're fine and happy the way you are. Christianity won't give you anything that you don't have already. Come on, let's go have a drink."

"No," the Indian said, and then he turned to leave with the rest of his friends. The trapper seemed too dumbfounded to answer. He just stood there staring after the young Indian. David quickly made his purchase, strode past the group of trappers, and followed the Indians out the door.

"That Brainerd is a deceiver," the man called after them from the open doorway. "I heard that he has a plan to gather as many Indians as he can and then sell them to England as slaves."

David turned and gave the man a bitter look. His face flushed as he struggled to control himself. One of the Indians put his hand on David's shoulder and turned him away from the store.

"Don't pay any attention to him," the Indian said. "We know it isn't true."

With a final scathing glance at the trapper, David walked away with the Indians. Once he had loaded his horse with his newly purchased supplies, he let out a deep breath. He didn't usually become so angry at the prattle of foolish men, but if anything would turn the Indians from Christianity it would be the threat of enslavement. They were a proud people and hated the thought of being enslaved. But David's anger subsided as the Indians reassured him that they did not believe the trapper's gossip. They trusted David and knew he wanted only the best for them. They remained committed to Christ, and no threats or deceptions from men such as those at the English settlement would change their minds or turn their hearts from God.

As he rode his horse back to Crossweeksung, David thanked God for protecting the Indians from the lies of others. The Indians had no reason to trust him; after all, he was a stranger among them. But despite all the obstacles, God continued to preserve His people at Crossweeksung.

"If God will work, who can hinder?" David said to himself.

Waving goodbye to the Indians who had walked back with him from the village, he turned down a snow-covered trail that led to the cabin he had built just before winter. He had gone only a few yards when a young Indian woman intercepted him on the path. She was covered from head to foot with furs, but her nose was red and her eyes were swollen. David recognized her immediately as one who had been deeply affected by his sermon the previous day. She had come to him afterward and confessed that she had been very fearful of God's judgment because she knew she would go to hell if she died. But that was all she had said. David was glad to have the opportunity to speak with her again.

"Hello, can I help you?" David asked, bringing his horse to a halt.

"Me try, me try, save myself, last my strength be all gone," she replied abruptly, as if a dam had suddenly burst. "Me could not me stir bit further. Den last, me forced to let Jesus Christ alone, send me hell if He please."

David tried to follow her broken English as best he could. He put his hand on her shoulder and asked her to calm down and walk with him down the path.

"But you were not willing to go to hell, were you?" David asked after he had untangled her muddled sentences.

"Could not me help it. My heart he would wicked for all. Could not me make him good."

"You mean that you saw that it was right that you should go to hell because your heart is so wicked and would continue to be so even after all your effort to change it?"

She nodded and sniffed back tears.

"But I find comfort," she said.

"How did you find comfort?" David asked, a little surprised, considering what she had just said about going to hell.

"By my heart be much grad," she said.

"Why is your heart glad?"

"Grad my heart Jesus Christ do what He please with me. Den me tink, grad my heart Jesus Christ send me hell. Did not me care where He put me, me lobe Him for all."

"Your heart was glad that Jesus Christ would do with you what He pleased, right?" David asked, making sure he understood. "And even if Christ sent you to hell you do not care, but you would love Him anyway?"

She nodded. David stared at her in amazement. He had never met anyone so desirous to submit to God's will that she was willing even to go to hell if that was what He wanted. God had clearly given her a desire to serve Him and be conformed to His will no matter what that might be. She obviously loved Jesus more than anything and wanted His will to be done.

The young missionary smiled as he thought of the comfort the woman had found in submitting to the will of God. David stopped walking and looked down into the woman's shining face. Her tears had dried.

"You cannot change your own heart, but Jesus Christ can," David said gently. "I think He already has. If only all Christians could abandon themselves so completely to the will of God, the church would know the comfort that you have found. If you trust in Him, and love Him as you say, He has promised not to send you to hell. Go now in peace."

The woman smiled, then with a wave of her hand she headed back down the trail. David watched her buckskinned feet crunch through the snow until she rounded a bend and went out of sight.

Grinning with delight, David turned his horse toward home. Not far ahead he could see his cabin through the bare trees. After securing his horse in a shelter near the cabin and putting away the feed, he hurried up the snow-covered steps of his humble home. Lifting the icy latch on the door, he stepped inside. His breath billowed in the chilly air. Setting his Bible, which he carried with him everywhere, on an oak table near the fireplace, he lit a candle that he kept on a shelf beside the door. The flickering light revealed a sparse room with only a cot of corn shucks and a table. David placed the candle next to his bed and started a fire in the small fireplace. The cabin warmed up quickly. He took off his jacket, hung it on the back of the door, and then splashed his face with some water from a wooden bowl beside his cot. Pushing aside his books and papers with partially translated psalms, he spread out some clean paper in front of him on the table. He needed to make some additions to his journal.

David dipped his pen into a jar of black ink and reflected on the past few months. Every day he had visited the Indian camps and preached to those who gathered. The Indians welcomed him whenever he arrived at their camp and even encouraged him to continue his teaching on into the evening. Sometimes he would preach two or three times a day. When he wasn't preaching, he would visit from hut to hut, talking with people, helping them in their business affairs, and counseling them.

As he had done at Kaunaumeek, he taught the Indians through catechism classes. He would ask them questions, and they would repeat the answers back to him. Young and old would gather around him, inquisitive and ready to learn. He would ask, "What is the chief end of man?" The Indians would then answer as they had been previously instructed, "The chief end of man is to glorify God and to enjoy Him forever." This method of instruction helped him cover a wide range of topics in a way that the Indians would remember.

Whenever David was teaching or preaching, many Indians were stirred in their hearts with a new understanding of God and of Christ, a new awareness of their sins, and a desire to be saved. Often, when he would preach to large assemblies, not a dry eye could be seen. One time after a sermon, an Indian woman whom David had never met before told him that she was going to travel forty miles to call her husband so that he, too, might be awakened to the knowledge of the true God.

The English who had gathered for that day's service were excited to see the conversion of so many Indians. To David's delight, not all the white settlers were like those he had met on the boat at the Susquehanna or like those at the trading post. The English people who attended the worship services supported him and encouraged him in his work. And most of all, they praised God for bringing the Indians into the kingdom of heaven that they might have sweet fellowship with them as brothers and sisters in Christ. By early November 1745, David had baptized forty-seven people, thirty-five from Crossweeksung and the rest from the Forks of Delaware.

After recording the number of baptisms in the ledger of his journal, David rubbed his cold hands together. He got up and stoked the fire with a long branch, then threw another log onto the flames. As the fire licked the crackling wood, someone knocked at the cabin door. David opened it, letting a gust of winter wind steal inside. The dim light from the cabin flickered across the wrinkled face of an Indian woman whom David recognized as one who attended his meetings quite often. He had tried to speak with her many times, but she seemed to be unable to communicate. In her old age, she could not remember things nor could she think clearly. She seemed to be like a small child, and David had almost given up hope that the woman would be able to comprehend anything about Christianity.

He stared into the childlike eyes that peered from the deep folds of the woman's face. She had to be more than eighty years old. David was surprised that the woman had walked from the camp to his cabin. Then he noticed a young girl in the darkness behind the old woman. Slowly she stepped into the light, a little hesitant about coming to his cabin at night. She explained that she had led the woman by the hand to meet with him. Not at all disturbed by their unexpected visit, David invited them inside out of the cold.

The old woman shuffled into the cabin, her buckskin tunic slapping against her laced boots. She kept wringing her hands, and her eyes darted back and forth. Trying to calm her, David asked her to sit down.

"What is wrong, friend?" David asked.

With some help from the young woman, she told David that her "heart hurt very much," and that she was afraid she would never find Christ. She explained in a childlike way that she had heard David preach many times, but never understood what he was talking about and never "felt it in her heart," as she put it, at least not until the previous Sunday.

"And then it was like a needle had been thrust in my heart," she said. Then one night before Christmas, a number of Indians gathered in her house to worship and pray together. Their talk about the Lord pricked her in her heart, as she described it, and she could not sit up. She simply fell down onto her bed.

"Then I went away and it was like I dreamed," she said thoughtfully. "But I do not think I dreamed."

She went on to explain that while she was "away" she saw two paths. One appeared very broad and crooked, and it turned to the left. The other appeared straight and very narrow, and it went up a hill to the right. She traveled for some time up the narrow right-hand path until something seemed to block her way.

"It was like a darkness," she said. Then, shaking her head, she corrected herself. "No, it was more like a block or a bar across the road."

She went on to explain that as she stood looking at the bar, she remembered one of David's sermons in which he had urged the assembly to strive to enter in at the straight gate. She was about to climb over the bar when she suddenly came to herself. Since that night, she had been very distressed that she had turned her back on Christ and, as a result, would never receive His mercy.

Because the Indians were prone to be deceived by trances and tricks of their imagination, David was very concerned that the woman was not truly convicted of her sins but merely terrorized by her own doubts. He had warned the Indians many times that

Satan often deceived people through dreams and trances. To make sure that was not the case with this woman, David asked her questions about her own sin and need of salvation, the sufficiency of Christ and the ability of God to save. After talking with her awhile, he discerned that she seemed to understand her sinfulness and that Christ was the only way to eternal life, but she remained convinced that she could not be saved because she had refused to take the narrow path in her dream.

"Christ is able and willing to save the old as well as the young," David told her. "Your sins are not so bad that Christ is not able to save you. If you come to Him, He will surely save you. A dream cannot keep you from Him."

Immediately, she began to beat her breast and cry, "But I cannot come. My wicked heart will not come to Christ." She cried even harder and struck her breast again and again. David tried to calm her.

"I do not know how to come," she sobbed. "I do not know how to come."

"You're right," David said gently. "None of us can come to Him on our own. God must change our hearts and bring us to Himself. If we were left to ourselves, not one of us could climb onto the narrow path on our own. We need Christ to bring us into the way of life. Only through Him and by His power can you be saved. Trust Him and depend on Him to save you. Let us pray that God will give you faith in Christ, that He will bring you to Himself and save you from your sins. Let us ask Him to help you onto the narrow path."

David took her hands and prayed that God would

change her heart, that He would draw her to Himself and adopt her as His child. As David prayed, the old woman grew more calm, but she still did not believe her heart could be changed. She thanked David for listening to her and for his prayers. He encouraged her to continue to seek Christ, to rely on His grace in salvation, and to listen to the preaching of God's Word.

As David watched the two women disappear into the night, he thanked the Lord for bringing the old woman to a conviction of her sin and prayed that she would find forgiveness in Christ. Closing the door and locking out the winter chill, David returned to his journal. Dipping his pen into the ink, he paused in thought. In just one day, he had seen three very different manifestations of God's power and grace. God had protected the Indians from the lies of the English trappers. He had given the young Indian woman whom he met on the path such a love for Christ that she would submit to His will in anything, even if it meant her going to hell. And He had brought this woman of more than eighty years to a fearful conviction of her sin, something that he had rarely seen among the elderly.

"God will be glorified among these people," David said to himself. "And I am thankful to be a witness to it."

19

A Community Takes Root

As the cold winter marched on at Crossweeksung, David continued to preach to swelling crowds. Indians came from far and near to hear him. Bundled in furs and huddled around campfires, they would gather every day to listen to the Word of God. Many travelers from distant regions decided to remain in the Crossweeksung territory so they could hear about Christ daily and meet with other Indians who had been awakened to a love for God. The camp, which once housed about three families, grew to more than twenty, located only a quarter of a mile from David's cabin. The close proximity enabled him to teach more often and help them in their business affairs whenever they needed him. And because many of the Indians had expressed a desire to learn English, David arranged for a schoolmaster to come and live among them.

Day by day the community of Crossweeksung settled into a routine of prayer in the morning and evening, catechism lessons under David's instruction, and study of the English language with the schoolmaster. On Sundays, entire families, from wailing babies to the most frail grandparent, would gather for worship. Hardly a week went by when someone was not baptized during the afternoon service. Many who had remained staunchly opposed to Christianity for months confessed faith in Christ and were baptized before a teary-eyed assembly.

In early January, David baptized the woman he had met in late December who had completely given herself up to the will of God, even if it meant going to hell. Not long after she had spoken to David, she had become convinced that Christ had saved her from her sins and given her eternal life. The fear that had held her in its firm grip disappeared, leaving joy in its place. Thanksgiving filled her heart as she found peace resting in God's grace. After the baptism, she spoke with David through an interpreter.

"I have heard it said that some people who live far away sent you to us," the woman said, her eyes filled with tears of joy.

"Yes, some very good people in Scotland," David replied.

"When I heard that some people far away sent you here, I could not help but pray for them all night," she exclaimed. "Last night my heart went out to God for them. I love them so much for making it possible for my people to learn about Jesus Christ."

The woman reached out and wrapped her arms around the young pastor. Tears streamed down her shining face. David gave her a gentle hug back.

"Thank you, dear sister," he whispered. "You are a blessing from the Lord, and I praise Him for the grace He has shown you."

"I could never love unless God had shown me how," she said as she withdrew from his embrace. With a smile on her face and her eyes bright with joy, she waved goodbye and walked back to her hut.

The day being nearly over, David returned to his quiet cabin nestled under the drooping branches of an ancient oak. He felt quite peaceful and content, encouraged by the work God was doing among the Indians. But he was exhausted and weak. He could not even summon enough strength to read the Bible as he always did before turning in for the night. So without changing his clothes or removing his boots, he sunk into his bed and fell fast asleep.

After just a few hours, he awoke with a burning fever. No matter how hard he tried, he could not get back to sleep. Every joint in his body ached from the fever, and whenever he shut his eyes he felt as if he were swirling on a swift current down river. He shivered in his buckskin blankets until morning, but when dawn arrived he was too weak to get out of bed. Tucking a pillow behind him, he struggled to sit up, groaning with the effort. After taking a deep breath, he leaned over and pulled a tin cup from a small bowl of water beside his bed. He sipped the tepid water, but as soon as it passed his lips, nausea swept over him. Turning over on his side, he tried to calm his stomach, but it was too late. In one violent rush, he vomited into the bowl of fresh water. After a few minutes of hanging over the side of his bed, he fell back into the folds of his blanket, hoping the churning in his stomach would ease.

He remained curled in his bed until late morning. The nausea had passed, but the fever raged on. Keeping himself wrapped in a thick blanket, he sat up and reached for a barrel of water at the edge of his bed. After dipping his tin cup into the fresh water and taking a few sips, he leaned back on his pillow and reached for his Bible and writing pad that were tucked under the bedding. He tried to prepare a sermon, but found that he could not concentrate. The letters on the page before him blurred as his eyes refused to focus. His hands shook as he tried to jot down notes on his writing pad. After about fifteen minutes of fruitless effort, he closed his Bible and reached for some cloths that had been soaking in the barrel. He draped the cool rags across his forehead and settled back into his bed. A few minutes later he was fast asleep.

Some of the Indians dropped by throughout the day to see if he was all right. But they found him either asleep or too sick to speak. An older woman from a nearby camp left food, but when she offered to stay with him, he urged her to go. Alone, with only his Bible to bring him comfort, David remained curled in his bed throughout the night and the following day.

Too sick to venture outside, he stayed inside his cabin for nearly a week. As the days passed, he could walk around his house, tend to the fire, and sip from his barrel of water, but he could only remain standing for a few minutes at a time. Finally one day his fever broke, and he felt strong enough to walk outside. When he opened the door, a cold, refreshing breeze brushed against his face. Closing his eyes, he breathed in the frosty air. Moving like an old man, he walked down the path, stretching his stiff legs and drinking in the winter sun. When he stood very still with his face lifted to the sky, the sun felt like a warm blanket against his skin. After walking a few yards from his cabin, he began to tire. Sighing, he returned to his lonely cabin, feeling like a prisoner who had been given a few moments of freedom only to be forced back into his stuffy cell. Filling his tin cup with water and dishing some hominy into a wooden bowl, he sat by the crackling fire and ate his breakfast. After scraping the bowl and draining his cup for a second time, he climbed into bed and for the first time in many days slept in peace.

Once he fully recovered, David was able to return to his pastoral duties. Most nights, as the wind howled outside, his cabin would be filled with people. It brought David great delight to see his home turn from a house of sickness to a house of praise. Late into the night the Indians would sing, pray, and listen to their pastor teach from the Bible. Often the entire assembly would be moved to tears as David told them about the mercy and goodness of Christ. Knowing there were those among them who had not been converted, he would warn them to flee the coming wrath of God, to seek the covering of Christ's righteousness. When the Indians would hear words about Christ's giving up His life for them, about His perfect obedience even to death on a cross, they would weep because of their unworthiness to receive so great a salvation.

By late March 1746, the congregation at Crossweeksung had grown to about one-hundred and thirty people. More Indians had moved into the region, and as the numbers grew David had to deal with new problems. The land they were then living on was not the best of the Indians' lands. Some of the tribe's leaders had told David the previous year that the better part of their lands was to the north at a place called Cranberry. Until the time David had arrived, the Indians did not care about cultivating their land because they had been, as they admitted themselves, lazy. One of the challenges David had faced was to teach the Indians that God is honored in hard work. Preaching from the Proverbs that condemned sloth and laziness, he had urged the Indians many times to work hard so they could provide for their families and trade with the white people. The tribe, once being awakened to God's ways, was anxious to begin tilling its lands and bringing in the harvest. To prepare for the upcoming planting season, a group of Indians set out to Cran-berry to clear it and make plans for moving the entire tribe to that area.

As soon as word reached the English settlements that the Indians were moving, some of the white people spoke out against the Crossweeksung tribe. They spread rumors that David was inciting the Indians to cut the throats of helpless travelers, and they viciously urged the white community to forbid the Indians from trading at the villages. David soon discovered that the root of the white people's hatred for the Indians of Crossweeksung was a desire for their land. Once the Indians decided to clear and till their fertile lands, the English settlers wanted to claim the land as their own. David reminded the Englishmen that the territory was clearly the Indians' because part of the tribe had been living on the land. A mandate had already been set throughout the colonies that any land inhabited by the Indians was not neutral territory but must be purchased from the Indians who lived there. Some of the white people in New Jersey, however, claimed that the Cranberry property was theirs and insisted that they had plans to establish a settlement of their own on it. But when

David pressed the point that they had no legal claim to the land, the settlers could do nothing except watch the move take place.

Despite that fact, the white people continued to complain and spread rumors that David and the Indians could not be trusted. Undaunted by the hostility of the settlers, David encouraged the Indians to go ahead and prepare to move when everything was ready. Surprisingly, the move went forward without any serious conflicts with the settlers. David and the Indians considered this to be a testimony to answered prayer because tense situations such as this did not always end peacefully. There were many stories of white people and Indians fighting, even killing, over land.

Just as friction with the white settlers seemed to be dying down, David's plans to help the Indians prepare for their move were delayed. The day the Indians began tilling the land in Cranberry and packing their meager belongings at Crossweeksung, the schoolmaster fell deathly ill. David had to stop his work among the Indians to tend to the man's needs. For more than a week, David watched over him, brought him water, and fed him. He understood all too well what it was like to be sick and alone in the unfamiliar wilderness. But unlike his own illness just a few months earlier, the schoolmaster's seemed worse, and David feared for his life. So throughout the warm spring days and cool nights, he lay on the hard floor, staying close in case the schoolmaster needed him.

When it was late and the cabin was still and silent, David would lie awake, tired but unable to sleep, his

thoughts churning like a swirling river. The struggle
with the English settlers, the demands of caring for
the sick schoolmaster every night, and his own weariness dampened his spirits. He could not pray with
the zeal he once had, and so he felt separated from
God, isolated and alone. His old enemy, melancholy,
had laid siege to his soul, draining his strength with
each passing day.

One morning, however, after more than a week of
caring for the schoolmaster, David awoke to find him
sitting up, his fever gone and his strength returned.
Seeing David's weary face, he immediately urged him
to go home and get some rest so he would not fall prey
to the same illness. The missionary excused himself,
thankful that the schoolmaster had recovered and excited to be able to return to his work among the
Indians. As the spring morning passed into afternoon,
David's spirits brightened. He took a stroll in the
woods and prayed to God with an earnestness and zeal
that had eluded him for days. According to his private
custom, he knelt on a bed of fallen leaves under the
massive forest boughs and asked God to protect His
people as they established a community at Cranberry
in the name of Christ.

In early May, after many weeks of preparation, the
Crossweeksung Indians moved to their new lands
where they could live, work, and, most importantly,
worship together. As the caravan of Indians crested a
hill that bordered the Cranberry territory, they
paused to bask in the beautiful display before them. A
babbling stream skipped through a vast meadow
adorned with wildflowers of every color. Crimson
tulips swayed in the gentle breeze, their deep hues

overshadowing all others like rubies on a bed of diamonds. The cheery daffodils and delicate bluebells, while unable to compete with the striking richness of the tulips, cast a glimmer of subtle elegance across the meadow. Along the edge of the gurgling stream, the tiny white blooms of Queen Anne's Lace shimmered in the sunlight, creating the illusion of a dainty hemline that stretched into the distance until it disappeared under the shelter of knotted trees. Looking beyond the meadow to a region over the next hill, the Indians spied their partially tilled farmland. The dark, rich soil stretched for miles until it too disappeared into the cool shadows of the forest.

The Indians hurried to unload their supplies. Many of the older children ran into the woods, scouring the forest for bark and branches to build their homes. David watched the bustling scene with delight as children scurried underfoot and parents twisted limber saplings into frames for their huts. The day passed quickly, and soon the sun began its timely descent behind the mountains.

Once everything began to settle down during the next few days, David baptized an Indian who had been a powwow at the Forks of Delaware. The old man first became genuinely concerned for his soul when he saw David baptize Moses and his wife the previous summer. Soon after that, the Indian had followed David to Crossweeksung to hear him preach. Convicted by the teaching of Scripture, the man gave up his witchcraft, but at that time he still did not believe God would save him.

"My heart is dead, and I can never help myself," the man had told David. "I realize now that I must go to hell."

"Do you think it is right that God should send you to hell?" David had asked.

"Oh, it is right. The devil has been in me ever since I was born," the man had cried. "I have always served the devil, and my heart has no goodness in it now, but is as bad as ever it was."

Throughout the winter, the man had been very anxious to hear David preach. He told the missionary that he loved to hear him speak the Word of God even though he was convinced that he was going to hell. No matter how much David told him about the mercy of Christ, the man could not believe that God would save such a great sinner as himself.

Not long after the move to Cranberry, the Indian seemed to listen to David's preaching with new ears. His heart melted, and he grasped for the first time the grace of the Lord. God could and would forgive him of his many sins, no matter how terrible they were. Since that day, he felt at peace and knew that he had been saved from his sins by the mercy and love of Christ his Savior. Following his baptism, he often traveled with David to the Forks of Delaware, where he proclaimed the Gospel boldly, especially to those who were still powwows just as he had once been when he lived among the Delaware Indians.

The more Indians who were baptized, the more there were to train and instruct through catechizing. David would spend many hours instructing them privately and encouraging them to guard against temptation. The work was difficult because he was not able to live as near to them as he had before they moved to Cranberry. Since the move, he had to board with an

English family who lived a few miles from the Indian settlement. Despite the distance, he remained faithful to meet with the Indians every day, to encourage them when they were down, to pray for a sick child, or to answer their questions about Christianity.

In early May, David had to leave his congregation to travel to Elizabethtown where he attended a Presbytery meeting in which all the pastors of the region gathered to decide on issues concerning the church and to examine men for the ministry. Presbytery meetings gave him the opportunity to catch up with old friends and to fellowship with ministers like the Rev. Edwards of Northampton. Whenever he had the opportunity to talk with the esteemed minister, he would inevitably ask about Jerusha. Mr. Edwards would often comment on how alike David and Jerusha were. They had the same serious, thoughtful personalities and an unusual desire to live for the glory of God. He never mentioned this to David, but he often thought the two would make an excellent couple if they were ever to marry.

As David rode back to Cranberry after one of his journeys to the Presbytery in Elizabethtown, he reflected on his brief meeting with Mr. Edwards and seriously thought about settling down among his flock, building a home, and taking a wife. He had always been committed to being a missionary to the Indians, traveling into the distant regions and telling others about Christ. But did God want him to become a permanent pastor at Cranberry instead? Did He want him to stop traveling and settle down? But even as he asked himself the question, he knew his heart's desire was to go forth and preach the gospel along the

Susquehanna River. If God wanted him to remain at Cranberry permanently and start a family, he would trust God to direct him.

"Lord, if it be most for Thy glory, let me remain as a pastor to these people," David prayed quietly. "But if Thou see that this will hinder my usefulness in Thy cause, prevent me from making any plans in that direction. All I want, respecting this world, is to live in such a way that will allow me to serve Thee best."

During the following days, David continued to consider whether or not he should remain at Cranberry and start a family. But eventually, he became resolved to the contrary. Being convinced that God had prepared him for a solitary life by having him live alone in the wilderness for the past few years, he began to put the matter behind him. Even though a life of comfort and rest, in which he could enjoy the fellowship of believers and the companionship of a wife, was appealing, he could not shake the conviction that God did not intend for him to live such a life. If God meant for him to live without a home and common comforts for the sake of bringing others into the kingdom, he would wholeheartedly give up everything to fulfill God's will.

"Here I am, Lord, send me," David prayed. "Send me to the ends of the earth. Send me to the rough, the savage pagans of the wilderness. Send me from all that is called comfort. Send me even to death itself, if it be but in Thy service, and to promote Thy kingdom."

David's decision to remain a missionary to the Indians was affirmed when he witnessed another person enter Christ's blessed kingdom. The old woman who had come to his cabin that winter, distressed by her dreams and afraid that she would not be able to come to Christ, was baptized on a warm summer day in June. From the time she had talked with David in late December until the beginning of the summer, she had grown in her understanding of Christ and had come to realize that He was willing to save even an old woman of eighty years. She still saw things in a very childlike way, for her mind was not the same as it had been when she was young, but God changed her heart and gave her an abiding faith in Jesus Christ.

As David poured water over the woman's gray hair, he looked into her wrinkled face. Where there had once been fear, confusion, and dread, there was peace. At that moment, David had never been more certain of God's will for his life. As the gentle currents swirled around him, he peered up river to where the dark trees dipped their aging limbs into the sparkling water beneath. The time had come for him to make another journey to proclaim the gospel of Christ on the shores of the Susquehanna.

20

Preparations

"David, someone is here to see you," Moses exclaimed as he stuck his head through the entrance of the bark-covered house. David was sitting in front of a small fire, eating some boiled corn and talking with two Indians who directed the affairs at Cranberry. They were in the middle of discussing future trading plans with the white settlers when Moses interrupted them.

"Who is it?" David asked.

"He says that he's your brother," Moses responded. "Do you want me to bring him to you?"

"No," David replied, standing up quickly and dusting off his pants. "I'll go to him."

David could barely contain his excitement. No one from his family had ever visited him before, and he couldn't wait to see his younger brother. John had written that he might visit, and David had given him directions, but he wasn't sure if he would be able to make it before summer. It appeared he had found the time.

The Indian settlement at Cranberry had grown quiet as the sun set behind the western mountains. David hurried from the hut toward the riverside trail where Moses had met John Brainerd. Just as David reached the edge of the settlement, he saw his brother's horse through the trees. He quickened his pace.

"John," David yelled, waving his hand.

The horse galloped toward him. John waved back and pulled the reins. He slid from the horse and ran to greet his older brother.

"It is so good to see you, John," David said with a smile.

John gave him a warm hug. "It's been a long time," he said as he took the reins of his horse and walked beside David toward the village. "The entire family has missed you dearly, but you have been in our prayers constantly. I am thankful that I found the time to visit you."

"I am, too," David replied. "The last time I saw you was at Yale. You had just begun your second year. And now you have graduated. How has it been?"

John looked down at the ground as he walked. He knew how troubling David's dismissal from Yale had been, and he did not want to bring up painful memories by talking about his own years at college.

"It's been fine," John said. "God used my classes to bring me closer to Himself. Anything short of that would have been a waste."

David nodded. John quickly changed the subject and asked where he could get some dinner. He had barely eaten anything all day, and he was famished.

"I'm sure one of the families would love to share their meal with us. It will give us time to talk. I'm looking forward to hearing any news," David replied, anxious to talk to his brother about everything that was going on back home.

As the evening sky grew dark, the two brothers walked to the Indian camp. John told David about his brothers and sisters in Haddam and about friends in New England. His sister Spenser had been sick but had recovered before John left to visit David in New Jersey. The young missionary paused for a moment. He had not even known that his sister had been sick. So much of the outside world seemed to be passing him by. For a moment, he felt a tinge of regret that he did not live among his family and friends, but as quickly as it came, the feeling disappeared, replaced with confident resolve that nothing was more important for him than the work he was doing among the Indians.

David paused in front of a large wigwam and pushed back the flap of a spacious hut.

"This is where we will eat," David said as he motioned his brother to wait and come in behind him. He didn't want to startle the Indian family by barging in on them. Once inside, David introduced his brother to the husband, his young wife, and their three children. The family often provided David with meals and welcomed John to share their dinner. As they ate, David explained to John how the Indians had recently moved to the area, despite complaints from the white settlers.

David also told him about his plans to travel to the Susquehanna River. John shared his brother's desire to see the pagan Indians come to know Christ, and he was excited to hear how God had been using him in the advancement of His kingdom. David admitted that his previous journeys along the Susquehanna had not been easy, but he had scattered so many seeds that he knew he must return to teach the Indians more about Jesus Christ; he hoped that during his absence some of those seeds might have taken root.

"Have you considered settling down here and being a permanent pastor to these people?" John asked.

"I have, but that is not God's will for me," David replied. "I could never remain here, knowing that there are so many Indians who have not heard the Good News. I pray that the great work God's Spirit has done among these people will spread to those along the Susquehanna and beyond."

"I understand," John said, crunching into another ear of corn.

"What are your plans now that you have finished college?" David asked, changing the subject.

"I think I will go to Bethel in New Jersey to minister among the Christian Indians there," John replied. Like his brother, he wanted to spread the message of the Gospel to the Indian nations. "I would appreciate any advice you might give me."

David thought for a moment. "The most important thing is that you continue to pursue personal holiness every day of your life. That is the foundation to everything you do in ministry. Never grow weary of being conformed to the image of Jesus Christ. As you labor among the Indians, work solely for the glory of God, not for your own interests. Labor for God's interests. Also, learn to distinguish between true and false religion among your people. It is so easy for people to be deceived. Look to the Spirit of God for discernment and compare your own experiences, as well as the experiences of others, to the Word of God. I have found that white people and Indians alike can easily have a false assurance of their salvation. They assume they are saved just because they pray or attend church, but that is about the extent of their devotion to God. Some think that as long as they have made a profession of faith, it doesn't matter how they live. I cannot tell you how many people think they are saved just because they have prayed a meaningless prayer or professed Christ to be their Savior, even though they clearly have no love for God, no desire to worship with His people, and no commitment to obey His sovereign will. They hang on to a profession instead of examining their lives for the fruit of the Spirit—love, obedience, goodness, self-control, faith.

"You must also watch out for those who seem to live as Christians, but inwardly they are trusting in their own righteousness instead of relying on the grace of God for salvation. Just because someone says all the right things and seems to do all the right things does not mean he is saved. Those who have a heart for God love not just what Christ has done for them, but they love Christ for who He is. Many people will say they believe Christ died for their sins, but they have no love for Him as their Savior and their King."

David paused, reflecting on what he had just said. After staring into the fire for a moment, he looked over at his brother. "Keep a close eye on your flock and guard your own heart," David said. "That is the best advice I can give you."

Following dinner, the two brothers walked outside and sat down before a sputtering campfire. They talked all evening as the stars brightened the clear sky above them. After a couple of hours, they rode back to the English settlement where David was staying, and as if they were young boys again back home in

Haddam, they read some Scripture, said their prayers, and turned in for the night. John would have to get up early and ride for New Jersey. Even though he would have liked his visit to last longer, John could not remain at Cranberry because he had appointments with some ministers the next day.

As first light touched the corners of the gray countryside, John secured the saddle on his horse and loaded his gear on its back. Having finished preparing for the day's journey, he embraced his brother. David felt John's warmth and strength and wished he could stay longer, but he understood that he had work to do. Releasing his brother, John stepped back and gripped David's shoulders, holding him at arm's length so he could get a good look at him.

"Take care of yourself and write often," John said with a smile. "You won't do anybody any good if you don't look after your health."

"I will try," David replied. "And you do the same."

John climbed onto his horse, and, with a snap of the reins, he rode briskly down the dew-covered trail. David stared after him until his slim figure faded into the trees. When David could no longer see him, he picked up his tattered Bible from a bench in front of the cabin, climbed onto his horse, and rode to Cranberry. As his horse trotted across the rocky fields and through the woods, he prayed, for his heart was filled with love and adoration for God. Reflecting on his brother's brief visit, he thanked God for giving him the desire to remain in the lonely wilderness even when the outside world seemed to beckon him back into its fold.

"I wish I could give something back to God for all that He has done among these people," David said to himself. "But I have nothing to give. All I can do is rejoice that God has done the work Himself, and that none in heaven or earth might pretend to share the honor of it with Him. All I can do is be glad that God's glory has been advanced by the conversion of these people."

That day and throughout the following months, David continued to help his people set up their new village. Sometimes, though, he would leave them and travel to distant towns to tell other ministers about his work among the Indians. In early June, he rode to Freehold to assist the pastor there in the administration of the Lord's Supper. In the afternoon, he preached to the white people and told them about the great work God was doing at Cranberry. He informed them that he had been keeping a journal of the details of his missionary journeys, including the conversion of the Indians at Crossweeksung. The Missionary Society David worked for wanted the journal to be published so people from far and near could become more interested in missions work among the pagan Indians of America. If more people could hear about the desperate need of the Indian people to hear the Good News of Christ and be encouraged by the work God had done among the people of Crossweeksung, maybe more people would be willing to enter the mission field as David had done.

The Sunday afternoon following his return from Freehold, David spent most of the day with a family who had been caring for their sick daughter. She had been deathly ill for a week, and her parents had feared that she would not live to see the next Lord's Day. But God had been merciful and had preserved her life. When David entered the dimly lit hut, the husband and wife greeted him warmly and led him to where the girl slept in the back of the room. The child looked pale but seemed to be stronger than when he had previously seen her. Slowly, the girl opened her dark eyes, blinking in the dull light of the hut. Wearily, she smiled at her pastor who knelt beside her, concern and relief etched into his kind face. David took her small hand in his own and prayed that God would continue to restore her health. She smiled again, closed her eyes, and slipped into a peaceful sleep. David quietly prayed with the girl's parents, then returned to the English settlement where he had been staying. He had been feeling ill himself and needed to rest before returning to the Indians that evening.

David's health remained poor for the rest of the month. He tried not to let it interfere with his duties, but it was a burden nonetheless. As the days passed without any change, he began, as he often did when he became ill, to struggle with depressing thoughts about himself. More than once he wondered why God would use a feeble sinner like himself. But despite David's melancholy moods and persistent weakness of body, God continued to prepare him for his trip to the Susquehanna. His zeal for the lost never diminished, and his certainty of God's call to carry the Gospel to the Susquehanna only increased as the days passed.

After weeks of eager expectation, David rejoiced that the time had arrived for him to begin his final preparations. On a Saturday in early August, weak but anxious to begin his trip, he met with the Indians to help them with some of their secular business. He would not be with them for many weeks, and he wanted to make sure their affairs, especially those that involved trading, were in order before he left. They were still very dependent upon him for guidance in their business. David had tried to train some of the men so they would not be taken advantage of by foreign traders, but they still relied on him to intercede on their behalf.

Once the Indians' business affairs were in order on Saturday, and after having baptized six more people on the Lord's Day, David was ready to begin his journey to the Susquehanna. He selected six men to go with him, including Moses. Each man had a strong desire to see others come to know Christ, and David was confident that those he had chosen would not be easily tempted by the pagan tribes they would meet along the river.

The day before the company planned to leave, he and the Indians at Cranberry spent the day in prayer. When they were not praying, David read from the Psalms. Both children and adults hung on to every word as he read from Psalm 2: "Ask of Me, and I shall give thee the nations for thine inheritance, and the uttermost parts of the earth for thy possession." Before leaving them for the afternoon, he read from Psalm 72: "Blessed be the Lord God, the God of Israel, who only doeth wondrous things. And blessed be His glorious name forever; and let the whole earth be filled with His glory. Amen, and Amen." In one chorus, the Indians exclaimed, "Amen, Amen." After David left them to rest before his travels the next day, the Indians continued to sing praises to God and offer up prayers for the protection of their beloved pastor and for the conversion of the Indian people.

The morning of his departure, a large group of Indians came out to see him off. They prayed and loaded their pastor with supplies. He would be traveling toward Philadelphia and then to a white settlement on the river south of the Indian country—a longer route, but safer. From there, he would travel up river to visit the various Indian tribes. His six companions planned to ride with him for the first part of the trip, but then they would head off to the Susquehanna through the mountains to take care of some business on their own. David would meet them later at the Susquehanna River. He decided, on account of his health, that it would be best to take the long way around and avoid the hazardous mountain trails that had given him so much trouble in the past.

In the pale morning light, the small company of seven headed off down the mountain trail. They traveled through the wooded terrain all week until they came to Charlestown, which was located about thirty miles west of Philadelphia. The first leg of the journey was uneventful, and David arrived at Charlestown in good spirits and fair health. Because the family he was staying with was spending Saturday in preparation for the Lord's Supper, he decided to remain through the weekend. The pastor of the local congregation asked him to preach on Saturday afternoon, which he gladly did, never able to pass up an opportunity to proclaim God's Word to willing ears. The next day, he and his friends participated in the communion service, and David preached again in the afternoon. That evening, the tired missionary spent time alone in prayer until midnight, then climbed into bed confident about the work God had called him to do.

That Monday, David parted with his friends who would rejoin him at the river. After saying his good-byes, the young missionary set out alone toward the white settlement of Paxton. Once he reached the town, he decided to keep going and lodge that night by the side of the Susquehanna. At dusk, he drew his horse up alongside the quiet shore. The glistening river stretched into the night, blending with the darkness of the far bank. It was hot and humid. David's shirt clung to him and perspiration dripped down his face. The long ride had left him tired and weak, and all he wanted to do was sleep. He quickly ate a light meal, read his Bible, and prayed.

The night grew still as David lay curled on the hard ground with a jacket stuffed beneath his head. The sound of his steady breathing became lost in the buzz of insects and the slow beat of the river against the shore. He tried to sleep, but his head began to ache, keeping him awake. Chills swept through his body as his fever soared. His clothes became soaked partly from the humid night air, partly with perspiration from his fever. He tossed and turned throughout the night, the moon and the stars unaware of the missionary's misery as they continued their relentless march toward the dawn.

Finally, morning came, but the dawn brought him little relief as he woke up coughing. Sitting up on his knees, he bent over, his head nearly touching the ground. He coughed until his chest ached and blood dribbled down his chin. After a few minutes, the coughing eased, and David made his way to the shore where he washed his face and hands and changed his wet shirt. Tired and weak, he walked back to his camp and readied his horse for the long day's ride. Even though part of him whispered to turn back, to return to Crossweeksung where he could rest, he refused to allow his physical frailties to interfere with his mission. Putting the previous night behind him, he climbed onto his horse and followed the Susquehanna north to the Indian territories.

21

A Final Journey

Overhead the stars twinkled in the clear night sky. In the surrounding forest, the beasts who hunted their prey by the light of the moon scampered through the brush just beyond the fire's hot glow. Beside the crackling flames, David and his company from Cranberry rested. Five had already drifted off to sleep, but David and Moses remained bright-eyed as they discussed their trip to the Susquehanna. Not far from their camp, the village of Shamokin slept, unaware that the light of God's Word would once again come among them. Would they see it and understand at last, or would their hearts remain hard and their minds closed? David couldn't wait to find out.

After having talked for nearly an hour, the two men grew quiet. David leaned back against a moss-covered tree. Moses lit a pipe.

"Are you sure it was such a good idea that you decided to make this trip?" Moses asked a little hesitantly. He had seen the young man's strength fail with each journey to the Susquehanna, and he had also seen the delight in David's face as he preached to the Indians of Cranberry. Moses had often wondered why he had not just remained in Cranberry instead of insisting on traveling to the tribes of the Susquehanna.

"I know it's what God wants," David replied. He

smiled as a look of confusion crossed Moses' face. "I know you do not fully understand. I don't expect you to. All I can tell you is that I am not satisfied doing anything else except what God has called me to do."

"But don't you know that it's killing you?" Moses insisted. "This journey is bad enough for a strong man, but for you—well, I do not mean to offend, but you just don't have the strength for it. Are you trying to be a martyr?"

David smiled again. "No," he said gently. "I'm not purposely putting myself in harm's way. I don't want people to remember me as a martyr. I'm just doing what I know is God's will for my life. It's a matter of my calling. I cannot in good conscience do anything that is contrary to what God has called me to do. We must realize, Moses, that God does not always call us to do things that are easy. Sometimes they take sacrifice. Sometimes our service is very costly. It means giving up comforts that might be good for another man, but for you, well, they're just not meant to be."

Moses sat quietly, staring into David's haggard face as his friend spoke. For the first time, he caught a glimpse into the soul of this servant of God. In it, he saw no pride, no deceit, no insincerity. It was a picture of simplicity, of unwavering devotion to a single purpose—that purpose being the glory of God. David's only concern was to travel the path God laid out for him, to bring glory to Him through the preaching of His Word. Some men might think that path too difficult to take, or him too foolish to venture upon it. But to David, it was a matter of loving obedience, of willing sacrifice, and of unwavering faith.

"Ever since God changed my heart," David con-

tinued, "I have not felt comfortable in any other setting except in the preaching of the Gospel to those
who have never heard it. Whenever I have been at
ease in this world, I have not felt free. It is difficult to
explain, but all I can say is that God has not given me
the liberty to live comfortably. I haven't had that kind
of liberty since I began to preach. Some might call it a
madness. Maybe it is. But it is a madness given to me
by the Spirit, and I will never ask Him to take it from
me."

"But what if the tribes along the Susquehanna
refuse to believe?" Moses asked. "Won't all your sacrifice be wasted? They have not responded to your
preaching so far."

David did not answer immediately, but considered carefully what Moses had asked. He harbored no
ill thoughts toward his interpreter. He knew the
Indian was not trying to be critical. His question was
born more out of frustration than criticism, and David
understood that frustration all too well.

"I know it has been an uphill battle this past year,"
David said. "I have preached so often, but the spiritual darkness remains. Sometimes I can't sleep at night
because I am so distraught by the hardness of the Susquehanna Indians. But it's because of that darkness
that I must go on. I cannot turn back because the mission seems hopeless. The success of my preaching is
not my concern. That is God's work. However, I
must admit that I am the first to become frustrated
when the natives do not turn from their pagan ways
and put their faith in Christ. Nevertheless, I cannot
turn my back on them. I must press forward. Unless
they hear the Gospel, they will never be free. I must

go, and even if no one is converted, I will know that I have done what God has called me to do. I can do no more than that, and I can certainly do no less."

Moses found that he had no more to say. He was moved by David's passionate commitment, but he still failed to understand why it was necessary to push so hard. Still, he resolved to remain by his friend's side, to support him in his work, and to stand by him as he carried out his mission. In the past, Moses had continued to travel to the distant tribes only because it was his job as an interpreter, but now the motivation was rooted deep in his soul. He was a Christian, and he wanted others to see the light of Christ just as David did.

Through a trail of smoke that hovered above the dwindling campfire, David smiled at Moses. It was as if he could read the interpreter's thoughts. The Indian might not fully understand David's devotion to his calling, but Moses did sympathize with him in his desire to see others come to know Christ. Catching the meaning behind David's grin, Moses simply puffed on his pipe, blew smoke into the night air, and returned the smile. He finally resigned himself to the fact that David would never give up the call to be a pioneer missionary, no matter the cost.

The next morning came early for the travelers as a bright and cheery dawn stirred them from their sleep. The path to Shamokin lay ready to be trod, and the fields of the Susquehanna lay in wait for the harvest. As David rode quietly down the mountain path, he wondered whether he would be the one who would reap that harvest or if his work would be the sowing of more seed, seed that would one day blossom into glorious fruit to be gathered by others.

By the time they reached the village of Shamokin, the sun was high in the sky and the Delaware Indians were busy hunting, preparing meals, and off trading with other tribes up river. David looked into the faces that glanced at him from behind half-built wigwams and billowing campfires, and his heart overflowed with love. He sensed desperation within him, a degree of urgency to proclaim the Gospel that he had never experienced. He felt as if he were running out of time, as if at any moment the opportunity to preach Christ would be ripped from his grasp. For the past eleven days, as he traveled to the Susquehanna, he had prayed fervently for the power and freedom to preach the Gospel. Now that time had arrived, and the task seemed overwhelming; and indeed it was. But David knew he could do all things in Christ, and that God would give him the confidence to preach to those who remained closed to the Gospel.

Once the company from New Jersey reached the most populous part of the village, David slid from his horse's back and greeted those Delaware Indians who had left their work to welcome the strange group to their camp. The Delawares thought the travelers from Cranberry strange because they had never seen so large a group of Indians in the company of a white Christian. The odd ensemble piqued their curiosity. What could the Indians of New Jersey have in common with the white preacher? They, of course, knew David; he had visited their village in the past, but only with Indians who were either guides or interpreters.

David noticed the curious glances in the direction

of his companions. He and Moses exchanged a knowing look; it had been a good idea to bring converts to the Susquehanna. Nothing could make more of an impression for the Gospel than for natives themselves to proclaim the glory of Christ to fellow Indians. This made perfect sense to David. The Indians were more inclined to trust their own rather than an outsider, and they would be much more moved to hear the testimony of someone who understood their own beliefs and traditions rather than someone who didn't.

The impact of the Cranberry converts was striking from the very moment they arrived. As David began preaching, the Delaware Indians gathered quietly. They sat on the ground before him and listened without yelling out any objections as they had in the past. When it came time for the Cranberry Indians to give their personal testimonies, the Delawares were transfixed. Could it really be true that these Indians had found something that their own traditions could not offer?

Even the Delaware king became curious and asked for David to come and speak with him. Two young braves dressed in simple loin cloths and with blue feathers in their braided hair led the missionary to a smooth, stone platform that extended into the rushing Susquehanna. The Delaware chief sat cross-legged at the very edge with his back to the river. Before him a pile of twigs and branches smoldered over a circle of stones. On either side, two women sat stringing brightly colored beads into long strips.

Without a word, the king motioned for the missionary to sit before him. David obeyed and settled himself on the stony surface not far from the edge of the platform. Below, the river roared its way past the wooded shore. Above, a flock of birds screeched its way from treetop to treetop. On the platform, there was only silence. David did not presume to speak first. The Indian king took his time, looking David over from head to foot. It was not the first time he had met the missionary. David had asked for an audience with him when he had visited Shamokin on previous visits. But those times were brief and were mainly for the purpose of giving David permission to speak with the rest of the tribe about Christianity. This time, David hoped to have more of an impact on the king personally.

"My people tell me you are here again to speak of the Christian God," the king said. His voice rumbled, making him seem older than he appeared. David could not guess the king's age. The deep lines across his forehead and gray in his hair erased the bloom of youth, but the strength in his broad shoulders, the bright gleam of his eyes, and his nimble movements kept his true age a mystery.

"Yes, I have come from across the mountains to speak of Christ," David replied respectfully.

"And what would you have us know about your religion, about this Christ?" the king asked.

"I would have you know that He is the only God, that Jesus Christ is the only way of salvation, that all men are lost unless they have faith in Him," David replied.

"And do your companions believe this teaching?" the Indian asked, referring to the Cranberry converts who had received so much attention.

"Yes, they do," David said.

"It is a serious thing to turn one's back on one's own traditions," the king said gravely.

"You are right," David replied. "But if you discover that those traditions are not true, then wouldn't it be best, and right, if you reject what you have always believed and embrace the truth?"

"A man would be a fool to believe that which is not true," the Indian agreed. "But what is true? Isn't that the question we must ask?"

"Yes, and you are not the first to ask it," David replied. "Many have asked the question. Some do so with a sincere desire to know the truth, but some ask because they do not really believe that you can know the truth. They ask, 'What is the truth?' without expecting to receive an answer."

"But you believe there is an answer?" the king asked curiously.

"Of course. That is why I am here," David said. "Jesus Christ is the truth."

The king did not respond. He merely stared at the ground before him as the breeze stirred his long hair and the gurgling river continued its steady course below. The smell of freshly-scaled fish drifted up from the shore where some women were busily sorting the day's catch. On either side of the chief, the two women continued to bead, first a blue, then a red, then green, then yellow, then blue again. Over and over they repeated the same pattern.

"Why must we believe in this Jesus Christ to be saved?" the king asked suddenly.

David thought for a moment, trying to find the words that would best explain this important truth.

"Do you know how your tribe sometimes has

conflicts with other tribes in the area?" David asked. The Indian nodded. He knew all too well the conflicts that often erupted between the tribes of that region. Some even led to bloodshed.

"Well, sometimes the only way you can be reconciled or come to a peaceful agreement with another tribe is through a mediator, someone who will go to them and speak on your behalf," David explained. "Without that person to intercede for you and come to an agreement with the other tribe, you would continue to fight. Is that not right?"

The king nodded thoughtfully. But then a look of skepticism crossed his face.

"But I am not at war with God," he replied. He spread his arms wide in a gesture of peace.

"But you are," David said earnestly. "We all are. The Bible says we are by nature enemies of God. We do not serve Him and worship Him as we ought. We lie, we steal, we think bad thoughts, we grow angry. All of that is rebellion against God. The only way we can be at peace with Him, the only way we can be cleansed of our sins is through the mediation of Jesus Christ."

"How, then, do we get Him to speak for us?" the Indian asked.

"You ask Him to," David answered.

"You mean we do not have to conjure the spirits or dance or sacrifice animals?" the king asked.

"No, Christ is our sacrifice," David replied. "His work is enough. All we have to do is to have faith in Him, to believe in Him, and to rely on Him for our salvation. We must trust in Him, confess our sins, and follow Him as our God and our Savior."

"You speak many words great with meaning," the king replied. "You have given me much to consider. For now you may go. Speak as you wish to my people if they will listen."

Without another word, the king held up his hand, and the two young braves stood beside David, signaling that it was time to leave. David stood up between them, nodded to the king, and returned to the village. As he walked down the rocky path dimmed by afternoon shadows, his heart soared with hope that God would open the king's eyes to his need of Christ.

For the rest of the day, David and the Indians of Cranberry preached and testified to the mercy of Christ. Finally, by evening David was too exhausted to utter another word. Leaving the others to continue speaking with the Delawares, he retired to a small wigwam and fell asleep as soon as he lay down.

The following morning, he awoke to pounding thunder and pouring rain. A northeasterly storm had brewed during the night and was blustering its way through the river region. David looked outside at the steady rain with weary eyes. The smoke that was trapped in the wigwam because of the moisture outside began to irritate his lungs. His throat was beginning to close up, making it difficult to breathe. He wanted to go outside, but the storm was too fierce. So, trapped like a caged and wounded animal, David paced up and down in the wigwam. As morning turned into afternoon, he began to lose all strength. He couldn't pray or read or speak. All he could do was lie on the cold floor and try to breathe. His chest heaved up and down, and every time he coughed blood would dribble down his chin.

David felt as if each passing hour would be his last, but finally the storm broke, the smoke cleared from the hut, and he was able to go outside. By that time, however, it was evening, and most of the Indians could not be found. Tired and sore, he returned to the hut and tried to sleep through the night. When he awoke the next morning, he could breathe more easily, but he felt weak. Still, he refused to allow his feeble body to keep him from preaching. So, with dark circles under his eyes and his face pale from sickness, he stood boldly before the Indians and proclaimed the name of Christ.

After several days of preaching in Shamokin and still no converts, David and the others traveled up river to the Great Island. There he suffered from continued weakness of body and lack of response from the Indians. Try as he might, he could not open the eyes of the Indians. This proved to be a much-needed reminder of David's dependence upon God for the conversion of sinners. Just as David had told Moses from the very beginning, all one could do was preach. It was up to God to change hearts.

But even with that in mind, David grew discouraged. His body failed him at every turn. He could barely summon the strength to preach, and when he did the power and freedom that he so cherished in the pulpit escaped him. This struggle plunged him into a depressed and melancholy mood. One night as he lay shivering from a fever and gasping for every breath, his mind clouded with doubt. "Oh, what a dead, heartless, barren, unprofitable wretch am I," he complained to himself. "I am so weak and ill I can hardly do anything to help these poor people who so desperately need Christ."

Another night when he and his friends camped in the forest, his thoughts grew even darker as he thought of the many people back home praying for him. The night had turned chilly, and dew blanketed the forest. Trying to keep dry and warm, David covered himself with branches and pine needles. In the distance, wolves howled at the moon. They seemed to draw closer with each passing hour. Beneath his blanket of twigs, David grumbled to himself. "So many people are praying for me and expecting me to carry out my duties with zeal and steadfastness for God," he thought bleakly. "They think I am here to do something for God among the poor Indians. They think I am fervent in spirit, but, oh, what a heartless frame of mind I am in! If only God's people knew me as God knows me, they would not think so highly of my zeal and resolution for God as perhaps they now do! I wish they could see how heartless I am. Then they would not be deceived and would think no more of me than they ought. But, if they saw how unfaithful I have been, the smallness of my courage, they would be ready to shut me out of their doors as unworthy of the company or friendship of Christians."

It was in this state of mind that David returned to Shamokin. As he slowly walked through the village, he looked into the faces of all he passed, just as he had done when he had first arrived. In the eyes of each, he saw hopelessness, confusion, and pride. Even in the faces of the youngest children, with their rosy cheeks and playful smiles, darkness broiled beneath the surface. Silently he cried out to God for their salvation, to bring light to their eyes and life to their souls. He prayed that God would use his meager efforts to bring the Indian people to a saving knowledge of Jesus Christ.

As he prayed, he grew more confident, and his desire to preach could not be contained. He hurried to the center of camp, and possessed with a newly found zeal he began to preach. The freedom, the power, the fervency that had eluded him for so long came flooding back, spilling into every word and gesture. So passionate were his pleas, so bold were his proclamations that anyone who heard him would never have guessed that he had suffered so long both in body and in spirit. Tears streamed from his eyes and his voice shook as he used every ounce of strength to declare the glories of Christ and to invite the Indians of Shamokin to dine at the table of the living Lord.

But despite his efforts, no one turned, no one confessed Christ. Some left the village that day filled with thoughts about the destiny of their own souls, but none put their faith in Christ. The miracle of Crossweeksung would not be repeated here. David finally resigned himself to that fact. So that night, as he looked into the weary eyes of his companions, he decided to return to New Jersey. His mission to the Susquehanna was over, and it was time to return to his beloved family at Cranberry.

As David and his friends traveled the road toward home, he reflected on the past few weeks and hoped the journey had not been a failure. He could not guess what God's purposes were in bringing him to the Susquehanna. Maybe God would eventually convert the Indians who had heard the Gospel through him.

Maybe God simply wanted to cause some of the Susquehanna Indians to come to his congregation in New Jersey, something a few of them were inclined to do. Or maybe his work was only the preparation for other missionary efforts in the future. David did not know. But he did know that God had called him to the Susquehanna, and that he had been obedient to the call. Christ had been declared in the wilderness, light had burst forth into the darkness, and God had been glorified.

22

Saying Farewell

"Chop the trees into six-foot poles, then bring them to the far side of the field," David instructed one of the Indians who was overseeing a fence-building project along the borders of the Cranberry land. The young man nodded and echoed the instructions to a couple of men who were hacking away at a large pine tree on the edge of a trampled corn field. For the past few weeks, bears and deer had been roaming through the corn, damaging much of the crop. The Indians became concerned that there wouldn't be much left for the harvest, so David advised them to build large fences around their farm lands to keep the animals out of the fields.

Weakened by his prolonged illness, the twenty-eight-year-old missionary walked slowly across the field. Since his return from the Susquehanna, he had been shut up in his cabin, bedridden with a high fever and violent coughing. He looked frail and gaunt with his pale cheeks sunken and his eyes dark and swollen. The least effort seemed to leave him exhausted. Even preaching proved to be too much of a strain. He would often have to sit down to preach, and afterwards his people would carry him back to his house—a one-room cabin the Indians had built for him after his return from the Susquehanna. During those long nights as he lay shivering on his bed of corn shucks, he often wondered if he could go on, if he could get out of bed the next morning to prepare a sermon, if he could kneel on the hard floor to pray. But even as the fever raged, he knew he had to continue his ministry among the Indians. He could not bear the thought of his flock being left to wander without a shepherd.

As the sun rose high in the cloudless sky, David joined the others who had been fixing some of the broken fences on the far side of the field. Greeting him warmly, they offered him some water. The day was unusually humid for late October, and the men had taken off their tunics to work. David accepted the tin cup of water from one of the Indians and checked the work they were doing. He had built fences and mended them countless times back on the Brainerd farm in Haddam and was thankful he could use his farming skills to help the Indians protect their crop.

The men worked late into the afternoon. Finally, as the day drew to a close and the forest trees cast their long shadows across the newly erected fences, the men headed back to Cranberry where the women were waiting with hot meals. Tired and hungry, they gathered around crackling fires to eat. But no one touched his food until David prayed and thanked God for giving them strength for the day's work.

The next day, he visited the families of Cranberry, helping them with various spiritual struggles they had been having. As the afternoon wore on, David hoped he would be able to gather his flock together that evening to teach from the Scriptures and help them to prepare for worship the following day. But even though he had felt stronger that afternoon, more so than he had in many weeks, his strength began to fail as evening approached. Pain seared through his chest, and severe coughing shook his whole body as blood erupted from his lungs. He would have to wait until the next morning to preach.

But the morning did not bring any relief, and David was robbed of another opportunity to proclaim the Good News. All he could do was lie in his cot and pray that the fever would pass quickly. Some of the Indians stopped by to check on him, asking him whether he would be able to lead the services that day, but they found him too weak to stand. David was grieved and frustrated that he could not declare the truth to such willing ears. He had hoped to train some of the men to fill in for him when he was unable to preach, but none were ready. They needed so much more guidance, training, and instruction. If he would ever have to leave them, which he believed would more likely happen sooner than later, he knew someone would need to be sent to replace him.

Finally, toward evening, he felt strong enough to sit up in bed and teach from the Scriptures. He called all the Indians together to join him in his home. Everyone crammed into his cramped cabin to listen to him teach from the Sermon on the Mount in Matthew 5:1–16. There was very little breathing room, but the Indians didn't seem to mind. They were happy as long as they could hear the words of their dear pastor. Barely speaking above a whisper, David read, "Blessed are the poor in spirit, for theirs is the kingdom of heaven. Blessed are they who mourn; for they shall be comforted. . . . Blessed are they who are per-

secuted for righteousness' sake, for theirs is the kingdom of heaven." The Indians listened in silence.
They knew persecution. They were often laughed at
and ridiculed, even physically assaulted, because of
their newly found faith, and they clung to Jesus'
words to "rejoice, and be exceedingly glad, for great is
your reward in heaven; for so perse-cuted they the
prophets who were before you."

David exhorted them to let their light shine before
men that they might bring praise and glory to the name
of Christ. It would be so easy to hide their faith from
others, never to talk about it, to keep to themselves.
They would encounter less conflict and persecution
that way. But Jesus' words rang in their ears, "Let
your light shine before men, that they may see your
good works and glorify your Father who is in
heaven." David urged the Indians to tell others of the
Gospel and to pray that God would use them to enlarge His kingdom. Many were ashamed that they had
been negligent in this privilege and duty of telling
others about Christ. They admitted that they had
been intimidated by other Indians who scoffed at
them and made fun of them. But as they listened to
Jesus' teaching, they were filled with courage to
oppose those who sought to undermine their freedom
in Christ. They were inspired to proclaim the
Gospel, and encouraged to live without shame, without fear before others who hated the truth.

As the cool, autumn days passed, David ministered
among his Indians, teaching them, encouraging them
like a parent protectively caring for his children. But
as the weeks sped by, his health took a turn for the
worse. One Sunday morning he tried to get out of bed

but couldn't lift himself even to get a drink of water. All day, he remained curled in his cot, too weak to read the Bible, crippled by the pain in his chest. As he lay in the darkness of his cabin, perspiration poured down his thin body and his lungs heaved in piercing pain. Realizing that he had little hope of recovery, he admitted to himself that it was time for him to leave his flock in more able hands. As always, the thought of his people being deprived of a pastor who could strengthen them in their faith caused him more pain than his bodily illness. But, after much prayer and consideration, he came to the conclusion that if he could not serve them, another would have to be sent in his place. The time had come for him to join his friends in New England where he could be looked after in his final days.

That Monday, David called his congregation together. He sat outside his cabin wrapped in a buckskin blanket, waiting for them to arrive. They gathered quickly, concern written on their faces. Once David was sure everyone was present, he slowly stood before them, grunting with the effort and wincing at the pain in his chest. He cleared his throat. The crowd hushed.

"I have gathered you here today to bring sad news," David said weakly. "During the past few months, I have tried to serve you faithfully. But I have grown weaker by the day. I see now that I can no longer minister to you as a pastor should. You need someone who is strong and healthy, who can nourish your souls with sound teaching, help you with your business affairs, and comfort you when you are sick and suffering. My time here among you dear people has come to an end. It grieves me to leave you, but I know that God will always be with you."

He paused a moment to catch his breath. Sniffles rippled through the crowd as the Indians choked back their tears.

"I would ask only one thing of you," David continued. "That you continue to seek the glory of God in all things, that you serve Him with all your heart and grow in knowledge and understanding of Him. For as you grow in true knowledge of Him, you will become more and more like Him. Seek His will, His interests, and His honor in all you do. Pray that I will do the same even in the face of death."

Tears flowed freely as David sat back down, too weak to stand any longer. Weeping, the entire assembly knelt in prayer, and David quoted from Psalm 16: "Preserve me, O God, for in Thee do I put my trust. O my soul, thou hast said unto the Lord, Thou art my Lord. My goodness extendeth not to Thee, but to the saints who are in the earth, and to the excellent, in whom is all my delight. . . . I have set the Lord always before me; because He is at my right hand, I shall not be moved. Therefore my heart is glad, and my glory rejoiceth; my flesh also shall rest in hope. For Thou wilt not leave my soul in hell, neither wilt Thou permit Thine Holy One to see corruption. Thou wilt show me the path of life. In Thy presence is fullness of joy; at Thy right hand there are pleasures forevermore."

With what remaining strength he had, David spent the rest of the day visiting all the families in Cranberry. He ministered to each one according to their particular needs and encouraged them as best he could under the circumstances. He comforted them when they broke into tears, reminding them that he would see them all again one day and worship with them before the throne of God.

After he finished the visitations, he stopped by the home of the schoolmaster to say farewell. Knowing that David would be meeting with other ministers and members of the Missionary Society during his journey to New England, the schoolmaster asked him to have more Bibles sent to him. If the Indians were ever going to learn English, he would need more Bibles. David, of course, promised to urge church members to give generously so this need could be met. He and the schoolmaster then prayed together, after which David returned home, packed some supplies, and rode two miles to his former house in Crossweeksung. There he gathered together some personal belongings before beginning his long journey the next day.

The following morning, the weary missionary rode the twenty-one miles to Elizabethtown where he would stay at the home of Jonathan Dickinson before making his way to Northampton, Massachusetts. He had written Mr. Edwards, informing him that he would be arriving as soon as he could make the trip. The Edwards family had invited David on a number of occasions to visit them, and the day had finally come when he would accept the offer. He looked forward to seeing Jerusha again and spending many hours talking with her father.

After a short but tiring journey on horseback, David arrived at Elizabethtown in early November. The Rev. Dickinson and his family greeted him warmly, but they were apprehensive over his sickly appearance. The circles under his eyes were deep and dark, making him look like a mere shadow of his former self. Mr. Dickinson, who was a physician as well as a pastor, helped him to the guest room where David fell onto the soft, downy bed, exhausted from his travels and too sick to move.

For the next few days, Mr. Dickinson hardly left his friend's side. Ever since he had met David shortly after his expulsion from Yale, he had cared a great deal about him. The fifty-eight-year-old minister, who had been sympathetic to the revivalists, took David under his wing and was one of the many ministers who spoke on the young man's behalf to the board at Yale. Since then, he had kept up with David's missionary work through correspondence. He, along with all of David's friends, did not want to see that work cut short.

Throughout the winter, David remained too weak to move. His violent coughing continued, and he often ran high fevers. Mr. Dickinson feared he would not live to see the spring. But despite his failing health, David's spirits remained high. He did not fear dying but looked forward to the day when he would be free from the weakness of his body and able to worship God with all his glorified strength. In a letter to his brother Israel, he wrote, "Oh the blessedness of being delivered from the clogs of flesh and sense, from a body of sin and spiritual death! Oh the unspeakable sweetness of being translated into a state of complete purity and perfection!"

So it was with this attitude that he faced every day during that long winter. He read Scripture, listened to the godly conversation of his friends, and spent many hours in prayer for his congregation at Cranberry. He was greatly comforted that God had brought so many of the Indians into His kingdom and that He would care for them while they were temporarily left to make their pilgrimage without an earthly shepherd.

In late February, while David was still confined to his friend's house at Elizabethtown, one of the Indians from Cranberry came to visit him. David rejoiced at the sight of his Indian friend and asked him many questions about the state of his flock. The Indian gave him a number of letters from the congregation, which he read with much enthusiasm. Every sentence of broken English and every description of how God had been revealing His grace and love to the people of Cranberry were like gentle raindrops falling on dry and thirsty soil. David's spirits soared when he heard the news of his people's faithfulness. They continued to serve the Lord soberly, maintaining good behavior as they carried out the affairs of daily life at Cranberry. Anxious to hear any tidbit of news the Indian could remember, David visited with his friend late into the night. Before the Indian left, David asked him to encourage the congregation to persevere in their faith and to keep their eyes fixed on Christ.

For a brief period after the Indian's visit, David maintained a refreshed and joyful disposition, despite the constant pain and fever. But as the days turned into weeks, his old melancholy returned. One evening, as snow blanketed the yard outside his window and the fire burned brightly in his room, he complained to Mr. Dickinson that he wished God had taken him while he had been working on the mission field. He confessed that he despised wasting time in the doldrums of sickness. To David's surprise, Mr. Dickinson responded not with words of comfort but with a gentle rebuke.

"You say that you are trifling away time to no purpose, but who are you to question the purposes of God?" the older man asked gently. "Every hour that you live, you live to glorify God, even if all you can do is pray. That is not time wasted, and you should not treat it as such. God has determined that you should live, even as sick as you are. Because He has determined it to be so, you should not complain that you are living to no purpose. With every breath, you can lift praises to God. That is a high and lofty privilege. Do not cheapen that purpose with a flood of complaints."

David thought about what the pastor said. He did not think he had complained as much as Mr. Dickinson implied, but he accepted the reproof nonetheless and took the opportunity to examine himself for even more sin that might be hidden in his heart. The pastor's rebuke caused him to reflect on the many times he had been dead of heart and plagued with a complaining disposition. This humbled him and brought him to his knees in sincere confession and repentance before the Lord.

Throughout his illness, David's thoughts, cares, and prayers kept turning to his congregation at Cranberry. Every day he longed to see them, and when he finally began to improve, he decided to travel back to the village to visit his people. He arrived at Cranberry in mid-March, though the day-long journey proved to be more difficult than he had anticipated.

He could stay only a couple of days, but he wanted to see how the Indians were doing and offer any encouragement he could.

When he appeared through the trees at the edge of the town, some of the children sighted him on the trail and ran toward him, yelling out greetings with bursts of excitement. David smiled at them and slipped from his horse. They wrapped their arms around him, their pale buckskins brushing against his leather boots as they led him by hand to the middle of the town. A crowd swelled behind them as they walked. The news of his arrival spread, and everyone came out to welcome their pastor home.

As the Indians gathered around him telling him their news, David soon discovered that all was not well at Cranberry. Some of the Indians who had struggled with drunkenness had slipped back to their former ways. David immediately spoke with the backsliders and exhorted them to repent and return to the Lord. He warned them that the true child of God cannot continue to live in sin; he will either be severely disciplined by the Lord and brought to humble repentance, or he will be hardened in his sin, thus proving he was never part of the true flock of Christ. The Indians accepted their pastor's rebuke and appeared relieved to have his wisdom and spiritual strength guide them once more, even if it was for a moment.

Toward evening, as David warmed himself by the fire, Moses, David's faithful interpreter, joined him, having just arrived from the Forks of Delaware.

"It will not be long now," Moses said, as he stared into the fire.

David knew he was talking about his death and simply nodded.

"You will finally be home where you have always wanted to be," Moses said, turning to look at his sickly friend.

"Yes, but you will be left here to continue the Lord's work among your people," David replied. "Persevere in that work, even when everything seems to stand against you."

"We have seen plenty of those times together, haven't we?" Moses replied, smiling as he thought about their difficult journeys to the Susquehanna.

"We certainly have," David whispered. "You have been a faithful companion to me, and for that I will be forever grateful."

The small fire sputtered, and the village grew still. David and Moses stared into the night, the dying flames warm against their faces. The breeze smelled of newly budded trees and tender grass. Moses breathed in the fresh air. David coughed. Silence hung between them. The missionary leaned against a tree and closed his eyes. As the fire slowly died, the cool night air brushed his face. David stirred, and Moses glanced over at him.

"I think I need to turn in for the night," David yawned.

Moses stood up beside him and embraced the young man whom God had used to bring him into Christ's kingdom.

"I'll miss you," Moses said gently.

"We will meet again, my friend," David replied. Without looking back, he turned and disappeared into the night.

As much as his strength would allow, David spent the next day counseling and giving instructions to the leaders of his congregation. Before leaving Cranberry, he read a psalm to his people and explained its meaning. In response, the Indians sang a hymn together, clasping hands and weeping freely. As David rode his horse down the road that led to Elizabethtown, many of the Indians walked beside him, wanting to be with him as long as they could, knowing they would never see their beloved pastor again in this life. Even though many did not want to admit it, they knew it would not be long before he stepped over the threshold between this world and eternity.

23

The Light Grows Dim

The frosty days of winter had passed, and the warm beauty of spring was in full bloom as David traveled the long road to Massachusetts. He took his time, stopping at the homes of friends along the way. David knew in his heart that this would be the last time he would see any of them in this life. Their smiles, their warm embraces, their gentle words lifted his downcast spirit. Little did he know how much of an encouragement he was to them. His willingness to leave this world, but his longing to remain if only to preach the Gospel to the Indians touched their hearts. The ache of leaving the Indians behind could not be hidden from those who knew him best. Such love and commitment inspired all who saw him during those final days. Many commented that with his passing the church would lose one of its finest treasures on earth but gain one of its brightest stars in heaven. David knew he was dying, but he hoped that maybe, just maybe, God would preserve his life and send him back to the mission field, to his people at Cranberry who so desperately needed a pastor.

It was with this hope tucked securely in his heart that he made his way to the home of Jonathan Edwards. The day was still young when he pulled his horse to a stop in front of the quaint, two-story house.

Nothing stirred except the breeze through the grass, and David wondered if anyone was home. He was just about to dismount when the door to the house flew open. A young woman stood in the doorway wearing a plain, blue work dress and apron. Her long, dark hair was pulled back into a braid and tied with a white ribbon. She wiped her hands with a soiled dishcloth and walked down the steps.

David slid gingerly from his horse and pushed open the whitewashed gate. He took off his hat and nodded in greeting.

"Dearest Jerusha," David said gently. "It is good to see you."

Jerusha stopped an arm's length away and smiled. "I barely allowed myself to hope that you would make it," she said, her voice edged with a strained mix of delight and concern. Her modest blue eyes glimmered with tears as she gazed at the young man.

"You don't look well," she sighed. "Was the journey difficult for you?"

"Yes, but God has brought me safely here," he replied, fumbling with the edge of his hat. Before he could say more, Jerusha's father strode down the walkway dressed in simple field clothes and dusting hay off his cotton shirt.

"Mr. Brainerd, I am relieved to see that you made the trip," Mr. Edwards exclaimed, shaking the younger man's hand. "We heard discouraging reports that you had taken a turn for the worse. We feared you might not come."

"I had that fear as well, but God has seen fit to bring me into your company," David replied. "And I thank you for having me as your guest."

"It's our pleasure," Mr. Edwards replied cheerfully. "Jerusha, why don't you go inside and prepare
Mr. Brainerd some tea while I show him his room."

Jerusha hurried up the walkway, leaving her father
to help David with his supplies. Mrs. Edwards and
the rest of the family came out to greet the missionary
and welcome him to their home. As soon as his belongings were carried to his room upstairs, David accepted the tea Jerusha had prepared. He held the
dainty cup in his thin hand and let the steam wash
over him. The fragrance and warmth quickly chased
away the aches and pains of his long and exhausting
journey.

As he sipped tea and munched on biscuits, David
talked with Mr. Edwards for the rest of the afternoon.
He told the attentive minister about his delay in
Elizabethtown and his final meeting with the Indians
at Cranberry. As he reflected on his flock back in
New Jersey, he explained how he hoped someone
would step forward to carry on the pastoral work at
the Indian settlement. He had written to his brother
John about the possibility of his taking over the ministry at Cranberry, and David hoped to receive a reply before the end of the summer. That is, unless he
recovered and was able to return there himself.

But throughout the following week, David's health
did not improve. He continued to spit up blood and
run a high temperature. Anxious about the young
man's health, Mr. Edwards contacted Dr. Mather of
Northampton and asked him to come and examine
David. After looking him over thoroughly, the doctor
explained that he had tuberculosis of the lungs, or
consumption as it was commonly called. The case was

advanced, and there was little hope that he would recover. Ulcers and large blisters had formed on the
lining of his lungs, and when they would burst, the
discharge and blood would seep into his lung cavities.
This made breathing painful and difficult.

The doctor's diagnosis did not disturb David.
Unlike so many people who are terrified of death because they do not have faith in Jesus Christ, or because they have no assurance of their salvation, David
knew he would be with his Father in heaven when he
finally left this world. This brought him great comfort
and joy as he faced the final days of his life. Instead of
dreading the day of his death, he looked forward to it.
It was not a morbid hope, but the joyful expectation of
a son eagerly anticipating the day when he would finally go home.

Until that day arrived, David's temporary home
would be with the Edwards family. As the summer
days passed, Mrs. Edwards and Jerusha tended to his
needs, washing his clothes, preparing his meals, and
changing his linens. In the afternoons, after Mr.
Edwards finished his long hours of study, David
would talk with the older minister about the Lord,
about his longing to be in heaven, and about his concerns for the Indians at Cranberry.

Every day, David would thank God for allowing
him to live with the Edwardses. It was a blessing just
to be in the company of such a godly family. He took
great delight in seeing how each of them, and especially Jerusha, loved to serve the Lord. Often, early
in the morning when David would walk outside to
pray, he would see Jerusha strolling through the
fields, her head bent in prayer. Sometimes she would

stop and kneel, lifting her face to the heavens. Whenever she returned from those times alone with the Lord, her face would shine with an inner joy. David often thought that a man could not have a more godly and devoted wife than if he were married to Jerusha Edwards. He was continually struck by her piety, her devotion to God, and her freedom from the trappings of worldly desires and distractions. Even though she was only seventeen years old, she possessed a spiritual maturity that belied her years. She loved to pray and worship, and she never complained as she carried out her household responsibilities. Devoted and faithful, she honored her parents in every way and still found time to serve David by preparing his meals, cleaning his soiled clothing, and making notes in his journal when he was too weak to do it himself.

Every morning, after Jerusha had served him breakfast, David would ride his horse across the beautiful Massachusetts countryside. The doctor had advised him to keep riding even though it was painful. The exercise and fresh air would help to strengthen his failing lungs. David enjoyed his morning rides, despite the pain in his chest. The surrounding meadowlands were more glorious than he had imagined. A wide creek ran through the Edwards property, bordered by weeping willows, lush maples, and flowers of every color. The sweet aroma of summer grass filled the warm air, and miles of rich farmland reminded David of Cranberry. His heart ached to return to the Indian village, but he finally knew that day would never come.

In the evenings, when the Edwardses gathered for

family worship, Mr. Edwards would often ask David
to read from the Scriptures or lead the family in
prayer. The older minister would comment that his
praying brought comfort to everyone in the family because it was so empty of self-righteousness, so sincere
and humble. He would not pray as if he were giving
some eloquent speech that would impress the others,
nor would he pray with false humility designed to
bring attention to himself. Instead, his prayers were
simple and from the heart, giving God the esteem and
honor due Him. David expressed himself with the
humility of a sinner before a holy God and with the
reverence of a subject coming before the throne of his
great and glorious king. In his prayers, he would confess his utter dependence upon God for everything
and proclaim the sufficiency of God in meeting his
needs. He would also pray fervently for the advancement of Christ's kingdom in the world and the
spread of the Gospel to the Indians.

After being in Northampton for nearly a month,
David decided to go to Boston to meet with members
of the Missionary Society and to visit with other
ministers. He wanted to arrange for someone, perhaps
his brother, to take over the ministry at Cranberry and
to urge the New England congregations to send more
missionaries to the Indian people. Grieved that the
churches were not more faithful in fulfilling God's
mandate to tell every nation about the Good News of
Christ, David wanted to urge others to reach out to
their red-skinned neighbors, to put off fear and prejudice, and to embrace the Indians with the love of
Christ. Too much hostility had developed between
the white men and the Indians because many of the

settlers were more concerned about themselves than about the Indians' spiritual needs. While all white people were not guilty of such selfishness, and some of the Indians certainly played their part in the hostilities, there were enough rotten apples to give Christians a bad name among the Indians. David wanted that to change, and he hoped a visit to Boston would inspire churches there to support mission work to the Indian people.

When David first mentioned his desire to go to Boston, Mr. Edwards was not convinced the young man should take the trip. But once David explained why he needed to go and reassured Mr. Edwards that he felt well enough to travel, the pastor gave his consent.

"I will support you in this only if you take someone with you to care for your needs," Mr. Edwards told David in early June. "I think Jerusha would be honored to assist you as you make the trip to Boston, if you do not have any objections."

"No, I don't," David replied, thankful for the recommendation. "It would be a privilege to have her accompany me, but are you sure you don't mind her traveling with me alone?"

"I trust both of you," Mr. Edwards replied. "But for the sake of discretion and propriety, I will arrange for you both to stay at the homes of various ministers along the way so there will not be any raised eyebrows."

A few days later, David and Jerusha set out for Boston, traveling slowly and making frequent stops at the homes of ministers whom Mr. Edwards had contacted. They arrived in Boston three days later, where they were welcomed into the home of a local minister. During the following week, David visited with various pastors and members of the Missionary Society. Many had read the journal he had published about the outpouring of God's Spirit upon the people of Crossweeksung, and, as David had hoped, it had spurred many ministers to become more interested in missions to the American Indians.

David remained strong enough to speak on various occasions about his ministry among the Indians until one day in mid-June. While in a meeting with a number of wealthy citizens and ministers from Boston concerning the support of mission work in Indian territories and the establishment of English schools in Pennsylvania and New Jersey, he suddenly felt burning pain in his chest. Jerusha, who had been faithfully assisting him, called a physician. After an examination, the doctor said that ulcers were bursting in his lungs and advised him to go immediately to bed and rest.

Constantly attended by Jerusha, he remained in the same condition for weeks. Sometimes he would try to walk around the house where he was staying, but after only a few steps, he would grow so faint that he had to return to bed. Most of the time he could not even speak, except to say "yes" or "no." If he tried to say more than a few words, he would have to stop and take a breath. Many friends stopped by, gathering around his bed to sing, to pray, and, on those rare occasions whenever he had the strength, to listen to him tell about his ministry among the Indians.

Through it all, Jerusha remained by David's side, caring for him, offering words of encouragement and comfort. As he regained some of his strength, he and Jerusha would discuss Scripture and talk about the glories of Christ's kingdom, sharing the love and joy they both knew in Christ. With those who came to visit, he would always talk about Christ. He was impressed with the need to tell them that the essence of religion consisted in acting above all selfish intentions, living for God's glory, pleasing and honoring Him in all things. Often in a barely audible whisper, David would explain that a Christian was best motivated to love, adore, and worship God when he understood how worthy God is of such worship.

"When a soul loves God with a supreme love, he then acts like our blessed God Himself," David explained one day. "When our interests and God's become one, and we long that God should be glorified, and we rejoice to think that He is unchangeably possessed of the highest glory and blessedness, then we are acting in conformity to God. In the same way, when we are fully resigned to, and rest satisfied and content with, God's will, in this we are also conformed to His image."

Sometimes when he would speak, the ulcers in his chest would burst, sending him into unbearable agony. Jerusha would try to comfort him as he lay writhing in pain. She would dab his forehead with cool rags and lift his head so he could sip some water. It would often take a long time for him to grow calm again, but once the pain eased, David would inevitably continue to speak about Christ and His grace. During such times, Jerusha would take notes or jot down entries in his diary. But always she kept an eye out for telltale signs that another coughing fit was about to come on.

"One thing we must all remember is that we cannot be conformed to God's will, we cannot live wholly for Him unless it is by the power of the Holy Spirit," David said late one night, unable to suppress all that was on his heart. "Only those who rely on the grace of Jesus Christ will be like God. We must never think it is our own work and our own ability. A changed heart is God's own work, and He delights in His own work—not in the filthy rags of self-righteousness that we try to bring before Him. Because it is God's work, and not our own, it is steadfast and stable. God secures us by His unchanging power, and the work He does in us is rooted in that unchanging power. Therefore, if God works this marvelous change in our hearts, we do not fear that it will one day disappear, but it will continue even as God continues."

Whenever anyone stopped by, David would urge him to examine whether he had truly been saved, whether God had ever really changed his heart. He knew how easily people can be deceived, and he couldn't bear to die knowing he could have said something to make a difference in someone's life.

But his words were not only for the benefit of his visitors. Even as he exhorted others to search for the fruit of salvation in their lives, he would examine his own heart. "Do I have true religion?" he asked himself more than once. The answer would always be the same, "Yes." He knew in his heart that he sincerely longed to please and glorify God. Though he was by no means perfect, at the root David wanted to please God and be conformed to His will. Glorifying God was his utmost interest and his highest happiness. Even as he lay dying, he longed to be in heaven where he would glorify God perfectly, unhindered by the assaults of Satan and the temptation of his own sinful desires. Heaven meant more to him than his own happiness, it meant glorifying God in purity and truth.

At night when everything was quiet, except for the rustle of the breeze at his window, he felt the fullness of God's love, and, as so many times before, he wanted to be with Christ in heaven. He thanked God that his thoughts were clear at times, despite his fever, and that he relied, not on sentimental feelings that so easily change like shifting shadows, but on the promises of Christ that anchored his melancholy soul. How easy it would have been to drift along like a discarded boat, carried by the changing currents of emotion; but through the relentless days and nights of suffering, Christ held him fast.

While David remained bedridden throughout the summer, his brother Israel, who was a student at Yale College, came to visit, bringing with him sad news. David's sister, Spenser, had died at Haddam. He had been close to his sister as he grew up. She had been very devoted to God, a devotion that had always impressed David. During his college years, he would often stay with her whenever he returned home to Haddam. Sadly, he had not seen her in many years and did not know she had been seriously ill. The news struck him to the heart, but he was comforted by the confidence that he would soon be reunited with his sister in God's heavenly kingdom.

During David's final days in Boston, members of

the Missionary Society came to visit him. They valued his insights concerning missionary efforts to the Six Nations along the Delaware River, and they sought his advice on how to continue the work now that he would no longer be with them. Sick as he was, he did his best to help the Society in every way that he could. He selected two suitable candidates to go on the mission field and spread word about the need for Bibles and teaching materials to be sent to the missionaries and schoolmasters already in the field. Many wealthy people who visited David promised to send Bibles and supplies to the Indians at Cranberry. David was also able to persuade them to provide an additional schoolmaster to help in New Jersey. Even though he wanted to do more, he was pleased that, even as he lay dying, he was able to help his congregation at Cranberry and arrange for other missionaries to continue the work he had begun in the Susquehanna River region.

In late June, after taking care of some business concerning the Indians, David took another turn for the worse. Jerusha wrote a letter to her father, telling him about her friend's decline: "On Thursday, he was very ill with a violent fever, and extreme pain in his head and breast, and sometimes delirious. He remained the same until Saturday evening when he seemed to be in the agonies of death. The family was up with him till one or two o'clock, expecting every hour would be his last. On Sabbath-day, he was a little revived, his head was better, but very full of pain, and exceeding sore at his breast. He could barely breathe without terrible pain. Yesterday he was better, but last night he slept just a little. In the morning he was much worse. Dr. Pynchon doesn't think he will live much longer, though, he says, he might be able to come to Northampton."

Jerusha's fears, however, were soon eased as David suddenly began to grow stronger. His slight recovery surprised everyone. Dr. Pynchon explained that if the discharge from the broken ulcers in his lungs cleared from his system, he might recover for awhile. But the doctor warned that as soon as the ulcers burst again, he would be thrown into a high fever and more than likely never recover.

David took the short break in his illness to return to Northampton. His visit to Boston had been beneficial, even though it drained him of much strength. He had made arrangements for more missionaries and had secured more funding for his congregation in Cranberry. As he left Boston on a warm summer day to return to Northampton, David's heart felt lighter because he had been able to tie up loose ends concerning his plans for future mission work among the Indians. He left with the hope that more churches would reach out to the Indians of North America and proclaim to them the Good News of Jesus Christ.

24

Unto Glory

David's strength continued to decline after his return to Northampton. The ulcers did not break as they had in Boston, but he grew so weak that he could no longer walk down the stairs. To make moving about easier for him, Mr. Edwards moved him into a comfortable bedroom on the bottom floor. Whenever his strength would allow, he would make his way from the bedroom and join the Edwardses in family worship. One time, when Mr. Edwards had to be out of town, David led the family in its devotions. He could barely hold up his head, and yet he prayed and read from the Scriptures with remarkable fervency. But that would prove to be the last time he led the family or anyone else in the worship of God. He grew steadily weaker until he was no longer strong enough to leave his room. His legs and feet began to swell, and the pain in his chest and head increased, keeping him bedridden throughout the rest of the summer.

One night, as he lay half-awake, David heard a knock at the front door. Mrs. Edwards' footsteps echoed through the hallway as she hurried to the main room. David could barely hear her voice as she welcomed the visitor inside. The muffled tones of a man's voice drifted in from the hallway. Then footsteps came toward his room.

"He's in here," Mrs. Edwards whispered outside his door. David tried to sit up, wincing from the pain. The door opened and his brother John stepped inside. In the dim candlelight, the two brothers stared at each other, then a wide smile spread across David's face. John returned the smile with a distressed look. He barely recognized his brother—he had grown so thin and frail. Hurrying to his brother's side, John gently embraced him, his throat tightening as he struggled to hold back the tears that threatened to spill down his cheeks.

"It is good to see you," David whispered, his throat too dry to speak.

"It is good to see you, too," John echoed, helping his brother lean back onto the pillows. "I was afraid I would not see you before—" he couldn't finish.

"It's all right," David said softly. "I know I am dying. I, too, am thankful to see your face again before I leave this world. Don't worry, I am not afraid. Soon I will be with the Lord."

John nodded, sniffing back his tears. "I've brought you some things from your house in New Jersey: your diary and private papers. I thought you would want them with you."

"I do. Thank you," David said, taking the papers from his brother and placing them on the bed beside him. "Have you made a decision about taking over the ministry at Cranberry?"

"Yes, I've decided to accept your proposal and move there as soon as possible," John said.

"I couldn't be more pleased," David said with a faint smile. He had trouble breathing so he lay very still, trying to catch his breath.

"It is a comfort to me knowing that you will be shepherding my flock when I am gone," David whispered hoarsely. "When you return, please charge my people in the name of their dying minister—and mostly in the name of Christ—to live and walk as becomes the Gospel. Tell them how greatly they would wound the cause of Christ if they fell into sin. If they continue to live in sin while professing to be Christians, they will prejudice other Indians against the truth. Remind them that their religious affections will mean nothing unless the main principle of their lives is the pursuit of holiness and love for God."

"I will tell them," John replied. "Please, don't try to talk. You need your rest."

"How long will you be staying?" David asked.

"I can't stay long, but I hope to return to see you as soon as I can," John said, taking David's hand.

"John," David said weakly. "I must tell you something that has been on my heart lately. I see now, more than I ever have before, how wrong I was not to take better care of myself. I pushed too hard. Many people tried to warn me, but I refused to listen."

He paused a moment, reflecting on his own thoughts. "I'm ashamed of my pride, and it has cost me dearly. Please, John, do not make the same mistake. Be strong in body and in spirit so you might labor long among the Indians."

Even though he wanted to say more, he didn't have the strength. The pain in his chest was unbearable, and talking only made it worse. John tried to calm his brother and reassured him that his advice would be taken to heart. With this assurance, David seemed content. He had delivered his warning, and now he could be still and rest.

Holding David's hand, John remained by his side late into the night. As the hours clicked by to the sound of the clock on the mantle, John wondered if each labored breath would be his brother's last. He stared at David, wanting to remember every line and contour of his face, grieved by the pain he saw there. When his brother finally fell asleep, John left, shutting the door quietly behind him.

As the summer turned into fall and the trees exchanged their green raiment for burnished gold, David grew worse. At times, his breathing became so shallow that Jerusha feared the end had finally arrived. But whenever he seemed at his worst, his spirits lifted and he choked out praises to God. His love for the Lord and gratefulness for His mercy could not be contained within him. Whenever David had the opportunity, he would testify of God's grace to those who would listen—and there were always visitors willing to listen.

Early one morning, when his brother Israel was visiting with two ministers from a nearby town, David was able to talk to them about the hope that sustained him through the pain of his final days.

"I am truly happy because I know I will be going to heaven," David told them, his voice gaining strength as he spoke about heavenly things. "My heaven is to please God and glorify Him, and to give all to Him, and to be wholly devoted to His glory. That is the heaven I long for. That is my religion, and that is my happiness, and always was ever since I suppose I had any true religion. And all those who are of that religion shall meet me in heaven."

He paused to catch his breath and to sit up slightly in his bed. Jerusha tucked another pillow behind his head.

"I do not go to heaven to be exalted in myself, but to give honor to God. It is no matter where I will be stationed in heaven, whether I have a high or low seat there; but to love, and please, and glorify God is all. Had I a thousand souls, if they were worth anything, I would give them all to God. But I have nothing to give, when all is done.

"It is impossible for any rational creature to be happy without acting all for God. God Himself could not make him happy any other way. I long to be in heaven, praising and glorifying God with the holy angels. All my desire is to glorify God. My heart goes out to the grave, it seems to me a desirable place. But, oh, to glorify God! That is it, that is above all."

Those who listened remained silent, enraptured by his passion and zeal for the Lord. David paused to catch his breath, then continued: "It is a great comfort to me to think that I have done a little for God in the world—oh, it is but a very small matter, yet I have done a little. And I regret that I have not done more for Him. There is nothing else in the world that can yield any satisfaction besides living to God, pleasing Him, and doing His whole will. My greatest joy and comfort has been to tell others of Christ. And now in my illness, while I am full of pain and distress from day to day, all the comfort I have is in being able to do some little piece of work for God, either by something that I say to you, or by writing, or by some other way."

Nearly every day was the same as families from

the Northampton church came to visit the well-known missionary to the Indians. No matter who would visit, David talked to each person about his own relationship with God, including the children. He would take them by the hand and urge them to seek God and forgiveness in Christ, to consider how they would face death one day even as he was facing it at that moment. He warned them of how desperate and frightful death would be if they did not have the comfort and assurance of Christ's love and grace.

"When you see my grave, remember what I said to you while I was alive," he would tell them. "Then think to yourself how the man who lies in that grave counseled and warned you to prepare for death."

On those days when David was not receiving visitors, he would sit in his bed propped up on pillows in an effort to use his time for some good. He would write letters or work on various projects he wanted to complete before his strength gave out. One project involved editing a new work by Thomas Shepard that had recently been selected for publication. Mr. Shepard was the founder of Harvard University and a minister at Cambridge in England. He was a devoted minister of the Gospel, and David admired him greatly. During his own years in the ministry, David had studied Shepard's work thoroughly and had learned a great deal about what it meant to make a sincere profession of faith and to live a godly life in obedience to the commands of Christ. In honor of this famous minister, David spent his final days writing a preface to Shepard's diaries.

It is ironic that the very conclusions David drew from reading Shepard's journals would be the same that others would draw from reading David's. This is evident from a portion he wrote one morning as Jerusha placed cool rags on his swollen legs. Of Shepard's diaries he wrote, "For as it is a journal of the private experiences of that excellent and holy man, designed for his own use, so it contains, as it were, this true religion for a course of time, delineated to us in a very exact manner; whence we have opportunity to see with utmost plainness what passed with him for religion, what he labored after under that notion, and what were the exercises and difficulties he met with in pursuance of a religious life."

As David finished the last line, he leaned back on his pillows and sighed. "What a comfort it is to read of others who have labored so long and hard in the ministry, and who lived so fervently for the glory of God," David thought to himself. His thoughts were suddenly scattered as painful cramps shot through his swollen legs and ankles. This only added to the pain he already suffered from the ulcers in his lungs. His body was beginning to shut down, and David knew his time was running out.

Through all the days and nights when David was tortured by bursting ulcers in his lungs and the spitting of blood, Jerusha tried to make him comfortable by bringing him hot tea and fluffing the pillows behind his head. In the mornings, he would lie half awake and listen to the rustle of her skirt as she walked into the room. It sounded like a spring breeze through the maples. As she moved about the room, tending the fire and changing the wash basin, he would remain very still, basking in the comfort of the sound. Then she would sit beside him and wait until he asked for something to drink. Every morning, she would read the Bible to him, and even though he couldn't always speak, just having the Word of God spread open before him brought him great joy.

One morning, when Jerusha came to bring him some water, David struggled to sit up in bed. She sat beside him as she always did, concern etched into her young face. He took her soft hand in his own and gently asked, "Dear Jerusha, are you willing to part with me?" She was about to respond when he continued, "I am quite willing to part with you. I am willing to part with all my friends. I am willing to part with my dear brother John, although I love him the best of any creature living. I have committed him and all my friends to God, and can leave them with God. Though, if I thought I should not see you and be happy with you in another world, I could not bear to part with you. But we shall spend a happy eternity together."

Tears flowed down Jerusha's cheeks as she squeezed David's hand tightly. Dabbing her eyes with a linen handkerchief, she tried to smile through the tears, wanting to say something meaningful. Her heart ached within her at the thought of no longer enjoying David's company, of no longer sharing with him her hopes and dreams, her delight in serving the Lord. She had never known anyone who understood her so well, who looked at everything with an eternal perspective, who saw life as a gift from God to be used for His glory. As she gazed into David's pale eyes, she thanked God that she would be with him again one day. Squeezing his hand again, she whispered, "I look forward to that day."

In early October, John returned from New Jersey
to find David much worse but peaceful and comforted
by the hope that he would soon be with his heavenly
Father. John reassured his brother many times that
everything was in order for him to begin his ministry
among the Indians at Cranberry. David's people
would be taken care of, and the news brought him
much joy, making him even more ready to depart and
be with Christ.

Soon after John's arrival in Northampton, the ulcers in David's lungs began to break more frequently,
causing him to cough up large amounts of blood and
discharge. The pain was unbearable, and David knew
the end was near.

"People have no idea how agonizing dying can be,"
David said to Jerusha one night as he writhed in pain.

As the cool, October wind howled outside, he became delirious, twisting and turning in anguish all
evening until a faint numbing sensation began to
spread through his arms and legs. Steadily, his mind
cleared, but his body seemed to drift. He could no
longer feel the sheets that were wrapped about him or
the cool perspiration that covered his skin.

"Please pray that God would give me patience,"
David whispered to Jerusha. "I think I will die
tonight, but I am afraid God will delay it."

That evening, he felt a surprising burst of vigor,
and he spoke again to his brother about ministering to
the needs of the Indians. They talked for nearly an
hour, much longer than John had expected. David
seemed to gain strength whenever he thought about
the spiritual needs of his people in Cranberry. But
soon his strength gave out, and no more could be

summoned. He tried to speak, but words failed to come. As dawn approached, he lay very still, his breathing barely noticeable. John held his brother's cold hand, and Jerusha sat next to him with her delicate fingers laced together in prayer. Her father paced slowly up and down the room, praying that God would be merciful and ease David's pain. Silence clung to the room like early morning dew, interrupted only by the steady tick of the clock on the mantle, an occasional crack of the fire, and David's faint gasps for breath.

Sitting on either side of the bed, John and Jerusha glanced at each other, grief mirrored in their eyes. The clock ticked on, drawing out the hours as David struggled for every excruciating breath. With the passing of the night, his mind became more focused on heavenly things, on Christ, on what it would be like to see Him in all His glory. The cords of this world were being cut and soon he would be free to fly into the presence of Christ and behold the face of God.

On Friday, October 9, 1747, just as the sun unfurled its glorious rays along the dark horizon, David's eyes fixed on an imperceptible point above him. Suddenly, there were no more painful gasps for breath, only the steady ticking of the clock. John, Jerusha, and Mr. Edwards waited for him to breathe again, but he never did. Jerusha closed her eyes, laid her head against David's still body, and let the tears flow onto his white linen shirt. Her beloved friend, who had sacrificed so much to see the Indians find new life in Christ, had finally arrived at the one place where he had always longed to be—in the glorious presence of his sovereign and most gracious Lord.

Epilogue

It was not long after David Brainerd's death at the age of twenty-nine that Jerusha Edwards joined him in that heavenly assembly. Her father wrote of her death:

It has pleased a holy and sovereign God to take away this my dear child by death on the 14th of February, next following, after a short illness of five days, in the eighteenth year of her age. She was a person of much the same spirit with Mr. Brainerd. She had constantly taken care of and attended him in his sickness, for nineteen weeks before his death; devoting herself to it with great delight because she looked on him as an eminent servant of Jesus Christ. In this time, he had much conversation with her on the things of religion; and in his dying state, often expressed to us, her parents, his great satisfaction concerning her true piety, and his confidence that he should meet her in heaven, and his high opinion of her, not only as a true Christian, but a very eminent saint, one whose soul was uncommonly fed and entertained with things that appertain to the most spiritual, experimental, and distinguishing parts of religion; and one who, by the temper of her mind, was fitted to deny herself for God, and to do good, beyond any young women whatsoever that he knew of. She had manifested a heart uncommonly devoted to God, in the course of her life, many years before her death, and said on her death-bed that "she had not seen one minute for several years, wherein she desired to live one minute longer, for the sake of any other good in life, but doing good, living to God, and doing what might be for His glory." (The Works of Jonathan Edwards, volume 2. Edinburgh: The Banner of Truth Trust, 1992, p. 385)

*　　*　　*　　*

Although David Brainerd did not live to see it, Yale University decided later to include him among its lists of esteemed students. The college that sent David Brainerd away in disgrace later honored him as one of its heroes. A tribute to him can be seen today on a house in Yale's Sterling Divinity Quadrangle, where there is an inscription: "David Brainerd, Class of 1743."

Appendix A

The most famous forerunner of David Brainerd was John Eliot, who served faithfully as a missionary to the North American Indians in the mid-1600s. The following is the introductory chapter from Jesse Page's book, *David Brainerd: The Apostle to the North American Indians*, written in the 1890s, which we will use to provide an account of John Eliot:

The North American Red Indian in his sprayed feathers and moccasins forms a conspicuous and well-known figure in the stories with which the young people on both sides of the Atlantic are familiar. He has always held a position of respectability compared with other wild men of the woods—living a life of freedom and sport, brave in conflict, solemn in council over the pipe of peace, fond of his squaw and the little red youngsters who gamboled at the door of his wigwam, a mighty hunter, and yet pausing in the prairie solitude to kneel in the presence of the Great Spirit; such is the Indian of literature. Perhaps the picture has been drawn a little fancifully, possibly the cruel torturing nature, the sly cunning, and the treachery of the warpath have not been truthfully disclosed, but in many respects the redskin was once, if he is not today, a noble savage with many fine characteristics, having a nature capable under Divine culture of many grand possibilities. Unhappily the white man has not improved the red man, except where the former has carried the message of the Cross, and by this time devastating wars and drink, the dreadful scourge of all the nations, has reduced this fine race of braves to a miserable group of exiles on their own land.

The story which is to be told in the following pages is of the early history of the Red Indians, and of one who gave himself up to the work of preaching the Gospel to them, and pointing them to heaven. The better however to understand what led up to the work which Brainerd took in hand so nobly, a brief glance at the experience of the earlier missionaries will not be out of place.

Although the gallant admirals of Queen Elizabeth in their visits to the newly discovered shores of America did not altogether neglect the Christian teaching of the natives with whom they came in contact, it cannot be said that mission work began with any enthusiasm until the seventeenth century, when religious intolerance drove the Pilgrim Fathers from their native land to seek a home in New England, where they might worship God according to the dictates of their own conscience. As will be seen later on, it was in the *Mayflower*, or one of the other ships of the Puritan refugees, that the ancestors of David Brainerd sailed for the new home across the wide sea.

But the first missionary was John Eliot, once a young schoolmaster in an Essex village, who in the year 1646 had gained the confidence of the Indians amongst whom he had taken up his abode, and succeeded in mastering their language, and constructing a grammar thereof, which has since been of much service to his successors. He worked with great industry in their cause, and actually secured so much interest and support in England that the House of Commons and the Universities of Oxford and Cambridge contributed money freely for his enterprise.

With this he bought land, built towns, founded a sort of Commonwealth like his own country had at home, and got the Indian Christians to express publicly their confessions, and testify to their faithful belief in the new religion. A very curious book he wrote, called "Tears of Repentance," dedicating it in this wise to Oliver Cromwell: "What the Jews once said of their centurion, he loved our nation, and built us a synagogue, the same may be affirmed upon a more noble accompt of your Lordship, and of those faithful centurions and soldiers under your control," etc. The work is now very rare, and as the original volume, in strange old type, and queer spelling, on yellow faded leaves, lies before the present writer, he cannot forbear making a quotation of some of the experiences of those very earliest labourers, as told by John Eliot, under the title, "The Day-Breaking, if not the Sun-Rising of the Gospel with the Indians in New England."

After the Gospel had been preached, we read: "They told us they were troubled, but they could not tell what to say to it, what should comfort them; he therefore, who spake to them at first, concluded with a doleful description (so far as his ability to speak in that tongue would carry him), of the trembling and mourning condition of every soul that dies in sin, and that shall be cast out of favour with God. Thus after three hour's time thus spent with them, we asked them if they were not weary, and they answered no. But we resolved to leave them with an appetite; the

chief of them, seeing us conclude with prayer, desired
to know when we would come again, so we appointed
the time, and having given their children some apples,
and the men some tobacco, and what else we then had
in hand, they desired some more ground to build a
town together, which we did much like of, promising
to speak for them to the general court, that they might
possess all the compass of the hill upon which their
wigwams then stood, and so we departed, with many
welcomes from them."

Then, after a time John Eliot and his companions
visited the Indians again on the 11th of November,
1646, and, having spoken once more upon the
Christian faith, paused to see the effect of their words
upon the ring of red-skinned listeners: "The first
question was suddenly propounded by an old man
then present, who, hearing faith and repentance
preached upon them to find salvation by Jesus Christ,
he asked whether it was not too late for such an old
man as he, who was near death, to repent or seek after
God. This question affected us not a little with
compassion, and we held forth to him the Bible, and
told him what God said in it concerning such as are
hired at the eleventh hour of the day; we told him,
also, that if a father had a son that had been
disobedient many years, yet if, at last, that son fall
down upon his knees, and weep and desire his father
to love him, his father is so merciful that he will
readily forgive and love him, so we said it was much
more with God, who is a more merciful Father to
those whom He hath made so. . . . Having thus spent
the whole afternoon, and night being almost come
upon us, considering that the Indians formerly

desired to know how to pray, and did think that Jesus Christ did not understand Indian language, one of us therefore proposed to pray in their own language, and did so for about a quarter of an hour together, wherein divers of them held up eyes and hands whenever all of them (as we understood afterwards), understanding the same, and one of them I cast my eyes upon was hanging down his head, with his rug before his eyes, weeping; at first I feared it was for some soreness of his eyes, but lifting up his head again, having wiped his eyes (as not desirous to be seen), I easily perceived his eyes were not sore, yet somewhat red with crying; and so held up his head for a while, yet such was the presence and mighty power of the Lord Jesus in his heart that he hung down his head again, and covered his eyes again, and so fell wiping and wiping of them, weeping abundantly, continuing thus till prayer was ended; after which he presently turns from us, and turns his face to a side, and corner of the wigwam, and there falls a-weeping more abundantly by himself, which one of us perceiving, went up to him, and spake to him encouraging words, at the hearing of which he fell a-weeping more and more, so leaving him he who spake to him came unto me (being newly gone out of the wigwam), and told me of his tears, so we resolved to go again both of us to him, and speak to him again, and we met him coming out of the wigwam, and there we spake again to him, and he there fell into a more abundant renewed weeping, like one inwardly and deeply affected indeed, which forced us also to such bowels of compassion that we could not forbear weeping over him also, and so we parted, greatly rejoicing for such sowing."

In due time Eliot obtained such influence over the Indians that he persuaded them to abandon their roving life and settle in a town which was built under his direction and called "Noonatomen," which is Indian for "Rejoicing." He framed laws, not unlike those which prevailed in Puritan England at home, and translated the works of Baxter and other sound divines of that age for them to read. Subsequently, the town of Nantick, on the Charles River, was founded in 1651, and on a solemn fast-day he gathered the Indians together, and, like Moses speaking to the children of Israel, he exhorted them to serve the Lord. But then as now, civilization brought some evils in its train, and the terrible effects of strong drink were so manifest that neither whipping nor heavy fines could restrict its traders, of whose business Eliot spoke as follows: "These scandalous evils greatly blemish and intercept their entertainment of the Gospel, through the policy of Satan, who counterworketh Christ that way, with not a little uncomfortable success."

Eliot was at this time the pastor of Roxbury, and endeavoured to raise a native ministry, sending to college two young converted Indians, who, however, never lived to be useful in the work. The Puritan missionary, therefore, had to labour single-handed, and the unremitting nature of his traveling and preaching may be told in his own words, where he says in a letter: "I have not been dry night nor day, from the third day of the week to the sixth, but have traveled from place to place in that condition, and at night I pull off my boots and wring my stockings, and on with them again, and so continue. The rivers also have raised, so that we were wet in riding through them. But God steps in and helps me. I have considered the exhortation of Paul to his son Timothy, 'Endure hardness as a good soldier of Jesus Christ,' with many other such like meditations.' "

Great trouble, however, came upon those "praying Indians," as they were called, for an influential chief managed to incite the various tribes against the English settlers, and a terrible onslaught was made upon the white men and their families, farms were ruthlessly burnt, and the people, including the helpless children, brutally murdered. Then came the inevitable reprisals; the government sent the military to avenge those outrages, and although the Christian natives had, with few exceptions, kept aloof from their fanatical comrades, and stood loyal to their friends, they were suspected of complicity and had to pay the penalty. It was a bitter experience for Eliot, now an aged man, to see the very Indian towns which he had established broken up, and this too carried on with relentless violence by the whites, who drove the Christian natives into hiding, and destroyed the work which the patient industry and endurance of many years had built up.

But this man was the grand pioneer of Christian missionary work among the Indians, and although he closed his career amid circumstances of much discouragement, John Eliot will always be remembered as bearing, not without tears and weariness, the brunt of the battle for the Cross, and making, like John the Baptist, a highway for the spread of the Gospel of the Lord Jesus Christ among the wild redskins of the New World.

Just two hundred years ago, as the flowers of the early summer were blooming, and the foliage of the Indian forest had burst forth into freshest green, this eminent saint of God lay dying. His thoughts were all for the Indians, and the work he loved so well. Here are his last words: "There is a dark cloud upon the work of the Gospel among them. The Lord revive and prosper that work, and grant that it may live when I am dead. It is a work that I have been doing much and long about. But what was the word I spoke last? I recall that word *my doings*. Alas! they have been poor and small and lean doings, and I will be the man who will throw the first stone at them all. . . . Welcome joy! Come, Lord, come!"

God was not unmindful of the prayer of his servant and within twenty years of his death a boy was born who was destined to take up the gracious labour he laid down, and whose life and work will be the theme of the following pages. But before restoring from the mist of past years the living figure and the brave deeds of his successor, it is fitting that we linger for one moment more over John Eliot's message and the fruits seen after many days. Once more turning over the pages of that ancient volume which survives, a pathetic memento, the wreck of more than two centuries, we catch sight of the last of those confessions or testimonies which he noted down from the lips of the North American Indians, the simple heartfelt utterance of those who had found in Christ a Saviour. It refers to the two little Indian children, three years old, whose father had already expressed his faith in the Lord Jesus. There is scarcely a more affecting incident in the literature of missions, and here, in John

Eliot's own words, after so many years, the story, for the first time, shall be told: "This spring, in the beginning of the year 1652, the Lord was pleased to affect sundry of our praying Indians with a grievous disease, whereof some with great torments in their bowels died, among which were two little children of the age above-said, and at that time both in one house, being together taken with this disease. The first of these children in the extremities of its torments lay crying to God in these words, 'God and Jesus Christ, God and Jesus Christ, help me,' and when they gave it anything to eat, it would greedily take it (as it is usual at the approach of death) but first it would cry to God, 'O God and Jesus Christ, bless it,' and then it would take it; and in this died. The mother of this child also died of that disease, at that time. The father of the child told me this story, with great wonderment at the grace of God, in teaching his child so to call upon God. The name of the father is Nishohkon, whose confession you have before.

"Three or four days after, another child in the same house, sick of the same disease, was (by Divine hand doubtless) sensible of the approach of death (an unusual thing at that age) and called to its father and said, 'Father, I am going to God,' several times repeating it, 'I am going to God.' The mother (as other mothers used to do) had made for the child a little basket, a little spoon, and a little tray, these things the child was wont to be greatly delighted withal (as all children will), therefore, in the extremity of the torments they set those things before it to divert the mind and cheer the spirit, but now the child takes the basket and puts it away, and said, 'I will leave my basket be-

hind me for I am going to God, I will leave my spoon
and tray behind me (putting these away) for I am going
to God'; and with these kinds of expressions the same
night finished its course and died.

"The father of this child is Robert Speen, whose
confessions you have before, and in one of them he
maketh mention of this child that died in faith. When
he related this story to me, he said he could not tell
whether the sorrow for the death of his child or the
joy for its faith were greater when it died.

"These examples," adds Eliot, "are a testimony
that they teach their children the knowledge and fear
of God, whom they now call upon, and also that the
Spirit of God co-worketh with their instructions, who
teacheth by man more than man is able to do." With
this sweet fragment, we bid John Eliot farewell. In
noting down for us the heartfelt testimony of these
Indian converts, he has indeed taught us how the
Spirit of God "teacheth by man more than man is able
to do." These stalwart natives, drawn from their dark
superstitions and ignorance to a knowledge of the true
God, like Peter, are ready to declare unto their
brethren how the Lord hath brought them out of
prison. Their simplicity and childlike faith are
beautiful characteristics, and the veteran missionary
is not slow to appreciate them. The good old man, who
looks from a portrait before us, of grave aspect, with
solid and determined countenance not unlike the
Lord Protector himself, his wavy hair falling upon the
broad white Puritan collar, and with his old-fashioned
bulky Bible in his hand, we see him standing by the
wigwams, while the Indians, in attitudes of deep attention, spread themselves about him listening to his

words. The little brown children venture near him and catch the name of Jesus, as the retreating sunlight fills the forest with a shadowy silence. The scene fast fades, the mist of many years rolls upon again, blots out the group of listeners, blurs the overarching trees, and again noiselessly envelops in oblivion the figure of the preacher, whose voice just now we could almost fancy we hear. For a moment it all was vivid to us, a breathing human group, and the other vision too of the little sufferers in their wigwams calling on God and Christ and putting their toys aside, because they were going to Him. Was it not all so real, so living, so heart-reaching? We will not willingly let the picture be dissolved in forgetfulness. Rather will we cherish its memory and keep it as a background as our eyes now turn to the approaching figure of a tall, spare young man with eyes lustrous and sad, *David Brainerd, the Apostle of the Indians.*

Appendix B

The following excerpt is the final chapter of Jesse Page's biography, *David Brainerd: The Apostle to the North American Indians*, in which he gives an account of other missionary work that had been done among the Indians up until the late 1800s:

Who besides Brainerd have laboured for the Indian's good? What in the past has been the history of mission work to these tribes of red men, and how far and with what measure of success is this noble toil pursued in our own day? Such questions as these naturally may arise in the minds of those, who, from reading the preceding record of a good and faithful servant, may be inspired with a deeper interest in the race for whom he gave away his life. The history of Indian missions is itself worthy of a volume, alive as it is with exciting episodes, and rich in martyrology which is not surpassed by any similar work for Christ anywhere in the world. But it may not be out of place in anticipation of the questions just put to briefly narrate something of what has been done, and in these later days is being achieved, for the salvation of these people.

To go back very far, even to the fifteenth century, we find the Jesuits first in the field. They followed closely in the wake of the haughty Spaniard who, by the galleons of his then unsurpassed navy, made for himself a footing on the shores of the West. It would be unjust to refuse a recognition of the heroic devotion and self-sacrifice of these missionary priests. The Gospel which they carried may have been a sadly corrupted message of God's mercy, but its propagation inspired these men with a zeal and self-renunciation which is worthy of all praise. When the great Catholic Queen Isabella gave special commands that "great care should be taken of the religious instruction of the Indians," many there were who in the name of the Church leapt forward to do her bidding.

England, the great religious as well as political antagonist of Spain, was equally alive to the spiritual needs of the Indians, and in the gallant ships which hunted for the Spanish fleet in distant waters were brave, good soldiers of the Cross, whose mission was to fight not carnal but spiritual foes. Thus we find on the deck with Sir Richard Grenville, of that famous little craft *The Revenge*, one Thomas Hariot, of goodly memory, who stepping ashore among the Indians preached faithfully the Word of God. "Many times," says he in his notes, which have come down to us, "and in every towne where I came, according as I was able, I made declaration of the contents of the Bible; that therein was set forth the true onely God and His mightie works, that therein was contained the true doctrine of salvation through Christ, with many particularities of miracles and chief points of religion as I was able then to utter and thought fit for the time."

Doubtless in those far-off days as in these present with us, the Protestant missionary found a double foe to fight in the united errors of Pagan and Romish superstition. With the Pilgrim Fathers came the first definite endeavour to speak amongst the Indian aborigines the saving truths of the Christian religion. When they landed and began to found their Plymouth colony, it was immediately declared that their aim was "a desire to advance the Gospel in these remote parts of the world, even if they should be but as stepping stones to those who were to follow them." In Massachusetts they adopted as a state emblem the figure of an Indian with a label from his mouth saying, "Come over and help us." Thus it has been truly said, "These Pilgrims and Puritans were the pioneers of the Protestant world in attempts to convert the heathen to Christ. There were missionary colleges—self-supporting missions—composed of men who went on their own responsibility and at their own expense to establish their posterity among the heathen whose salvation they sought." In the first chapter of this book [see Appendix A] a sketch is given of John Eliot, a famous and successful missionary of that day, one whose name and work is deserving of more complete and worthier memorial in these present times of missionary interest. His Indian Bible published at Cambridge, near Boston, was the first and for many years the only edition of the Holy Scriptures in the vernacular. The work of Eliot and Mayhew and their praying Indians on the island of Martha's Vineyard is a most interesting page in the history of these early missions in New England.

The opening of the eighteenth century brings David Brainerd into view, taking up the noble labours of his Puritan predecessors. What manner of man he was, and what through the grace of God he was enabled to do, is set forth in this book; it need only be affirmed that evidently upon him descending the prophet's mantle, and a double portion of the spirit of devotion and power.

We now come to the time when General Oglethorpe laid the foundations of the colony of Georgia, and took with him a pioneer band of Moravian missionaries, who were destined to make history and inscribe their names indelibly in the record of distinguished service for Christ. One of this number was David Zeisberger, a man of apostolic character, who seemed to have had a charmed life, so wonderfully was he preserved amid a perilous career. In common with all the Brethren he was a man of peace, refusing to bear arms, and having the rare courage to accept the doctrines of the Sermon on the Mount as his rule of conduct, for which godly offence he became the butt of the white man's jealousy and spite, who, indeed, seems to have done his utmost to undermine the confidence of the Indians in their meek and devoted friend. He mastered the languages of the Six Nations, and when by persecution his Christian Indians were driven forth from Shekomeko, he founded the settlement of Gnadenhütten or the "Tents of Grace." Everywhere the influence of his teaching was felt, and the Christian natives began to flock around him, and fresh settlements were formed, notably Friendenstadt, or the "Town of Peace," among the Iroquois, and Schönbrunn, or "The Beautiful Spring," near Lake Erie. Soon afterwards the American War of Independence began, and the Moravian Brethren, staunchly refusing to take part with either side, were caught in the fiery storm, and suffered by the inroads and attacks of both whites and

Indians. Drink had made the red men lawless and thirsty for outrage, and the Christian settlements were being constantly invaded, and the lives of the missionaries openly threatened. In vain did the friends of Zeisberger urge him to fly. He determined, even if it cost him his life, to remain loyally with his converts. "My heart does not allow me," says he in reply, "even so much as to think of leaving. Where the Christians stay I will stay. It is impossible for me to forsake them. If Edwards and I were to go they would be without a guide and would disperse. Our presence gives authority to the national assistants, and the Lord gives authority to us. He will not look upon our remaining here as foolhardiness. I make no pretensions to heroism, but am by nature as timid as a dove. My trust is altogether in God. Never has He put me to shame, but always granted me the courage and the comfort I needed. I am about my duty, and even if I should be murdered it will not be my loss but my gain." He lived long beyond the allotted three-score years and ten, and, like Eliot, saw in his last days the cruel obliteration of that work among the Indians, which he had given the energy of this lifetime to accomplish.

Besides Zeisberger many others might be quoted, as, for instance, Christian Rauch, who inspired the Indians with confidence and respect. One of them, once seeing him peacefully sleeping in a hut amongst them, remarked, "This man cannot be a bad man. He fears no evil. He does not fear us who are so fierce, but he sleeps in peace, and puts his life in our hands."

Among the Moravian missionaries who came out with General Oglethorpe was a young English clergyman, who with considerable high-church notions began to preach the Gospel to the Indians in Georgia. This was John Wesley, whose mission to Georgia was the means of bringing him in contact with the Brethren, and resulted in his own conversion and that glorious revival of religion in his own country, the fruits of which are being gathered in every part of the world today.

The commencement of American missions to the Indians dates from a little gathering of students of Williams College, under a haystack in the rain, to pray for the heathen and devote themselves to the work of their salvation. The outcome of this first missionary meeting was the establishment of the American Board of Commissioners for Foreign Missions. The New York Missionary Society had already, in 1801, sent Mr. Holmes to work among the Tuscaroras at the Falls of Niagara, to whom came the pitiful appeal from some chiefs: "We cry to you from the wilderness, our hearts ache while we speak to your ears. . . . Think, poor Indians must die as well as white men. We pray you, therefore, never to give over and leave poor Indians, but follow them in their dark times, and let our children always find you to be their friends when we are dead and no more."

In 1818 the American Board sent missionaries to the Cherokees and Choctaws; schools were founded, and there seemed every prospect of permanent success, when the Indians were driven back beyond the Mississippi, and in despair many became slaves to drink, and fell away. In 1836 three missionaries, Mr. Spalding, Mr. Gray, and Dr. Whitman, traversed three thousand miles to reach the Kayuses and Nez

Perce Indians, and found them remarkably ready to receive the truth. During ten years great progress was made; schools, printing presses, and a Christian church were founded; but suddenly the unchristian natives burst upon the little mission house, treacherously murdered the doctor, his wife, and his friends, and the whole community were brutally treated and dispersed. After this Mr. Stephen R. Riggs, and his wife, began work among the Dacotas and Sioux, and after much patient endurance, God gave these faithful witnesses great success, and, like Brainerd, they saw a remarkable revival of religion among the Indians. "A Dacota now began to think as an Englishman, Christ came into the language, the Holy Spirit began to pour sweetness and power into it." But upon this glad time there waited a season of persecution and distress; and murderous outrage destroyed the workers, and dispersed the converts. Here seems to have followed a time when, on every hand, a policy of retreat and discomfiture seized the mission societies. The mission to the Chickasees was abandoned in 1834; that to the Osages in 1836; to the Stockbridge tribe in 1848; to the Choctaws in 1859; to the Tuscaroras and Cherokees in 1860—twelve missions, and forty-five churches, which reached about one hundred thousand Indians, abandoned in twenty-six years! Dr. Beard, of America, who vouches for these facts, says, "The question now asks itself, Why were not these hopeful missionary efforts to these pagan tribes more permanent? What turned the tide of success, and left the missions stranded? Here comes the story of dishonour. . . . Unscrupulous greed has hovered about the Indian reservations as waiting buzzards hover near the wounded creature upon whose flesh they would fatten. Lands granted to the Indians were encroached upon by the white people. These encroachments resisted led to war. Savage nature, wrought up with a sense of injustice, and burning for revenge, swept down upon the guilty intruder and settler alike with indiscriminate massacre."

One of the most conspicuous instances of the mission work among the Indians being injured by the unchristian aggression of the white man was that of the treatment of the peaceful and enlightened Cherokee tribe, who had so far embraced civilised ideas as to found the town of Brainerd in Georgia. The efforts of the missionaries there had been crowned with much success; but the State authorities were jealous of their influence with the natives, and at one time imprisoned two of them until the pressure of the Supreme Court, to which the missionaries appealed, enforced their release. The Indians were oppressed, deprived of their native government, and treated with the greatest injustice. Finally, a treaty was agreed upon, and for consideration, wholly insufficient, the Cherokees were to be exported wholesale beyond the Mississippi. The way in which this was enforced, and its miserable results, is thus well described by one of the best and most impartial works of missionary history [Cassell's *Conquests of the Cross*]. "This treaty was bitterly opposed by the majority of the nation. They said, 'We feel it due to ourselves frankly to state that the Cherokee people do not and will not recognise the obligation of the instrument of December, 1835. We reject all its terms; we will receive none of its benefits. If it is to be enforced upon us, it will be by your superior strength. We shall offer no resistance, but our voluntary assent will never be yielded. We are aware of the consequences; but, while suffering them in all their bitterness, we shall submit our cause to an all-wise and just God, in whose Providence it is to maintain the cause of suffering innocence and unprotected feebleness.'

"On the strength of the treaty, however, preparations were made for their removal, and forts were built to guard against any opposition that might arise. The 23rd of May, 1838, was fixed upon as the day when the troops were to commence operations. When the day arrived few had made any preparations, and families were turned out wholesale from their houses and farms, and collected into bodies ready for their long march to the Arkansas country.

"For a period of ten months the work of emigration went on, and during this period 10,000 people, divided into fourteen companies, travelled a distance of six or seven hundred miles, old and young, male and female, sick and healthy; none were spared, all were compelled to seek a new home away in the west. Before starting some of the companies were detained for a considerable in their encampments, during which they remained idle, and were exposed to every kind of evil and temptation which proximity to the whites afforded. Often without sufficient tent accommodation they were greatly exposed to the inclemency of the severe winter of 1838–39, and many besides were very inadequately clothed. The result was a terrible mortality among them, not less than one-fourth of the whole dying on the journey, this being on an average twelve deaths a day.

"The work of the mission was greatly deranged by the embarrassed state of political affairs of the Indians; and when the missionaries were arrested and imprisoned, some of the stations became neglected and abandoned. Under the system of lottery by which the land was distributed, the premises of two of the mission stations were taken possession of by the men who had drawn the lots containing them, and the Board suffered considerable loss therefrom. The Cherokees, too, now imbibed a deep prejudice against the Christian religion. They found themselves robbed and despoiled of their most sacred and undisputed rights by a nation professing to be Christian! They saw that those who taught them were themselves American citizens, and as such were partly responsible for those injuries done to them. The result was that a spirit of laxity grew up among the church members, and caused many to fall back into heathenism and superstition. Their own political condition occupied attention to such an engrossing extent that little heed was paid to religion, and the morals of the people suffered accordingly."

One of the most celebrated missionaries to the Indians in the present century was Peter Cartwright, the Methodist backwoods preacher. His own conversion from a life of gaiety and gambling, and his subsequent call to go forth to preach to the Indians is full of interest. He married an excellent woman, who became his brave and faithful helpmeet, and with their little children they travelled hundreds of miles through roadless swamps and forests and swiftly flowing rivers. The influence of his preaching was almost as striking as that of Brainerd; at one revival service we are told three hundred people lay upon the ground under conviction of sin. He stoutly opposed slavery, and, after enduring the discredit of emancipation principles, lived to see, at fourscore, the black man free. Others nobly followed up the work. Space fails to recount the remarkable missionary experiences of those who, during the past half-century, have given themselves freely for the salvation of the Indians. Each name, of which a brief mention can alone be given here, deserves a record in the annals of holy enterprise. How nobly Riggs and his devoted wife laboured among the Dacotas, how he compiled an invaluable dictionary of 16,000 native words, and how, with a party of sixty Christian men and women, they retreated a hundred miles across the prairie from the fury of the Indians' maddened rage. How Finley formed a church among the Wyandotts, and had a grand helper in a converted chief, by name "Summun-de-wet," how Breck spent nearly forty years amongst the Chippewas, how Jackson and Mrs. MacFarland preached the Gospel in Alaska, how Wilson and his wife founded the native community at Sarnia, on the Garden River, what Case and Copway did in the midst of the Ojibways, the faithful service of Macdonald and Kirby in the Youcan district, and of Duncan at Fort Simpson. Besides these, mention must be made of three native Indian missionaries, Peter Jones, John Sunday, and Henry Sternheur, who were called upon to "hold the fort" for Christ among their brethren, and were much blessed in their work. Amongst missionaries of our own time, perhaps the name of the Rev. Egerton R. Young is most distinguished, one who has described his work among the Cree and Salteaux Indians in a volume of charming interest.

Nearly all branches of the Christian Church have been and are represented in this work of spreading the good news of salvation among the denizens of the wigwams. The New England Company, which, founded so far back as 1649, may be deemed the parent society, does still a great work among the Mohawks on the Grand River, and has there and elsewhere educational establishments for the young Indians. The Church Missionary Society established a mission station in 1822, and are now doing excellent work in the district of Saskatchewan, among the Plain Crees, Sioux, and Blackfeet. The missions of the Unitas Fratrum or Moravians with its honourable history is still doing good among the Alaska Indians and Eskimos and Greenlanders. Societies which are indigenous to American soil do not forget the claims of the red man; the American Board, Baptist Union, Methodist Episcopal, Reformed Episcopal, Presbyterian Board, Mennonites, Bible Society and Society of Friends are all more or less engaged in this work. The dispersal of the tribes, and the recent conflict at the Pine Ridge Agency, has, however, affected the progress of these efforts. In all his troubles and vicissitudes, the redskin is not forgotten by many who still believe that he has an immortal soul to be won for Christ.

One of the most intelligent and famous of North American Indians, the chief Sitting Bull, who perished recently in a conflict with the whites, once said, "There is not one white man who loves an Indian, and not a true Indian but hates a white man." The bitterness of this declaration cannot be measured. But it is hoped that the perusal of the preceding pages will show that in the case of David Brainerd and many others since his day, it is happily possible for a white man to have a heart full of Christlike affection for his red brother, who, on his part, is not slow in reciprocating the fellowship of a common salvation.

Appendix C

For Further Reading

Day, Richard Ellsworth. *Flagellant on Horseback*. Philadelphia: Judson Press, 1950.

Dwight, Sereno Edwards. *Memoirs of Rev. David Brainerd*. New Haven: S. Converse, 1822.

Edwards, Jonathan. *The Works of Jonathan Edwards, with a Memoir of His Life*. Vol. I. New York: G. & C. Carvill, 1830.

Five Pioneer Missionaries. Carlisle, Pa: Banner of Truth Trust, 1965.

Howard, Phillip E., Jr. *The Life and Diary of David Brainerd*, Newly edited and with a biographical sketch of President Edwards. Chicago: Moody Press, 1949.

Norris, Rev. William H., *The Life of the Rev. David Brainerd*. New York: Carlton & Phillips, 1853.

Page, Jesse. *David Brainerd: The Apostle to the North American Indians*. London: S. W. Partridge & Co., 1890.

Pearce, Winifred M. *David Brainerd*. London: Oliphants Ltd., 1957.

Pettit, Norman. *The Life of David Brainerd*. New Haven and London: Yale University Press, 1985.

Journal of the Presbyterian Historical Society published by the Department of History of the United Presbyterian Church in the USA. Lancaster, Pa. and Philadelphia, Pa. Vol. 38 (1960).

Sherwood, J.M. *Memoirs of Rev. David Brainerd, Missionary to the Indians of North American*, Based on the life of Brainerd prepared by Jonathan Edwards, D.D., and afterwards revised and enlarged by Sereno E. Dwight, D.D. New York: Funk & Wagnalls, 1884.

Smith, Oswald J. *David Brainerd, His Message for Today*. Edinburgh: Marshall, Morgan & Scott, 1949.

Styles, John. *The Life of David Brainerd*. Boston, 1821.

Thornbury, John. *David Brainerd, Pioneer Missionary to the American Indians*. Evangelical Press, 1996.

Wesley, John A. M. *An Extract of the Life of the Late Rev. David Brainerd*. London, 1800.

Wynbeek, David. *Beloved Yankee, A Biography of David Brainerd*. Grand Rapids, Mich.: Wm. B. Eerdmans, 1961.